THE TREES

Conrad Richter

T H E
TREES

OHIO UNIVERSITY PRESS ~ ATHENS

Copyright 1940, 1945, 1946, 1950,
© 1966 by Conrad Richter

The Trees was first published on March 1, 1940

Published by arrangement with
Alfred A. Knopf, Inc. 1991

All rights reserved

Printed in the United States of America

Ohio University Press books are printed
on acid-free paper ∞

95   94   5

Library of Congress Cataloging-in-Publication Data

Richter, Conrad, 1890-1968.
The trees / by Conrad Richter.
p.   cm.
Reprint. Originally published: New York:
Knopf, 1940.
ISBN 0-8214-0978-6 (pbk.)
I. Title.
[PS3535.I429T7   1991]
813'.52—dc20
90-19936
CIP

v

❋   ❋   ❋

Contents

* * *

Foreword

THE AUTHOR wishes to acknowledge his debt to Henry Howe's rich and monumental historical collection of Ohioana given him many years ago by W. T. Boyd which implanted the seed; to other rare books and manuscripts made available by a score of helpful librarians; and to the help and support of individuals who because of their number must be nameless here.

Included among these latter are the neighbors of pioneer stock the young author once knew in the hills of Pennsylvania and later in the Ohio Valley, in whose mode of thought and speech much of this story is told, approximating as it does the store of eighteenth- and early-nineteenth-century speech collected from old manuscripts, letters, and records, a speech quite different from the formal written and printed language of the time into which the talk of citizens, the testimony of court witnesses, and even the conversation of ladies and gentlemen in the privacy of their family circles had almost invariably to be translated before reaching the respectability of public print. This early, vigorous spoken language, contrary to public belief, had its considerable origin in the Northeastern states, whence it was carried by emigrants into pioneer Ohio and adjoining territories, where today it has largely disappeared, and, along with the Pennsylvania rifle, into the South and Southwest, where it has more widely survived and is sometimes thought to be a purely native form of speech but which, wherever found, should be recognized with its local variants as a living reminder of the great mother tongue of early America.

The author also wishes to set down his obligation to those who told him as a boy and man tales and personal accounts that gave him a passionate love for the early American way of life. Through them he was made aware of the great masses of men and women whose names never figured in the history books but whose influence on their land and times was that of the people itself. If this novel has any other purpose than to tell some of their story, it has been to try to impart to the reader a feeling of having lived for a while in those earlier days and of having come in contact, not with the sound and fury of dramatic historical events that is the fortune of the relative and sometimes uninteresting few, but with the broader stuff of reality that was the lot of the great majority of men and women who, if they did not experience the certain incidents related in these pages, lived through comparable events and circumstances, for life is endlessly resourceful and inexhaustible. It is only the author who is limited and mortal.

CONRAD RICHTER

T H E
TREES

For Harvey

CHAPTER ONE

❋ ❋ ❋

The Vision

THEY MOVED along in the bobbing, springy gait of a family that followed the woods as some families follow the sea. In the midday twilight of the forest, the father's shaggy gray figure looked hump-backed, but the hump was a pack. In that pack under his rifle were a frow and augur, bar lead and powder, blacksmith's traps and a bag of Indian meal wrapped up in a pair of yellow yarn blankets.

Sayward carried the big kettle and little kettle packed with small fixings, Genny the quilts thonged to her white shoulders and Achsa a quarter of venison with the bloody folded buckskin her father had taken since the last trader. Even the littlest ones, Wyitt and Sulie, had their burdens of axe, bullet mould and clothes. Only their mother, Jary Luckett, went light, for she was poorly with the slow fever and could lug no more than the old blue Revolutionary greatcoat with the mended slit in the right shoulder.

It was the game that had fetched the Lucketts out of Pennsylvania. Months before the chestnut burrs had begun to sharpen, Worth Luckett looked for a woods famine. It would be like nothing since the second winter after Yorktown, he claimed. He spent so much time in the woods with nobody to talk to but Sarge, his old hound, that when he opened his mouth Jary had learned to pick up her ears and listen. For a month he had been noticing sign. The oaks, beeches and hazel patches would have slim mast for bears and pigeons this year. Deer paths lay barer than any time he could recollect of fresh droppings. And now the squirrels were leaving the country.

He claimed he had stood on a log near the old Mingo hemlock and seen them pouring like a mill race through the woods. They ran as if a pack of black Seven Mountains wolves were on their tails, or, worse, red piney squirrels tearing at the bucks to geld them. The very floor of the forest was gray and black with them. When they came to Paddy's Run, they didn't wait to take up and over the trees but plunged in like beaver. And the live ones fought over the drowned ones' bodies.

If meat on the go wasn't likely to be tainted, Worth could have caught himself a club and laid out a hundred without the waste of a dram of powder. As it was, he just stood on his log like a duck in thunder, waiting to see if the old Harry himself was not on the tail end. And when the last came, there was nothing behind them; nothing, he allowed, but famine.

The Luckett young ones stood listening to the tale with open mouths. The homespun over their hearts plopped in and out like the flanks of those runaway squirrels. They would have given the last stitch off their backs to have seen it. They wanted to go up West anyhow, and now they couldn't wait till tomorrow. But they daren't show it in front of their father. No, they just stood there gaping and dying to hear what their mother would have to say.

Jary sat quiet on her homemade hickory rocker. Oh, she knew how bad Worth wanted an excuse to get away from here. Her eyes slanted down toward the clay floor. Her mouth rounded a bit as if she took all these things, good, bad and indifferent, and was running them quietly and around inside her lips. Her mouth was so gentle and yet could shut like a mussel shell. She looked up and there was no telling what lay in her mind.

"You're aimin' to cross the Ohio?" she asked, and her eyes glinted a moment dangerously at her man.

He gave a nod. Even her father, Sayward saw, didn't know what she'd say or do. He took out his clay pipe and made to fill it, but his eyes never stopped watching her face. The young ones could hardly stand the waiting now.

Their mother went on grimly.

"I told you I'd never go way back there." Hope died in the young faces. She dropped her eyes and stared a long time across the doorsill, then around the cabin room at the familiar slab stools and puncheon table, the hand-whittled loom and wheel, and across the doorsill again to the mite of a grave in the clearing. None of these things could they take along. After while she stared up halfways at them. "And yit," back in her mouth she complained, "what's a body to do if the game's left the country?"

The four younger ones turned and made stiff and pious passage from the cabin. Once out in the twilight, they threw themselves on the ground, rolling and summersetting, leaping and kicking their bare feet, whooping and giving vent to their feelings like a pack of young coon dogs let out of the pen for a night's hunt.

Sayward, the oldest, went back to the haunch over the fire, turning it on the hook, catching some of the drippings in a long whittled spoon and basting it with its own juices. She hadn't given away to her feelings since her small hands had guided her youngest brother into the world. He was the fairest babe any of them had ever laid eyes on and she had slapped his little body, naked as a wild squab, till her hand was lame, but never would he open his mouth to cry or his lids to clap sight on his brother and sisters waiting to lug him around.

She had been just a little tyke then. Now she was fifteen and most a grown woman with the fire playing on her bare legs and shortgown. It took no trying to carry her breasts and head up. Life flowed through her calm and strong as current down the river. She could throw the other young ones, four at a time, and hold them squirming to the ground. "Not so all-fired hard!" they would yell at her when she'd comb or scrub them. Once when Worth was off to the black forest for pine martens and they hadn't a sliver of meat or dust of meal in the cabin, she had seen a young white faced buck swimming the river and had run barehanded into the deep water, grabbed hold of his spikes and tried to drown him like the Black Hunter of the Juniata. For a while there they had splashing apenty while the other young ones and Jary ran helpless up and down the bank. But when Worth came home with a few skins and nothing more than a skinny possum for meat, he found three quarters of venison hanging up and a small fresh deerhide pegged to one of the trees.

Now they had crossed the Ohio on a pole ferry and the mud on their feet was no longer the familiar red and brown earth of Pennsylvania. It was black like dung. The young ones were wild over tramping the same trace their father had tramped as a boy with Colonel Bouquet. Here was where the army sheep had to be shut in for the night and here where the soldiers had axed the trace wider to let the army train through. It was a country of hills and Jary had said she could breathe again like on those mortal sweet hills of Pennsylvania. Now that those hills were so far behind her, it was easier to give them up. Perhaps it wouldn't be so bad out here like she thought. What was the use of living in the same state as your folks if you never saw them anyhow?

They rounded a high ridge. A devil's race course cleared the air of limbs below. Here was something Worth had not told them about.

For a moment Sayward reckoned that her father had fetched them unbeknownst to the Western ocean and what lay beneath was the late sun glittering on green-black water. Then she saw that what they looked down on was a dark, illimitable expanse of wilderness. It was a sea of solid treetops broken only by some gash where deep beneath the foliage an unknown stream made its way. As far as the eye could reach, this lonely forest sea rolled on and on till its faint blue billows broke against an incredibly distant horizon.

They had all stopped with a common notion and stood looking out. Sayward saw her mother's eyes search with the hope of finding some settlement or leastwise a settler's clearing. But over that vasty solitude no wisp of smoke arose. Though they waited here till night, the girl knew that no light of human habitation would appear except the solitary red spark of some Delaware or Shawanee campfire. Already the lowering sun slanted melancholy rays over the scene, and as it sank, the shadows of those far hills reached out with long fingers.

It was a picture Sayward was to carry to her grave, although she didn't know it then. In later years when it was all to go so that her own father wouldn't know the place if he rose from his bury hole, she was to call the scene to mind. This is the way it was, she would say to herself. Nowhere else but in the American wilderness could it have been.

The sun was gone now. Far out they heard the yelping of a wolf and nearer the caterwauling of a panther. Worth stood leaning on his long Lancaster rifle, his nose wrinkling like a hound's.

"You kin smell the game!" he said hungrily.

Sayward sniffed. All she could wind was the scent of wild herbs and leaves mingled with the faint strange fetor of ranker, blacker earth than she knew in Pennsylvania. She looked at her brother and sisters. They stood with young eyes drinking in this place and it was plain as if drawn on shell-bark that what they saw were otters coasting down muddy slides and gray moose crashing through the woods and fat beaver cracking down their broad tails on gat water like pistol shots. They could see skins drying on the log walls of a cabin yet unbuilt and skins in a heavy pack on their father's shoulders and skins handed over the counter of a trader's post along the Scioto or Ohio where the shelves hung heavy with black and white English blankets, Turkey red calico, bolts of Merrimac blue, shawls with fringes, brass bound muskets and buckets of white beads.

"We mought even git rich and have shoes!" Sulie spoke out.

That broke the tension. They all looked down on her and smiled. Little Ursula, the baby of the family, the one they gave in to the most. One time she could look at you with such a helpless mouth, and then when you least expected it, she was spunky as a young coon and said grand things that no one dared think of but she and her Granmam Powelly who had a story and a half chip log house across the road from Granpap's gunsmith shop along the Conestoga.

CHAPTER TWO

❋　❋　❋

The Dark Country

I T SEEMED STRANGE the next few days when Sayward recollected the vision and realized that now they were down under that ocean of leaves. A red-tailed hawk screeching high over the treetops would hardly reckon there was a road down here. You had to be a porcupine rooting under the branches to find it or the black cat of the forest that could see in the dark and that some called the fisher fox.

This place, Jary quavered to Sayward, must be the grandaddy of all the forest. Here the trees had been old men with beards when the woods in Pennsylvania were still whips. Sayward watched her mother puttering along between the great shaggy butts that dripped with moss and moisture. All day she could see Jary's sunken eyes keep watching dully ahead for some sign that they might be coming out under a bit of sky.

Down in Pennsylvania you could tell by the light. When a faint white drifted through the dark forest wall ahead, you knew you were getting to the top of a hill or an open place. You might come out in a meadow or clearing, perhaps even in an open field with the corn making tassels and smelling sweet in the sun. But away back here across the Ohio, it had no fields. You tramped day long and when you looked ahead, the woods were dark as an hour or a day ago.

Sayward could feel the woods most when the time came to step a few feet into the brush. Sometimes Sulie or Genny ran in after her. Sometimes she went alone. The family bobbed on in single file and in a lick or two the forest had swallowed them up. While she waited here with the green leaves brushing her skin, with the monster brown trunks close enough to touch and all around her those wild unkempt graves of ancient windfalls, she minded what her father had once told her.

He had been tramping with his gun in the black forest when he felt it. He was a grown man and had followed the woods since he was a boy, and yet something came over him in those dark pines and hemlocks where the sun never came so that he wanted to run. He had hardly seen even a piney squirrel all day, and he saw nothing afterwards.

"I was so afeard I broke out in a sweat," he said.

Two hunters from the West Branch told him they knew what he meant. What made it they didn't know. It came over them no place but the deep woods. When pressed, Worth reckoned it might be a panther following his scent, for panthers were curious about humans. A while back he had circled in a tracking snow and found where one of the long yellow beasts had been snuffing behind him on his trail.

But Sayward had the feeling her father hadn't said what lay deepest in his mind. Alone here in these woods sometimes she could feel it. The trace was gone as if it had never been. The only roads were the deer paths. They looked like humans had made them. They coaxed you to come on. They'd lead you to a clearing, they said. They'd take you clear out of the woods. But well she knew that once she followed, they would twist and turn and circle on themselves and peter out in the middle of some swamp. Nothing moved in here. Even the green daylight stood still. The moss was thick and soft as a pallet. It invited you to lay down, and yet Sayward's feet wanted to run.

"It's nothin' but the woods fever," she would tell herself and make that self stand there and count clock time before she let her legs go. She stood up so stout, the skirt of her shortgown flared out a little in front. Between strong cheek bones her eyes looked at you blue and straight as whortleberries, and her hair hung in yellow braids heavy as hawsers on a Monongahela keel boat.

It was good to get back to the Indian trace after that. Human feet had packed it and like human feet it was never still, turning and dodging to miss the butts of the big trees. It pleased her to catch up to the family and hear the young ones crowing and quarreling over the droppings of some fox, wolf, coon or fisher fox in the trace, or to see her father point where a beast had stood on its hind legs and sharpened its claws in long scratches on the bark of a tree.

Some of the young ones would guess "painter" and some "link," meaning the black-browed catamount with hair on the balls of its feet.

"I reckon it was no more'n a bobcat," Jary would say soothingly, for she liked to think there was no savage beast in these woods as big as Sulie.

"It was a big black bear!" little Sulie herself would call out and look quickly behind her. Nothing could ever come big enough for Sulie, though it might come too close.

Generally Worth would wait to tell them what it was until the pack had come down off his shoulders. Camp and household chores blew out of his mind like down out of a thistle, but he never forgot a lick that had to do with the woods. When his tongue was supple, he could sit on a log by the campfire and go back over the day's tramp, naming every sign and the beast that had made it together with the trees that stood by. Most times he even said whether it was made by a he or she one.

Once they came to a fork in the trace where a child's skull hung on a pole and the beech trees were carved with sign.

"Kin you read it?" little Wyitt asked, standing there with his fur cap askew high on the shock of his sandy hair.

"Oh, I kin read it all right," his father said evasively. He went from tree to tree, standing in front of each and rubbing his beard. He told them the lefthand fork kept to the woods and the righthand one, if he minded right, led to Sandusky and the English seas.

Sayward saw a faint light break on her mother's face here in this shadowy, shut-in place.

"I heerd," she said, "it's fine livin' in the open prairie by the English seas."

"It's too fur for you, Jary," Worth told her.

"I'm stout," she said, straightening. "I kin walk a long ways."

"The game's cleaned out up there."

"You mought git wild bulls in the open prairies," she told him.

But Worth didn't hold much to that. How could he swap talk with any of the foreign Indians up there? Now Delaware was second nature to him for wasn't he part Delaware himself? And Shawanee he could get along with.

In the end they took the lefthand fork, and the light faded from Jary's face. All that day and the next the forest continued to thicken. None but Worth had ever laid eyes on such trees. A black walnut stood along the trace and three of them couldn't reach around it. No, they had to get a fourth to span it. Still bigger buttonwoods stood rooted on a creek's bank. Worth reckoned the heaviest close to fifteen feet through. He bragged he could drive two yoke of oxen past each other and never get off that stump.

Jary's face had gone cruelly bleak at the talk of oxen in this wild place. She peered dully at the nameless stream. The giant trees reached over and covered it from either side. Even in the middle the water looked dark as old Virginia tobacco.

"Ain't it got sun in these woods, Worth?" she complained, her eyes hard on him like her enemy. And when he had shed his pack and gone moseying downstream with his gun and Sarge, "If anything happens me, Saird, don't let him always have his way. You'll never git the chance to see Pennsylvany again."

"I mought never want to go back," Sayward encouraged her.

"Don't talk about the old state thataway." Jary sat the log, her face slanted down, her head giving at every beat of the blood in her gaunt neck. "I knowed it that day on the ferry I made all your beds wrong for you. Now you'll have to sleep in 'em as best you kin."

A long time afterward they heard Worth faintly hallooing down the stream.

"What kin he see in here?" Jary muttered.

"He mought have found some riffles we kin cross without gittin' wet to our middles," Sayward said. Together she and Achsa managed their father's heavy pack between them. When they reached him, far off the trace, the stream was still deep and slow with flecks of brown foam.

"Hain't you got eyes in your heads?" Worth put at them, puffing on his clay, his own eyes sharp and knowing in his week's growth of beard.

Sayward expected at first the black soil where he stood was scattered with small gray stone. Then she saw they were the shed horns of deer. Most of them were broken up. Porcupines, squirrels and other woods creatures had eaten them through. And yet so many pieces lay around that at one place they made a thin drift like the gray leavings of last year's snow. It was plain even to little Sulie's wide eyes that herds of deer had been coming here for many winters to shed. Most every tree you looked at was rubbed smooth in places as their old axe handle.

Worth said little but the smoke came fast from his bearded lips. He showed them what he called a shovel horn and a blue horn and one on which he counted thirteen points. In the crotch of a tree where some Indian must have hung them he fetched out two unbroken gray moose horns. When he set them on the ground and put their tips together, all the young ones save Sayward could walk under.

"By the tarnal!" he kept saying.

He took them where the dark stream emptied into a log-choked river. Down the river path he fetched them to a small run and up that run to a strong spring cradled in the knees of an old beech. The ground hereabouts was black as charcoal and the timber the densest stand Sayward had yet seen. God Almighty, she expected, would have to take an axe here if He wanted to look up and see the firmament He made. The big butts stood shoulder to shoulder, and something came in Jary's sunken eyes as if she had found herself in a herd of those great foreign elephant beasts she had told her young ones a hundred times she had once seen splashing through the mud of a Lancaster street fair.

She looked around her in a sort of terror.

"You don't aim to stay here, Worth! Where'd you git sticks for a cabin? It'd take you all winter a-maulin' those big butts."

"Oh, it's got light timber here and yonder," Worth said. He looked up tolerantly at the wild grape and other creepers roping tree to tree with sloping leafy thatches that shut out every wandering speck of God's free air.

Jary opened her mouth no more except to swoop in what breath she could in this choked-up place. She had had her say and what good did it do her? The time to have set herself against this place was away back in the old state when Worth claimed the squirrels were leaving the country. Now she and her young ones were here and here likely they would stay.

The sun must have been straight overhead, for at one place a shaft of light filtered through. It was pale and thin but it looked golden as a guinea. For a hundred feet it fell straight to the ground. Woods flies were rising and falling in it. Jary watched them. When they dropped, they seemed to be falling down some deep, dark well. And she and her young ones, she told herself, were on the bottom.

CHAPTER THREE

* * *

Ridgepole

THE YOUNG ONES hailed the end of their journey like the start of a frolic. They threw off the packs they never need carry again and swarmed over the ground like young foxes or wolves at play, racing and tagging and yelping at each other. Genny was the swiftest. None of them could catch her. She'd tear around with her thin white legs, her torn shortgown and hair flying behind her. But Achsa could keep going when the others played out. Long after you couldn't see them any more, their shrill cries came like bird calls from the forest. Wyitt hid in a hollow log and it was a good while till they found him, though now and then you could hear a muffled bark like it came from the ground.

Little Sulie climbed a young tree, holding on to the ropy creepers.

"I'm up higher'n a chimly!" she yelled. "I'm up so high I kain't even see you."

Worth's square axe rang in the woods and small trees here and there began raising dust and twigs as they came toppling down. After the first few fell, Sayward saw her mother piddle over to peer up where they had stood as if they must have left a hole where she could see the sky. But the high roof of leaves stayed unbroken.

When he had the notion, Worth could be a handy man with

tools, and now the white chips spun from sunup to early forest dark. He wanted to finish this stint of a cabin and get at the more important chore of game. He hadn't even time to answer the questions of his favorite young one. Every so often during the day Sulie would come trotting over and stand by him until he stopped to wipe his forehead of sweat.

"Pappy!" she would begin.

"Wha-a?" he would encourage her in the patient tone that always came out of his growth of beard when he spoke to her. As she started to talk, he would nod understandingly and sympathetically and go on chopping, softly at first, then more strongly until the sound of the axe would gradually drown out the small earnest voice and off she would trot, halfways satisfied till the next time.

Oh, you would think Worth was the hardworking home body to see him. But once he winded a fox or the young ones came running in with news of a fresh bear track before Sayward could stop them, he would change right in front of your eyes. A sharp look would come in his eyes. He couldn't wait now till he got this out of his system. The axe handle slipped from his hand and the powder horn over his head, and likely they wouldn't see him again till the shadows were so mighty thick you couldn't tell if that thing coming through the big butts was a white man or an Indian. Most always he had on his back a skin or two wrapped around the choicest parts of the carcass.

The first time he had gone off without saying anything and left the cabin stand all day, Sayward expected her mother to sull and lay for him when he got back. But Jary took no more interest in the cabin than a squirrel hole in a tree. She went about like she didn't know it was standing there logged up no higher than Sulie's head with its top open to every gust of rain and wind and flying jaybird. This crib of saddled logs under these dark trees was no place she would ever live in. Daytimes she dallied around the cooking kettles and evenings she lay in their little half-faced leanto with the deep hollows of her eyes closed. She said she couldn't look at the young ones around the night fire. Here under the big butts they looked like little people. The black arches were mighty far overhead. Even when you threw bark on the fire, its light was swallowed up before it went a dozen poles down these dark forest aisles that ran on and on only God knew how many miles to the English Seas and the New Orleans river.

Now that the hunting was good, Worth ran balls at night

and wandered with his rifle all day. Pegged skins multiplied on the trees. The cabin had blown out of his mind light as a green gabby bird feather.

"You kin smell the fall," Sayward one day reminded her mother.

"I don't keep track of the days no more," Jary said.

"It's a gittin' late," Sayward went on. "Just goin' to the spring you can see a long ways under the trees."

"I hain't noticed," Jary complained. "My eyes kain't see so good in here."

"It'll give ice on the river one of these fine mornin's."

"Like as not," Jary sighed. "That's the way it runs."

Sayward went about her business. If her mother and father didn't care how soon the snow flew and them living in a half-faced leanto, it was nothing to her. The gums along the river flew their colored rags. Sassafras mittens hung a kind of red-yellow and the dogwoods flushed up like the wattles of wild turkey gobblers. Of a morning the pinch of frost nipped your legs, and acorns in the deer paths were mighty hard on bare feet. The woods air smelled fermented as cider. And the hill hooters of a night tried to raise the dead.

Not that the young ones minded it. They were drunk on fall. It was hardly daylight till they piled out of the leanto to hunt chestnuts and drag in shellbarks and look first at their snares for small game. Piles of walnut hulls rose by the big rock and their hands were stained darker than Shawanees. They hung to scarlet creepers and swung back and forward over logs that would have broken their backs had they ever let go. At deep dusk when they came in, they ate, yawned and lay down together in the shelter like a pile of wolf puppies for warmth till it was time to be up and rip and tear again.

When they wanted anything, they came to Sayward now rather than their mother. It took too long to get their meaning over to this slow woman sucked of her blood who lay abed or dallied around like a crone, though she was still in her thirties. No, they were too full of go for the likes of her.

It meant small shakes to them that the cabin wasn't done. They were tickled the leaves were coming down. They ran through them like it was the first snowfall, kicking them with their bare feet to stir up that tanyard smell. The birch and gum leaves were about the first to drop. The maples, ash and poplars shed not long after. You couldn't open your eyes without seeing the air full of leaves. They had no mind where they wanted to land. Some turned head over tincup till it made a body dizzy to watch. All night long you could hear them whisper when they lit. By morning the sleepers in the shelter were stitched with a hap of red, brown and gold.

Sulie spread her fingers like a fork and scratched herself a great pile to burrow in.

"I'm a white-footed mouse!" she yelled, sticking her head through. "And I'm not a comin' out till I come with young'uns a hangin' to my dugs."

"You're a young'un yourself still a hangin' to your mam's dugs!" Achsa mocked at her, jumping over and kicking at her pile of leaves.

"Don't you tech my house or I'll git a club and knock your noggin off!" Wyitt threatened.

Genny ran after Achsa and yanked her by the hair so she swore like a man.

"Kain't ketch a terrypin! Kain't ketch a terrypin!" she dared her and sailed off with Achsa hard after.

It was all over, Sayward knew, the morning it started to rain.

"Rain afore breakfast, quit afore noon," Genny said.

But Sayward reckoned they had a mortal late breakfast this morning. The cabin looked forlorn standing there roofless and only half raised in the rain and darkest day they had seen as yet in these parts. It put Sayward in mind of the deserted places Worth used to tell he saw in the Pennsylvania woods. Jary had always felt for those poor people, wondering had they died of a fever or was their hair lifted by the Mingos?

And yet, their own lonesome cabin Jary did not care a hoot about. No, she wouldn't even look at it. Not a word would she say to get Worth at roofing it. That night the rain kept on and the wind came up. Now the wind held its breath and now it tried to fetch down the trees. The logs in the half-raised cabin creaked and groaned. A cold, wet Sarge came in among the young ones deep as he could squirm to shut out the hullabaloo from his thin-skinned hound ears.

All night the wind rose. Now it came and now it went. This was a lull. You could hear the trees dripping. Then far off you could catch the next wave coming for you through the woods. You knew that all the squirrels in their nests were lying there listening and waiting for it like you. And when it came, you could feel the tall butts bending over you like fishpoles. Limbs cracked off like rifle shots. The wind, Sayward thought, dragged a long splint broom. First it passed over the tops of the trees, thrashing the branches. After while the splints reached down on the ground, rattling the leaves, twigs and sticks, and sweeping them in the leanto.

The wind and rain let up about dawn. None of the Lucketts had more than catnapped all night. Now they lay back in the quiet after the storm and slept.

Sayward dreamed she saw her mother standing outside.

"God help me!" Jary said.

When the girl opened her eyes, a bright light shone in her face. She sat up and saw her mother standing where she had seen her in her dream, her tousled hair down her rounded back. Then the girl saw that last night's storm had stripped the leaves from half the trees. Her mother looked like a half-blinded human that had lived all summer in a cave. She stood there peering up through the bare branches of an ash at sky so blue it hurt just to look at it.

"I never thought I'd live to see this day," she muttered to Sayward.

For the first time in days she had the girl comb out her matted hair, all the time warming herself in the sun, her wrinkled face held up to light and sky. Then she washed herself a little at the run. When Worth got up and fetched out his rifle from under the pressed leaves to see if it was dry, she was sitting on a wet log, and her mouth that could be so gentle was hard like a mussel shell.

"You started a cabin or hain't you, Worth?" she came out at him, her eyes cruel as death. "Or maybe you take us for woodchucks with a hole in the ground?"

It was good to hear the old Jary. Worth flushed up through his growth of beard. No more of the cabin was said between them. Worth ran a tallowed rag through his rifle and laid it carefully away. All day his axe hacked and slashed, hewed and chipped in the woods. It grew dark early this time of year. Sayward kept fires going for light. She and Achsa helped him lift the logs into place, locking saddle to notch and notch to saddle. After them came the rafters.

The days now were gray and cold. Sayward wedged in poles for chinking. The young ones carried white clay from the river bank for Genny to daub it. Jary helped. Worth was laying the rib poles now, turning the bows to the sky, for the weight of the roof would settle them straight. Soon as he got done at one end, the young ones scuttled up like piney squirrels, thatching it with shell bark that with the help of hides had to do till the black ash bark would run in the spring. If it turned out that they would stay, he would split out clapboards. Long top rib poles held the bark and hides down. They jutted out from the roof like steer horns, lashed to the under rib poles with leatherwood and hickory withes.

"You better move in the shanty tonight," Worth said late that afternoon.

All day a gray light like frost mist had hung and driven through the black butts and branchwork of the woods. Oh, this was winter now, anybody with half an eye could tell. As long as daylight lasted, the young ones fetched in fresh leaves from where the wind had raked them in windrows behind some bush or stump. Chips and log leavings they piled in the chimney corner. The chimney wasn't topped off yet with sticks and clay, but it drew fire. It still seemed the middle of the afternoon when dusk moved over the forest and settled down.

"It's snowin'," Achsa called out when she came back in that evening.

"Snowin'?" Jary quavered pleasantly.

Sayward watched her mother's eyes take a turn around the cabin. The firelight played sociable fingers on roof and rafters. The logs smelled clean, and the beds of new leaves made you sleepy. Everything was spick and fine as a newborn babe in a fresh log cradle. Piles of knobby hickory nuts and black and white walnuts lay hulled in a corner. Tomorrow or the next day Worth would take his old frow and split chinking boards for loft and shelves and puncheons for a table stand. Already he had an old windblown poplar log picked out.

The girl felt her mother's loving eyes rest on each one of them. All, except that little brother back in Pennsylvania, were here together. They had a roof over their heads and a bag of meal hanging from the rafters. A buckskin door weighted with a short green log shut out the dark and snow.

Her mother's eyes were mortal young and warm tonight in their deep sockets. So they must have looked, Sayward reckoned, when she had moved in their first cabin along the Juniata. Three of her young ones were to get born in the world there.

CHAPTER FOUR

❅   ❅   ❅

The Square Axe

O NCE THEY WERE IN THE CABIN, they had creature comforts
again. Worth set his gun up in a dark corner where he
wouldn't see it unless he had to and set to work splitting out three-
inch puncheons and hewing them smooth with the axe. With
these he made a table stand to eat off of, a bench to sit down on
and a door with hickory hinges to keep out forest beasts. The
bench wouldn't set even on the rolling dirt floor and he bedded it
in the tamped earth. But his stools were fine and steady any
place you put them, for they had only three legs.

Still Worth wouldn't say he had enough. No such thing. He'd
work till he was black in the face, splitting out clapboards and
laying them on the scalped joists for a loft. Before he was done,
they all had to climb the ladder and see how snug and warm a
place he'd made under the eaves where you could lay of a night
and listen to the rain on the roof over your head. Three of the
young ones fought to have their beds up there with the woods
mice racing over their legs in the dark and the chipmunks rolling
walnuts and hickory nuts over the loft floor soon as it began to
come daylight.

And still Worth wouldn't stop. Not till he had worked out his
mind. He had to make a last splurge. This would be a mortal
handy thing for a house, something you had to pay tax on if you
had one down in Pennsylvania. He steadied the logs with wedges,
marked them with a straight edge and chopped out a hole, dressing it smooth with axe and knife. Over the hole he plastered a
few cross sticks and fast to the sticks the marriage paper the
Conestoga dominie had given them. Worth had always plagued
Jary for lugging such a useless thing around with her. But now
that he greased it with bear's oil, he reckoned it might be of some
account. It let the sun through like glass. Oh, then it was a sight to
see in that dark cabin, a window light blazing up like it was a fire
and making all the cubbyholes and corners plain as outside till

you could see the marks the barkworms left on the logs.

Even Jary said it was a tolerable place to live. They had to blister their feet a long ways to get here, but now they were holed up snug and cozy as a bear in his hollow tree. Let the winter cut up his didoes. Let the king's men come down from the English Lakes if they had a mind to. They'd have a hard time finding the Lucketts in this shut-in place. The woods were wide and deep. The cabin stood hid in the trees like a piggin in a haystack.

But after some Indian hunters had foxed them out, Jary complained, what was the use of putting up a cabin fine as a fiddle if you let such kind make it a public house?

Down in Pennsylvania the whites were thick as dogberries and the few Indians left knew their place. Away back here the whites were scarce as birds' teeth and the Indians plenty as dogberries. Their sharp eyes picked up Worth's spent bullet patches and tracked him to his cabin where they drifted in with no more knocking than leaves in October. Their fusils they set in the chimney corner for the priming to dry and themselves on the floor under the bag of Indian meal swinging from a joist.

"Whoo-stink!" little Sulie cried, holding her nose with her fingers.

Worth gave her a clip over the head and told Sayward to make them some johnnycake. The warm smell of baking meal in the cabin soon thawed out their tongues. They swapped grave talk with Worth and felt polite hands over the window and the skins he showed them, blowing the fur expertly apart at the places it was thickest and finest.

But Jary eyed the emptying grainbag with ropy mouth and angry, rebellious eyes. Never had she been the one to take up with the red people. No, Worth was as much Indian as anybody she wanted to know. All the Delawares, Shawanees, Nanticos, Kanawas, and the nations of the Mingos she ever saw were different from her people as a night dog from a hound. Oh, whites weren't sinless, especially in the woods. Some went around bad as Indians holding a grudge. But they couldn't hold a candle to their red brothers when it came to paying it. If Indians couldn't get back at the white persons that harmed them, they'd take it out on some handy white women or poor young ones they happened to meet up with that had nothing to do with it. They'd hack off their scalps likely with some brains hanging to them and set their pitiful hair up on a pole and prance around poking firebrands at it and bragging and carrying on like they had licked General Wayne and his whole army.

No, Jary had little love for Indians in general and these digging in her meal bag in particular. If the Shawanees raised corn like Worth said, why didn't they stay at home and eat their own? It rankled her to have to sit by helpless and see them coming this way as long as her meal lasted and eating what was meant for her young ones. And when Worth told Sayward to shake the bag for the last dust of meal to feed some that had been feasting on her plenty before, Jary flared up. She took that meal bag and sat on it, her mouth tight. Her eyes dared them all to come and get it, and Worth too, if he reckoned he could.

Those red hunters from Shawaneetown didn't stay long after that.

"There you go, a makin' bad friends," Worth told her when they had left. "They feed me when I go to their place."

"You got no business a goin' to their place," Jary's eyes flashed at him. "You got a family to come on home to."

"They mought not be good enough for you," Worth said. "But they are for me."

The only sign that Jary heard him was her sewed-up mouth. He began to get mad as she.

"If the Injun has any ornery tricks, who do you expect he learned them from but the whites?"

That was too much for Jary.

"Bosh and moonshine!" she flared out at him. "Injuns was a scalpin' and massacreein' and torturin' and burnin' up their own brothers long before they ever heerd of a white person. They brag their own selves how they killed off all the Injuns that used to live around here. Did you ever hear of an Injun payin' even a fi'penny bit for land like the whites?"

Worth would say nothing more. There was no use trying to get the best of Jary. You might as well try to head off a gadd or talk back to a whaup. His eyes retreated ominously into his beard till you couldn't see much more than the whites. In the morning he took his gun and Sarge and did not come back that night. Next day it started a cold rain.

On toward dusk they thought they heard Worth coming and Sulie ran to open the door. A Delaware stood there with the firelight licking on his wet face and on the silver wheels in his ears that were stretched down halfway to his shoulders. He was ugly as sin, bedraggled in his matchcoat as a wet turkey hen, but in he tramped big as some redcoat major. The water ran off him in little streams and when he got to the fire, he shook himself like a dog. The drops rained all over. He sat himself down by the warm hearth to dry. You might have reckoned this was his own cabin, and his squaw and young ones could be mortal glad to see him home again.

Jary had stared after him with a tight-mouthed, angry look. Now she turned to Sayward.

"If I had my way," her eyes said, "I'd a seed him in the river first. But what's a body to do—turn him out in the rain?"

Sayward was sitting by the table when he came. Now she went on about her business, working a doeskin with her hands. They had taken the hair off with lye from fire ashes and tanned it with oak bark liquor in a log trough. Once the hide was worked soft, Jary would lay it on the table and cut it out with the cabin knife, and Genny's nimble fingers would sew up a shirt for Wyitt. He had some squirrel ready that he wanted it trimmed with. Every morning he made the rounds of his log and sapling snares, hoping for a mink or otter skin Worth could trade for buttons when he went to some post. Oh, with black fur trimmings and horn or pewter buttons, Wyitt was going to be a dandy and no mistake.

When their caller got too hot in front, he turned his side to the fire and Sayward had a good look at him. She had never seen this one before. His nose was big as a red Conestoga potato. It even had eyes like a potato. Put that nose in a dark place like a cellar, and it looked like it would grow white sprouts. But nobody could sit bigger at the hearth.

Sayward had nothing for the way squaws gave in to the men, waiting on them hand and foot, giving them the notion they were lords of creation. About all these men would turn a finger to was war and hunt. Let them kill themselves a fat deer, would they fetch it in? Not them. They'd hang it up on the nearest tree where the wolves couldn't get it and march back to camp with nothing but their fusils over their shoulders. No, their squaws could come out and skin it and fetch it in.

For all she knew, this one here had plenty meat hanging out in the woods right now. It looked like it, for mighty little of theirs did he eat that evening, though she had roasted it to a turn. Worth hadn't come home and he wasn't likely to any more to-night, for when Sayward went out, the rain on the door log had turned to ice. It was a black world but tomorrow, she reckoned, would be a white one. And then they would have a new job getting rid of their company, for if there was one thing an Indian hated worse than getting out in the rain, it was getting out in the snow.

"You kin sleep up in the loft tonight," Sayward told Genny. "I'll lay with Mam."

Genny had plenty to say to that. She wouldn't have a savage who never washed from one summer to the next sleeping on her and Sayward's bed. But Sayward shooed her up the ladder and that was an end to it. When the Delaware was out, she pushed the axe under the leaves where she and Jary would lie. She piled logs on the fire to give light till morning. Then when he came in she barred the door and lay down beside her mother in her short-gown. If this fellow had any red cronies hanging around outside, he would have to get up to let them in.

Overhead in the loft she could hear the young ones restless and wakeful. But Jary could doze off the minute her head touched the bed leaves. She lay there on her back with her mouth open. Little quiet snoring served to quiet those in the loft. Little by little their whisperings and turnings played out. After while the clapboards overhead lay silent for all the firelight that ran back and forward across them.

Now, Sayward told herself, there were only two left awake in the cabin. Oh, that red body on the hearth could lie there still as it pleased him. He could suck his breath in and out like he was dead to the world. But he couldn't pull wool over her eyes. She was shy of believing that a woods Indian would drop off to sleep like a baby in a white man's house.

The wind was coming up, driving sleet and hard snow like fine bullets against the cabin, hunting for holes, but it couldn't get in. Sayward lay there thinking of all the folks she had heard about who had taken in strangers on some cold or rainy night when they shouldn't. From the loft she could hear the young ones' soft breathing. In her mind she could see them lying close together with their arms around each other. Achsa or Genny would be on the outside. That one would be the first a tomahawk would reach from the ladder.

Once or twice she caught herself breathing heavy and mighty near asleep. After a long while a shadow told her that their company was moving. She lay still as a log, save for her breath, watching through her merely shut lashes. He was raising up like a possum that had played dead. Now he looked over at the bed with sharp black eyes. He took his knife out of his belt and

Sayward's hand found the axe helve under the leaves, sweating around it.

When she was a little tyke, Sayward recollected, Jary would tell her not to fret if an Indian came around the cabin. No, she could shut her eyes and go to sleep. Like as not the Black Hunter of the Juniata was outside in the bushes, watching over them like he watched over all mothers and young ones, and his ball never missed. But across the Ohio it had no Black Hunter. She would have to do this her own self. Should he climb for the young ones first, never would he know what struck him. But if he came first for her and Jary's bed, then she would rise up and cleave him straight between the eyes like the woman back on Dunkard's Creek in Pennsylvania. Oh, she wasn't as big as Experience Bogarth who had hacked out the brains of one red devil and the insides of another and cleaved the head of the third who tried to push himself in the door when she would shut it. But if a lone woman could do that much, she could drive her axe in one shaved head so it would take Worth to pull it out when he came home.

She flexed her muscles ready to raise up and that's the last she had to till morning. Now who would have thought this Delaware didn't like her roast? That big heavy body had pulled a hunk of meat black with dried blood from his hunting shirt and was cutting it in two on the hearth. Now he sat there big as you please roasting a piece to suit himself on a long sharp stick of kindling from the chimney corner. Oh, you could see he could hardly wait to gobble it down. He ate with the blood running down his chin, smacking his lips and licking his fingers. Then he lay down belching like one who had to wait a long time for a supper he liked, but now he was well fed and these white squaws with their burned cooking weren't any wiser.

Sayward wouldn't have felt surprised to find the door open and him gone next morning, but the snow was still coming down and that held him. Worth tracked in soon after with two deerhides and a fine black fisher fox. He scowled a little to see the Indian sitting there on the floor. They talked a while in Delaware till Jary ran out of firewood.

"I tole you many a time," Worth growled, "not to leave your axe out under the snow."

Sayward took it from the bed of leaves while her father eyed her close.

"You sleep here with Jary last night?"

She nodded. The Delaware was watching too. His sharp

black eyes ran from face to face for what he could read. He picked up the axe and ran his finger over the bit and you could see he was putting two and two together. Oh, you could see this was a joke to him, a young squaw taking an axe to bed against a stout, hearty hunter like he was. He laughed silently, his nose and belly both shaking like bone jelly. He gave her back the axe and felt the girl's arm and thigh.

"He don't know no better," Worth said.

The Delaware was like a big child now. He had to go over this joke till it was stale. But Worth didn't laugh.

"I don't want you takin' no more Injuns in when I'm off," he said darkly after the company was gone.

"I thought you liked Injuns?" Jary's mouth was grim.

"I kin git along with them, but you mought not," Worth said.

CHAPTER FIVE

❀   ❀   ❀

Bread

I F I HAD BREAD," Jary complained, "then I believe I could eat."

The young ones stared at her, avoiding each other's eyes. They had known for a long time that their mother was tottery, with one foot in the grave. What they didn't know was that her sense was failing. Never had she talked queer before. It was a sign her other foot was shuffling mighty close to the bury hole.

"Look, Saird, she got bread now and ain't teched it yit," Wyitt said, pointing to what Jary held in her hand.

Even Sayward had to think a minute what her mother meant. Then she recollected that it started back in Pennsylvania one of the times the meal bag had been empty. The young ones

were tired of meat. They had cried for a change. They wanted
johnnycake and mush. Now Indian meal was something unhandy
to get hold of in the woods, Jary told them, but if they were tired
of meat, they could eat bread for a while. Bread was better than
johnnycake or mush, everybody knew.

That opened the young ones' eyes. So they had bread! Jary
called on Worth to swear to it and he nodded his head shortly.
Now bread, she told them, was venison, turkey and such. Only the
dark flesh of bear, coon and such was meat. Bread was lighter and
went in the blood easier than meat. And from now on she wanted
to hear them call things by their right names, bread bread and
meat meat. Even Worth had to say bread for venison, though for
a while the word stuck in his throat. And now the young ones had
grown so used to seeing bread on their mother's table, they
thought her weak in the head to be calling for bread and standing
there with an untouched turkey wing in her hand.

What the young ones didn't know, Sayward told herself.
wouldn't hurt them. But this was something too good for Genny
to pass by. Sayward could hear her now up in the limbs of the
hung elm with the younger ones still as possums around her.
Genny had a knowing mind. And now she was telling them the
bread their mother hankered for wasn't turkey or venison. No,
turkey and venison weren't bread at all. Their mother had made
that up. Bread was something settlement people had on their
tables. It was a little like johnycake, only bigger and better. She
and Sayward had tasted it when they were little tykes on a Conestoga visit. It made her mouth water now just to mind it.

All the others' mouths were watering, too. They spat to the
ground lushly with Genny.

"Ginny, go on!" they told her, but all Genny could tell them
was that once on a time a chit of a girl had sat up to a shaved-
board table. She was pretty as a settlement lady tricked out in her
white church gown and neats leather shoes made over a cobbler's
last. And in her hands was a big piece of bread white as gray
moose milk—

Sayward moved away. You wouldn't reckon, she told herself,
that that girl pretty as a settlement lady had been their mother.
Not to look at her now, puttering around this cabin in her old
walnut shortgown that hadn't been washed since Genny's fingers
had taken it in again. And still it liked to fall off Jary's bones. Oh,
her mother's days were numbered. The slow fever burned off
mortal flesh like a fire cooked meat off a bone. All day it never let

you rest. Jary had four stout girls to do all the cabin chores and yet her bare feet kept scraping over the earthen floor that had been damped and tamped and topped with white clay to match the daubing on the chinking. Talking did no good. It went in Jary's one ear and out the other. Her hair kept sliding down the side or back of her head, coming apart like a hanging bird's nest in December. It made her look like she was in her second childhood and her mother only thirty-six or seven.

"I'd thin it out, Mam," Sayward told her. "It's a mortal weight to lug around. Hair kin suck your strength like a blood sucker."

But Jary Luckett wouldn't part with any of her hair. Not her. Once her hams had been plump as Achsa's and her skin white as Genny's, and Sayward's breasts were no firmer than her's once were. All she had left that hadn't shriveled up was her hair. When one of the girls tended it of a morning, it swept down from the bench over the earthen floor, heavy as China silk before it went to the loom. You couldn't find a gray thread. No, she still had her hair and by Jeems' cousin, she meant to keep it.

"They kain't be much wrong with me or it'd a fell out," Jary told them, gaunt and jandered. "If I just had some wheat bread, I know I'd pick up."

Sayward had been shaving Worth to go to the Shawanee-town trading post. He sat on a stool with his head thrown back against the table, the sides of his face yellow with soft soap made from game fat and white hickory ashes. Not a word did Worth say, but when Jary cast up twice that they had no bread, Sayward could feel his face settle into sharp grooves as if the lye had stung him. When he came in from renching off the soap at the run, his naked cheeks were flat as a man's who has had enough of a woman's complaining for a while and is glad to be off to the woods.

The young ones watched him pull his spring furs from trees and stretchers and work them in a pack with his knee. Jary came shuffling out.

"I wa'n't a sayin' that at you, Worth," she said apologetically. "You got your faults but nobody can make you out a poor provider. Few has better meat than us. Most times we have venison a hangin' up. Then you give us special treats like gadd or duck. But a body that's losin' flesh is like one that's a luggin a young'un. It hankers for queer victuals."

Worth strapped up his pack with whang leather thongs.

"I mought be off five or six nights," he told Sayward.

It took no more than a long day, the girl knew, to tramp to Shawaneetown where Hough had a log house, a squaw wife and goods for the Shawanee and Delaware trade. Where Worth aimed to go with his pack of skins that would keep him five or six nights she couldn't make out, unless it might be Bannock's Mill on the Ohio. It came to her the Shawanees once said it took three days to go and three to come.

The same notion must have crossed Genny's mind, for she bent down and whispered to the younger ones who licked their chops and pushed up around their father, their eyes bright on him as young coons', their lips shut tight so he wouldn't see their mouths water.

"Well, what do you want?" Worth demanded of them.

They nudged little Sulie, for she was his favorite.

"We don't want nothin', Pap," she said, pleased as all get out, but before opening her lips she had to swallow a mouthful of spit.

"Git off now before I take a gad to you!" he stormed at them. They scattered like a covey of Conestoga field quail, but not very far. Worth came in the cabin and fooled around like there was something he wanted to do or say before he went. Seemed like he couldn't fetch it out, for he looked beat as he went outside where the hound leaped up and tongued at the sight of powder-horn and rifle.

"You git back and stay back!" he ordered harshly.

Young ones, older ones and sad-eyed hound stood together on the log step or by it and watched him go down the path. After a little the spice bushes cut off his legs, and he seemed to be just head and shoulders swimming through the brush. Slowly the great butts of the woods swallowed him up. But for a long while Wyitt held on to the loose neck of the hound so he wouldn't go after.

"Now nary me nor Mam nor any of you'uns knows where he's a goin'," Sayward told her sisters and brother. "Maybe he don't know right hisself yit."

But that evening when they were all in bed, she thought she could see her father lying out in the forest with no more than the shelving back of a rotten log to keep him warm and the pack of furs under his head for a pillow. And next morning when gray showed through the oiled paper window light, she had the notion he was up this long time, hunched forward on the trace, making tracks for whatever place he was going. A night or two afterwards she dreamt she saw him sleeping under some strange roof, snug as a mouse in a mill, while a soft dust powdered his buckskins like fine, dry snow.

Till it was over, she wished he had gone only to Shawanee-town. The third evening Jary coughed like it was spittle in her windpipe, and when she fetched it out, it was heart's blood. Sayward reckoned it would have filled a wooden cup but she had no chance to measure. Her mother went to the door and spat it outside and next morning it looked as if a hunter had cut the throat of a buck there. When the others got up, Jary said she expected she'd lie abed that day. She made as though nothing had happened, but the face on the pallet was white and waxy as the corpse plants that come up under the beech trees. You could tell by looking at her that, had she tried to stand on her feet today, her legs would have buckled under her like wild cherry whips.

Sayward didn't look for her father till the sixth day. She was down in the cabin alone with Jary tonight, for Genny couldn't stand the sight of blood and Sayward had sent her up in the loft. The fifth night she heard Sarge get up. His nails rattled across the hard dirt floor to the door where he growled. Settlement folks claimed the night air was poison and night swamp air gave you the shakes, but Sayward had left the puncheon door open a crack in the hope that Jary could catch her breath. The girl reckoned some beast was around, drawn by the firelight shining out in the forest, for it couldn't be Worth. A man would have to own lynx eyes to hold to the trace through the pitch-black woods night. Every step it had branches lying in wait to gouge the eyes out.

Then Sarge pushed the door open with his nose, wormed out and bawled like a bell. Sayward lighted a pine splint from the fire and went to the step. Holding the fire above her head, she waited. Up the path something formed itself slowly out of the gloom, and when it floated closer, it was the face of her father.

"You all right?" he put to her, not meaning her at all.

"Oh, we're just a middlin' fair," she said in a low tone.

Holding the light well off so Worth wouldn't see too much at once, she moved ahead to the bed and tucked the cover high over Jary's neck. Her father could run his knife into any forest beast and watch the red sap run. His hunting shirt was black from the veins of quartered deer he had fetched home on his back. But he wouldn't take it easy to see the dark blots on Jary's bed gown from what had spilled up out the past days before one of them could catch it.

Worth took the candle wood out of her hand and held it over the bed. Always, Sayward reflected, her mother seemed better after she bled. Tonight her face was gentle and the skin fair. Oh, an old body couldn't go back to the cradle again. And yet tonight she had something fresh and mortal sweet about her as a young girl.

Many a time had she looked like this when Sayward was just a little tyke. She would sit genteel as a settlement lady on her homemade rocker, listening to Worth, her face slanted down a little, her eyes on the doorsill and a faint smile on her lips. She was that way now, propped up on her pallet. You wouldn't hardly expect that for two days and nights she had to be waited on hand and foot.

Worth threw the candle wood with a shower of sparks in the fire. His pack of furs was gone but he let to the floor a tightly-woven grain bag that bulged with a soft fat look. From out of his hunting frock he took a bladder that had a thong around its neck.

"The miller woman sent Jary some risin'," he said to Sayward. "Next time, you kin raise with sour dough. Now you better git some on the fire— if you know how." A rattle of chinking boards made him glance up at the hungry faces by the loft hole. "You young'uns git back to bed," he told them shortly.

Sayward lifted the bag up to the table. It felt mighty heavy. Here was not just a cupful for her mother to taste but plenty for all. It would last weeks if the Shawanees didn't come around smelling it out. She spilled the gray white meal soundlessly in the little kettle, hoarding every pinch, feeling of it between her fingers. Not even the fur on the belly of a mink or beaver was soft and velvety as this. They must have run it through a deerskin sifter. Never had she baked wheat bread before but she well knew how, for the day after her father went she had wormed out of Jary the way it was done, just in case he came home with meal. Now the girl's firm hands mixed the flour and some water together, working in a little precious salt and maple sugar with the miller woman's yeasty stuff. By the time she set it by the fire to rise, her father had taken off his buckskin leggins that were wet from the fording of streams and had lain across her and Genny's bed, some of the quilt over his bare legs, dead as a log from his long tramp.

Twice during the night the girl lifted Jary to ease her sluggish coughing, but Worth did not wake up. Sayward thought her mother felt cooler, as if the fever she had not been free of since the girl could remember had let up. A while before daylight she expected the dough had risen enough. Anyhow, it would have to do. She worked it into small loaves to bake the quicker and set them deep in the hearth, covering them on top and sides with hot ashes and sitting by to keep a slow fire.

It was time for daylight when she roused herself from a half doze. A pleasing smell filled the cabin like a cloud. She scraped the ashes aside. Her small loaves lay round and brown under their grime. She brushed them with a turkey feather and wiped them clean with a greasy rag. When she looked up, her father was standing there clad only in his deerskin hunting frock that came halfway to his knees. He was sniffing hungrily.

"You better give her a piece of the crust first," he said, and Sayward saw it fall away white and beautiful under the whetted edge of his hunting knife.

Up on the loft the young ones had crawled to the hole and were watching greedily.

"It's bread!" Worth said, holding the crust under Jary's nose to smell.

Her lips held that faint smile as if he had said, "Here I got two fisher fox skins for you." Jary had always wanted a cape of those mahogany black skins. Never could you get anything finer to prank yourself out in. If a man wanted favor in a girl's eyes, that's what he would try to get for her. But one prime fisher skin was worth seven buckskins and a cape of skins would be worth a whole year's kill of deer.

"Jary!" Worth said louder. "You said you hankered after wheat bread. Here 'tis."

She nodded faintly but made no move to take it. He broke off a piece and put it between her lips.

"Chew it. Swaller it down," he coaxed at her, making his own jaws and throat move. He might have been showing how to a babe that had known naught but its mother's milk.

Her mouth smiled a little now as if she understood. Faintly she went through the motions, pressing with her lips and tongue and gulping, but it would not go down. Under her chest bone she started to cough and while they looked, the white of the bread stained a bright red in her mouth like somebody had dipped it in wine.

Worth's long buckskin-clad arms helped Sayward raise her to let the blood run where it would not choke her again. Under the scraggle of fresh beard his face was bleak as an old wagoners' trace when black frost has hardened the ruts and hoof marks. The grooves across his cheeks had deepened and his eyes drawn nearly shut as if here was something they did not want to see. Her father, Sayward thought, could face a bear, even an old she-bear with cubs. He could tramp the woods three days going and three coming to give his woman a taste of wheat bread. But this was something it took a woman to stand.

When they let her back to the bed, Jary was light as a pack of dried and brittle fox skins. Through the folds of homespun Sayward thought she could feel a coldness like stone. After this last bleeding her mother looked different. Her eyes stared at Worth like he was a stranger in her cabin and she had never shared her bed with him or given him four hearty girls and a lusty boy, not counting the babe back in Pennsylvania.

He turned and went to the open door and looked out at the black forest where gray daylight was just beginning to come. No use turning your back on this, Sayward wanted to tell him. Whether you looked or no, death would come and life would go. Up in the loft all signs of the young ones had vanished. Sayward reckoned they were lying face down on their beds.

A whole cabin couldn't go to pieces this way, she told herself. No, if her mother couldn't take hold of things now and her father wouldn't, some person had to. Her voice came out hard to hide her feelings.

"Don't you want to come down and see your mam die, Ginny?" she called up to the loft.

Like a slow wraith with her white legs and whiter face, Genny moved down the ladder. Behind her pushed Achsa, dark and mask-faced as a young squaw in coarse black pigtails and dove-gray bedgown. Last and slowest, holding on to each other when they could as if it would help, came the two youngest, Wyitt who fumbled and Sulie who held back now like the baby of the family she was.

She was the only one her mother recognized. A tender look came in the worn out face.

"Little Ursula," her lips spelled out. "Don't be afeard. I ain't a goin' to hurt you now."

Their father did not turn from the door. The dying fire flick-ered on the clumps of herbs Jary's hands had gathered and hung to the joists with leatherwood withes for string. There were boneset for fever and dittany for supper tea and pennyroyal to purify the blood. They were all dried up and withered now. Never would they stand and wave their leaves in the wind again. For a little while they had bloomed. They had seen a mite of this world. Then their day was done.

If Death was heading for this cabin, Sayward asked herself, where was Death now? Could they see or hear it when it came? Some claimed the wolves and corbies knew death. Once, Sayward recollected, they had sat in this cabin cracking walnuts and hickory nuts while the night dogs howled. All evening they had been bad. Jary had raised her head. Her mouth was ropy and her eyes like when one of them had done wrong.

"Must be some Injun a dyin' in the woods," she had said. "Them varmints kin smell death furder than a she-creater in heat."

Now while they waited, Sarge began to growl deep in his old throat. He got to his feet and stood in the middle of the floor. He looked at nothing but the hair kept raising on the back of his neck. Sayward would give no sign that she saw or heard, but she felt the sweat chill on her body like she stood in a winter wind.

CHAPTER SIX

❀ ❀ ❀

Riddledy Me

As I was walking down the lane
Out of the dead the living came.
Four there were and five to be
Now tell me this riddle or set me free.
— OLD RIDDLE

DAYLIGHT WAS RUNNING through the trees when Sayward took Jary's bedgown and shortgown out to wash. You hadn't dare wait too long, she told herself, to do something for a body you loved. Here, Worth had tramped that long ways after a bag of meal for Jary, and it turned out that all he could have fetched her was a length of domestic for a lonesome winding sheet. Oh, they could make out without it, she expected, ripping these and stitching them together in one piece. But it would not be pleasing as bought goods. She beat the gowns with a paddle and scrubbed them with soap and sand. Never would her mother rest easy in her bury hole with her bedgown fit to turn the stomach from lying abed these days.

When she came back from the run, Wyitt and Sulie were off somewheres. Only Genny and Achsa stayed in the cabin, going about their chores with cruel young faces. The bed was covered over. What lay there might have been no more than a long hump under the quilt. But you couldn't mistake the taint that hung in the cabin and outside, too, if you had a nose sharp as a beast to tell it. Jary used to tell how back in Pennsylvania they would lay out the dead in a room without a fire and with the window open to keep that taint from getting any worse till men could ride far as they could with news of the burying. One time Jary was in such a house when they heard a fearsome screech at night in the room where nobody but the dead was. The men pushed in with candles and found that snow had drifted in over the box set on saw horses under the window and it showed tracks where a bobcat had come in and tramped over the corpse.

She shook out the two wrung knots and hung the washed gowns by the fire. They would have to drip and dry before you could rip them. A living person might put on either one and its body would warm and dry it by its own self, but never would Jary as much as warm her bed again. The girl dipped hot water from the big kettle in the little trough Worth had hollowed out from a poplar log. Then telling Achsa and Genny they could help, she hardened her heart and laid back the cover.

Genny and Achsa came slow enough. This was no easy stint for young girls to lay out their mother's body for the bury hole. But whether you liked it or not, Death was something you had to go through life with. Plenty times you would meet up with it if you lived long enough, and you might as well get used to it as you could. Not often did Achsa open her mouth but today she talked to hide her feelings. She had run the black haw comb through her mother's matted hair and it reared up like Jary was still alive. Did they mind, she said in her low, heavy, boy's voice, that Conestoga girl they heard of, who before she died had her hair sheared close against the fever, and when they took her up to move her grave, her hair was grown long and shaggy again as a winter wolf's?

Sayward talked, too, but mostly under her breath to guard her face from showing to her sisters the pity she felt. It was no use sopping her soapy rag so easy, she told herself harshly. This wasn't little Sulie she was washing. There would be no complaining, "Not so all-fired hard!" from the body she had to wash all over today.

Out in the woods they could hear Worth's homemade mallet whamming the rusty iron head of his frow. He was splitting out chinking boards for a box. That was likely where Wyitt and Sulie were, watching him make this thing they hadn't seen before. Down in the settlements men yoked boards together with pegs the blacksmiths hammered out of iron. But Worth needed only to whittle out oval wooden pins and drive them with the grain in round augur holes, where they would hold a box together so long as the wood lasted.

When noon came, the young ones took a long time coming in, for there was Jary's bread staring them in the face. The way a thing turned out, Sayward thought, was seldom the way you reckoned. Here, less than a week back the young ones' mouths watered for wheat bread. They couldn't sleep for fear Worth wouldn't fetch meal for it. And now that it was on the table in front of them, they could hardly swallow it down. Mighty soon Worth went back to his mauling and Genny to the pillow she was sewing out of fine calico leavings. She would stuff it with feathers so her mother's head need rest against no hard and splintery chinking boards.

It was dark till Worth got his box and lid boards fixed to suit. They had to dig the hole by shellbark light. It was dug more with the axe than with the shovel Worth had hacked and whittled out of a piece of dead oak. The black ground was all roots. As far as their hands went down, the roots lay atop each other, this way and that, thick and thin, like a great den of snakes froze up for the winter and not knowing it was long spring. Sayward hated having to put her mother in a place like this. Those greedy, flesh-minded roots would slink around that box trying to get in. But what she minded most was Worth pounding the wooden pins through the clapboards on the box after her mother lay inside. He squatted there swinging his battered mallet, and it seemed with every smack he was hitting at Jary. Oh, he never meant it that way. He had worked all day making as good a box for Jary as he knew how. Some of the chinking boards stuck out a little from the others like rib poles over the cabin. But down in the ground it would lay plumb and true. It beat forty ways the split hollow logs some woodsies buried their women and young ones in back from the Juniata.

"It's good as a settlement box, Pap," she told him. "Mam would be proud could she see it."

When he was done they all lent a hand carrying it over to the white oak. Even little Sulie and Wyitt helped, for this was the last thing they could do for their mam. They let it down in the ground with Jary's feet toward Pennsylvania. Worth had dug the hole east and west like settlement graves were so the sun would shine in the faces of the dead when they sat up on resurrection morn.

Worth didn't sleep in his and Jary's bed that night. Likely he was cold, for he took a blanket to break the hardness of the floor and lay by the fire though it was warm enough for whippoorwills to call. One came so close they could hear it suck the air back in its windpipe. Tonight it kept saying, "Pray for Jary! Pray for Jary! Pray for Jary!" Next morning Worth looked as if he hadn't slept much. After breakfast he took down his rifle.

"You be all right here for a spell?" he said.

"I kain't see why not," Sayward told him. "We always have been."

She knew well enough he was running off. God Almighty had made a man free that way. When things got out of kilter at home, he could take his gun and go to the woods. Maybe Worth would hunt today and maybe he would make his way to Hough's post where it had a man or two like himself to play with the Deil's cards. Should he meet some Shawanee or Delaware hunters on the way, they would swap tobacco and hunting tales all day.

But a woman had to stay home and mind the big kettle and the little kettle. It wasn't likely she'd get away far as a whoop and a holler till the littlest one, was he son or brother, got big enough to take off by himself. And by that time she'd have forgot all about that mess of troubles and have plenty new ones.

"But it's no use a cryin' you ain't a man," Sayward told herself calmly. "God Almighty done it this way and you kain't change it."

She set to work to keep her mind off what it shouldn't fret over. She washed Jary's quilt and yarn blanket till her fingers got water parched. It was mighty hard to get that smell of Death out. It still hung in the cabin though she cleaned what she could. Her mother's old broom was worn till it wasn't more than a club, and she cut a green hickory stick, her knife splitting a splint at one end. This she turned back and split another, and another. When she was done and the handle whittled down, she had a fine, new broom. Tommorrow or next day she would have to make a little one just like it for Sulie.

The young ones did their own forgetting. They had been shut up with sickness and death so long. Now nothing was left of that save a grave, and that they could jump over. Oh, today they would make up for lost time. Back by the old gats each had his own sapling that nobody dared touch but he. They all climbed up at the same time like treed coons, swinging first one side then the other till some would bump and screech. In the afternoon they fixed houses with sticks and made out they were great folks dressing and undressing inside, pinning together with locust thorns the big sapling leaves of their fine, new green gowns and hunting frocks. You could hear them quarreling a long ways off who was pranked out the seemliest or if this small stone was a bed or a whortleberry biscuit.

Oh, those young ones had as much go as ever they had. But it got worked out in time. For a spell they would rip and tear through the brush, then it would peter out. After while, if Sayward took a kettle out for water, she would see them wandering up and down the run like they might be looking for someone. Sooner or later when she was back in the cabin she could hear them out in front. It was plain they hated to come in, for they would first hang around a long time. Mostly Genny would take the lead. You couldn't tell anything from her or Achsa. And Wyitt wouldn't look to the right or left to show what was on his mind. But little Sulie would give it away. Never came she in that door any more without looking hasty from the bed where her mam had died. She would scruch down her shoulders till she passed and then push a stool around so she needn't look at that bed quilt with the rising sun on it.

"What you a doin', Sairdy?" she would fetch out and sit there watching her biggest sister solemn as a hoppy toad.

No, you couldn't tell those young ones minded a lick when their mam died. But they could feel that something wasn't right around here now. It hadn't so many of them against the woods any more. Never of late had Jary been the lively one and yet it wasn't so bright around this cabin like it was once on a time. Worth must have felt it, too. He stayed off for longer stretches. Sayward guessed he knew plenty Indian men with sisters whose black eyes would glitter up at this chance to comfort him, for such looked up to a white man.

He was gone a long while this time. The young ones had looked for him back these two days. Tonight they said they would stay up and Holler Fortunes till he came.

"This is how you do—" Wyitt began to Genny who had sang out she was the first.

"Are you a doin' this or me?" Genny settled him.

She went outside, but no further from the door than she had to, for the night was black as thunder.

"Go on, Ginny!" little Sulie prodded her, she being the next.

"Hesh up!" Achsa told her.

Genny stood there, a slight, hopeful body in the shaft of firelight from the cabin. After while her voice sang out to the dark silent woods lying all around.

> If I am to die a maid,
> Let me hear my grave box made.
> If I am to wed and sing,
> Let me hear a little bird sing.

When she got done they all waited with big ears. Even Sayward came to the door. The last few nights the whippoorwills had been loud enough to wake the Seven Sleepers around the cabin. This night for some reason had no more whippoorwills than the day. You could hear nothing but the river over yonder talking to the woods. After while an air stirred from somewhere clacking together the leaves a little and fetching with it a faraway sound like Worth made when he fixed up Jary's box. Four or five fearsome strokes came slow and clear. Then you could hear only the river again.

Genny's face was like tallow when she turned back in the cabin. The others followed quick, for none of them reckoned they wanted to holler for their fortune right now.

"It was just an old woodpecker, Ginny," Sulie comforted her." "Wa'n't it, Sairdy?"

"If a woodpecker ever pecks in the night time, I never heerd him," Sayward said grimly. "But whatever mortal thing it was, I wouldn't think no more about it."

"It sounded like an axe to me," Wyitt said.

They stood mighty still and sober at that. It had no axe

nearer than Hough's post, they all knew, and that was a good day's tramp. Oh, there was no ripping and tearing around now. They stared at each other, feeling for Genny. Something was hanging over their sister's head. Any day or night it might come on her, the gripes, the cold plague, the bloody flux or only God knew what. She was the skinniest of the family anyway. Never would she eat enough to keep a lizard alive.

Genny looked behind the door where at dark Sayward always fetched in the axe. There it stood, its helve smooth and dark from handsweat.

"If that whacking was a axe," she marked her words, "it was a makin' my box."

"Maybe then you won't go racin' like a whitehead through the woods ready to tromp on a copper snake any minute," Sayward told her calmly. After a while she added, "It mought a been a Injun down the river. He could be a cuttin' off shellbark to mend his canoe."

A little color fell back in Genny's face, for this was the time of year when bark would run. But Sayward in her heart knew the sound too heavy for a tomahawk. She got them all in bed soon after and lay down herself with her shortgown on.

When she woke up it was getting daylight and Genny was shaking her.

"Kin you hear it?" she whispered.

Sayward lifted her head. Through a crack in the chinking she could make out mighty far off a faint hacking. The sound died out during the middle of the day but came again faintly at nightfall. Early next morning it was loudest of all and Genny looked like it was Granmam Powelly's clock ticking off the minutes she had left to live. She wouldn't come in for breakfast. No, she wasn't hungry she told Achsa. Sayward kept going about her business till the morning chores were done. Then she picked up the axe in her strong quiet hands.

"Now that's plagued a body long enough," she said.

It was a good thing, she thought, to have an excuse for going off from your cabin. A woman got tired of seeing the same big kettle and little kettle every day, the same gourds and chinking board shelves, feeding the same fire and going down for water to the same run. You wanted to drink water sometimes from some other run. The path down the river was beaten out little more than a deer path but you could tell the way it ran that no wild beasts made this. No, these were human feet. They knew where they were going. A foot path was a pleasing road to travel on, for it came to all things in the woods in time, the rotten log worn through in the middle to let you by, the bed of moss that had brown spots from feet, the sandy runs and cold spring, the narrows where the path clung to the sidehill, the hickory flats, the buck laurel and big whortleberry bushes in the swamp—the path got to all of them in time. Once it even came out at a half open place on the river where the sun on the water blinded you and a big old gandersnipe waded on his stilts in the shallows.

They couldn't hear that whacking when they started, only after they went a ways. The closer they got, the plainer it beat through the woods, making little Sulie stick close to her big sister. Now it had almost the ring of blacksmith iron. And now where the path climbed over a hill, the woods and river bluff below began to answer it. The echoes flew every which way till you couldn't tell if they had passed it or where the real sound came from.

"I tole you!" Genny said.

Little Sulie pulled on Sayward's shortgown.

"Let's go back and see if Pappy's home, Sairdy," she whined.

What this thing was, Sayward told herself, she didn't know. But too long had she lived in the woods to be scared of owls. She had come so far. Her legs had no notion of turning back now. Her naked feet slapped down on the cool path and on the drifted, curled-up leaves of last year's oak crop. Now they were going downhill. And now they could see something down there on the bottom. It looked yellow and kind of bright through the trees.

"You young'uns stay here," Sayward told them. "I want to see that'ar."

To herself she said, plagued if it didn't look like peeled logs. But the young ones wouldn't stay behind. No, they kept close after her, pulling at her clothes. Something was moving down there, bumping among the tree butts. When it came out, it looked like a forest beast none of them had ever seen before. Then it turned into a gaunt old blue-and-black spotted ox snaking a log, with a boy no bigger than Wyitt jumping that log first on one side then on the other behind it.

Now who, Sayward thought, would have looked for something like this! The young ones stared like they were beat out, for this was the first white human they had seen since they came in these woods. Oh, they had no notion to turn around and go back home now.

"Wow-wow-wow-wow-wow-wow!" Wyitt greeted that boy defiantly, patting his hand to his mouth like an Indian.

Like a shot the strange boy dropped his gad and jumped behind the back side of his ox that was glad enough to rest his weary bones. A grown man came running out of the woods with a gun and got behind the crib of peeled logs. One look at that musket and the Luckett young ones scattered like a bunch of squirrels on the far side of the handiest butts. Only Sayward stood calm and half-angered in the path.

"Don't draw no bead on us!" she called out. "We're nothin' to be afeard of. We're neighbors to you."

CHAPTER SEVEN

❋ ❋ ❋

Maidenhead

S O IT HAD WHITE FOLKS living in these woods and they never knew it, Sayward told herself on the way home. A pity Jary couldn't have lived to see this day. If anything could have made her hang on to breath a while longer, it would have been to lay eyes on neighbors. Never did Jary give a hait about how many paces a panther skin stretched from tip to tip or the points on the rack of a buck. All she cared about were humans. Back in Pennsylvania she would sit quiet on her chair and ask Worth a world of questions about some family he met up with in the woods. Worth would scratch his head and answer the best he could, and all the time Jary would sit there with her mouth rounded a little at what Worth didn't know. Give her five minutes with those folks, it said, and she would tell you more about them than Worth could take notice of from All Souls' night to Martinmas.

The young ones' tongues were loose enough now. Before they got to the top of the first hill, little Sulie turned her face, smart and sharp as a young coon's, over her shoulder.

"We got a winder light at our place!" she yelled back at them.

But when she had stood down there, she hadn't opened her mouth, neither she or any of the young ones. You might have thought they never had laid eyes on other white people.

"Well, kain't you say something to that boy?" Sayward had complained to Wyitt.

Not that it did any good. All he and the stranger boy could do was scowl at each other over the ox's rump. She didn't know what they'd have done without that ox. She tried to scrape up some talk with the boy's pappy but with a woman he was froze stiff as steelyards. Most of the time the Lucketts had to just stand there, first on one leg and then on the other, visiting with their eyes, waiting till a proper time had passed before they took their leave, saving their opinions till they got out of earshot. And when it went too long without a word, she or one of the girls would talk to that ox, running their hands down his soft neck. Oh, he was the most sociable one there, reaching out his snout for the fresh sassafras leaves they picked for him and talking a soft "Mmm-mm-mm-mm," deep in his gullet when they would neglect him. The beast's eyes were mild and patient as summer but you could see a world of power lay in his thick neck and the wide flare of his horns.

Now if it had a woman down there, Sayward thought, things might have been different. A woman would have been glad to see girls and young ones out here across the Ohio. Such wouldn't have lacked for words to talk, bidding them sit down on a log and maybe giving them a bite to eat to show them a hearty welcome. It would have been a comfort to look in a woman's face today and hear woman's talk. But it had to be enough just to know a second place in these dark woods was now marked with the sociable, human slashes of the axe. Their own cabin didn't look so lonesome any more when they came back to it standing by itself under the trees.

Worth heard about it from the young ones before he got in the house that afternoon. They told him all that had happened and some that hadn't, quarreling over how it was and wasn't. Supper done, he looked up at Sayward.

"Don't he have a woman?" he wanted to know.

"I didn't ast him," Sayward said shortly.

Worth had a look on his face as he pushed back his stool.

Most times Sayward could read her father's face like Jary could a book, but this look she didn't recollect seeing on him before. Now what, she wondered as she lay in her bed with Genny that night, did he have on his mind?

One day not long after she heard Sarge bark and after while the bass mumble of men's talk. When she went to the door, there sat their settler neighbor and Worth on the chopping log together. The ox they must have left down the river, but he and his boy had come up the foot trace mighty soon to see what the Luckett place looked like. And now that he was here his hair stood up curly all over his head like he was astonished with what he saw. It came over Sayward this must be Sunday for his boots had been freshly charcoaled and his linsey shirt was clean, though his neck and tow britches looked like neither had seen water for a long time.

His boy stood around like a lost sheep. Oh, Sayward told herself she would feed that man and boy well today, for they had no woman folks to look after them like Worth and Wyitt had. She would pick those wild pigeons and bake a deep pigeon pie in the kettle. The four youngest ones could squeeze together on the bench at the table. She called Genny to help. Genny told her those freshly blacked boots made her feel half naked and that's why she had stood off a little ways with her bare legs hid by the bushes.

After dinner it rained and the young ones had to stay in the cabin. The two men moved their stools back against the logs and filled the place with smoke from Worth's tobacco, telling where each hailed from in the old state and how he had made his tracks through the woods. The neighbor called himself Mathias Cottle. He was a little fellow who sat up big as one should who owned a cow and a mare back on his brother's place along the Youghiheny. But he was too full of twist and go to sit still long. His hands like those of a body with more pressing business on his mind kept cutting on the floor little squares out of a stick from his pocket. And all the time Sayward could feel his bright black eyes watching her chore around the cabin as they had watched her bare legs that day down at his improvement.

"Is her married?" he asked after while.

"Her?" Worth repeated, a little surprised, looking at Genny who was fair-skinned like Jary as a girl.

"Her!" little Mathias said, pointing his knife blade-foremost at Sayward, and she felt a strange sensation as if that blade had painlessly pierced one of her strong breasts.

Worth stared stupidly at his eldest daughter, and by his face she judged he thought as if he had blurted it out, which he was like as not to do. He was beat out that here in this Northwest Territory where men were scarcer than birds' teeth, a man with an ox, a mare and a cow had looked on her for marriage. Now Sayward, he always said, was more like Jary's sister, Beriah who could throw any boy head over tincup. The Conestoga settlement boys looked up to Beriah and told her their troubles, but when it came to walking home with a girl after meeting, it hadn't been Beriah. No, she could go home safe alone for no man or beast would dare molest her. The girls they saw home safe, bundled up with after, and stood up in front of the dominie or squire with in time were the cunning little wenches who held their ears shut when it thundered and pressed close at the rattle of small vermin in the bushes. Once Worth had said he wondered if a strong-minded, hard-waisted girl like Beriah wasn't like the third sex of the bees that did all the work and were neither male nor female.

"She's not married," he shook his head.

"Is her promised?"

"Not to my knowin'," Worth said.

Little Mathias jumped up and went outside where they could hear him priming himself with water from the gourd at the run. He came back in and tramped up and down and it was plain when he started to talk he was full of words to tell.

"Yesterday I says to myself, Mathias, do ye need a yoke of oxen back here? I says, no, I got a ox. I says, do ye need yer mare and cart? I says, no, they ain't no roads back here for a mare and cart to go on. I says, Mathias, do ye need yer cow? I says, no, I ain't got a little bitty'un wantin' mush and milk. I says, Mathias, do ye need a woman back here? I says, by Jeems' cousin, that's what I need! kain't cut down all these yere trees by myself."

He flashed his eyes at Sayward but she was listening to the rain on the roof, aware that her own sisters and brother sat in a row on the bench in the firelight staring at her with respectful eyes. What the stranger boy thought she couldn't tell, for he stayed by himself in the chimney corner.

Sometimes Worth Luckett was set in his ways as a pignut tree, and sometimes you could get no more out of him than an Indian. But it was plain that this was an unusual occasion and not lightly to be set aside. A man for his oldest girl had never showed himself before and might never again, anyhow not one with a cow, a mare and an ox to his name.

"You hear what he had to say, Saird?" he asked her.

"Oh, I heerd him all right," Sayward told him mildly.

"Well, kain't you say something?"

"I hardly knows him yit."

"You don't need to live with him tonight."

She gazed at her father curiously.

"Oh, Pappy," she thought, "you might hate just a lick to see me go, for Genny is mighty young to take over a cabin and cookin'!"

She tried not to read her father's mind too hard, for she would hate to think he had reasons of his own for wanting her married. A year and a half was mighty long time, she knew, for one like Worth to be fixed and settled in one place. But she wouldn't like to think that all that held him now with Jary under the ground was having to get meat for his young ones' bellies and skins to tan for their feet and trade for their backs. If she had a man it might change all that. He could off and forget to come home and they would be all right. Never would they starve or go naked, for their married sister would take them in. He would be free as a bird to wander. He could see those far places they told about where the deer had strange black tails. He could skin the striped tiger cat and the queer mountain ram that some called the bighorn. Even could he cross that far river they said was a river of flowing mud and see those Indians with blue eyes and hair yellow as a panther's. And when he tired, he could rest in the Spanish Settlements of the Illinois and listen to the women whose talk, they said, was like singing. Oh, he would console himself by telling in his mind what presents he would fetch them home from these foreign parts: a gold ring for Genny's white finger; a comb carved from a turtle's back for Achsa's black hair; a lump of blue gold to lay in Sulie's small hand. Presents for all would he have in his hunting shirt when he came back. But it wasn't likely he would come back, Sayward thought, for some Spanish woman who sang when she talked would get him.

"I heerd you say," she said politely to little Mathias, "about a goin' to the Youghiheny this fall after your stock and fixens. Hain't it some nice woman you know down 'ar?"

"Oh, it has plenty down 'ar. I know a fine one and her name's Maggie Bradley," he said.

Sayward nodded at him.

"Why don't you make her your lawful wife and fetch her home with your stock and turnip seed? I'd like to see a nice woman away back here."

Little Mathias looked at her but couldn't make her out. No, you could see he thought she held herself not good enough for a man with a cow, a mare, a cart and an ox when all her father had was a cabin with a paper window. It made him stand high as a little fellow could. When the rain slacked off, he and his boy went friendly home.

They were hardly over the door log till Worth turned on Sayward.

"What's got over you?" he grunted.

She took down a gut of bear's oil to fry some dodgers for supper, for the company had eaten all the bread, waiting till little Mathias and his boy were plenty out of hearing.

"I'm a standin' up with no Tom Thumb," she told him.

"You mought not git another chance," Worth said.

"He mought be the first," Sayward told him. "But I have a feelin' he ain't the last."

She stood there mixing meal with meat scraps, a forebearing, independent figure with the firelight playing on her long yellow braids and muscled legs that were bare above the knees.

Her father watched her through his brushy eyebrows.

"Next time I go to Hough's, I'll fetch you back goods for a new shortgown. You're too old to be a runnin' around any more like some young Injun with his backside stickin' out." He spoke gruffly but Sayward could see the respect in his eyes.

He meant it, she knew, but when he would remember there was no telling. So she pieced a hem on her clean shortgown that week and went down to the river to wash. The river was the oldest road through the forest there was. Big yellow butterflies traveled it all day. Now and then slow, green and gold gabby birds or some swift water birds flew up or down. The wind liked to use it, too, but this day it was calm. The only ripple in this smooth stretch moved straight across where she stood. It was like a swimming stick with its head sticking up but she knew it was only a water snake getting tired of one side like Worth and coming over to the other. Well, she would send him back where he belonged.

She waded in driving a flock of water bugs in front of her and stopped in some sandy shallows fetched down by a run. Here it had two or three old water logs on whose mossy top it was handy to lay your clean clothes and your gourd of soft soap. River foam had piled up in between the logs, dark brown behind and light in front. It would take a miller's bag to hold it all but little Sulie could hoist it to her back and never know it was there.

She pulled her dirty shortgown over her head and laid it on the logs. Nothing could be pleasanter than to stand here without a stitch on and feel the sand come boiling up between your legs and the whole river pushing at you downstream. Bubbles rose. Some claimed they were the breath of catfish and lamper eels in the mud, but Worth said it was the old earth herself breathing from some hollow place. The trees covered her over here like a green roof. Down in the amber water she saw a picture of her naked body shaking soft and delicate as a young tree in the spring wind.

A porcupine nosed out of low leaves along the bank and stood peering at her with its beady black eyes.

"Go ahead and look all you like," she said to it. "I wouldn't trouble to duck myself from a porkypine."

She tied her braids up over her head and scrubbed her body well with grease and sand, rinsing it off in the fresh current. Then for a while she stood to dry, inspecting with matter-of-fact criticalness her strong breasts and hams.

Yes, she was a woman now, she told herself, a white woman in this country of the men of the Western waters. It was good enough being a woman. She didn't know as she'd change it now, had she the chance.

CHAPTER EIGHT

❃   ❃   ❃

Settlement

T HINGS WERE LOOKING poorly in this Northwest Territory, Worth complained early next spring to Sayward; yes, mighty poorly. A man had to be afraid of not making his lead and powder by another year. Only a little while back it was as fine and rich a country as a man could clap eyes on. Game was plenty as pigeons in the woods. Deer shed their horns within gunshot of your cabin. The Indians didn't trouble much, for most of them lived further north and west. And it had no white hunters nearer than the forks.

Then the government had to go and cut that fool trace through the woods across the big bend of the Ohio.

Worth had taken it for a kind of surveyor's line at first, for they let the trees lay where they fell. Now, the Delawares told him, white men and women from the old states were beating along this line, their mud sleds, carts and once in a while a wagon pitching like crazy over the logs, stumps and rocks in the trace. You wouldn't expect, Worth said bitterly, these same whites had whole counties of new land left back in the old states if they wanted something to break their backs on. No, they had to come out here, first the Cottles last spring and the MacWhirters in the fall. And now the country was at the Deil's door, for a trader, his bound boy and a kind of runner had come poling up the river with a boatload of goods and plagued if they weren't fixing to start in the store trade where Indian trace forded the river!

"I'll thank them none for that," he said. "They'll draw more squatters than carrion kin flies."

Wyitt sat in a dark corner listening to his father. Not a word dare he say, but the news of a trading post right here along the river bobbed up like a float in his blood. His young back, stiff with import, pointed straight up to the roof and gable where his small pelts skinned with Sayward's cabin knife were. Oh, he had taken to the woods already like a young gadd to wind and water. His hand could make snares and deadfalls shrewd as a man. Already he smelled so heavy of skunk that the girls complained of him sleeping with them up in the loft.

Then tonight of all times didn't Sulie have to shoot off her mouth about a thing she had been told in secret.

"This here trader got any knives, Pappy?" she piped, innocent as all get out.

Worth lifted his head and threw a look around.

"Who's a needin' any knife?"

Wyitt in his dark corner would have liked to get his hands on that blabbing tyke of a sister. He'd tend to her in the loft tonight yet if his father wouldn't hear.

"I didn't mean nothin'," she whined.

"Which of them's lost your cabin knife?" Worth demanded of Sayward.

"It's right up 'ar on the shelf," she said, placid as could be.

His eyes retreated suspiciously into his two weeks' sprouts of beard while Wyitt's eyes burned at his youngest sister. Oh, he wasn't finished with her yet. He would fix her in the brush tomorrow. When he woke up early next morning, she lay so small, warm and helpless beside him, all his hate melted. He cared about nothing now save how soon his father went to the woods again. For three days he sat around still as a stone but inside he had never been on such tenterhooks. If his father didn't clear out soon, he told himself, he'd have to push him. That trader might change his mind and go somewhere else before he could get there. He might sell out all he had, for Worth said some Shawanees passing on the trace had already stopped and looked over his stock.

The morning Worth went after fresh meat, Wyitt watched every move he made. His father had hardly crossed the run till the boy was up throwing down his skins in the bushes. In the cabin he pulled on his hunting shirt with the black squirrel trimming and sopped his hair so that sandy corn shock of his would slick down.

"Where you reckon you're a goin'?" Sayward put to him.

"I ain't a goin' no place much," he said shortly.

He didn't fool her for a minute. When he went out, she took her work and sat on the doorsill with one eye on him, and he hung around fooling with Sarge a while like he was in no hurry. The hound had aged fast the past year. Even the gunpowder Worth fed him sometimes wouldn't liven him any more. All winter he lay in the cabin where he could feel the chimney heat. Now that it was getting to spring he liked to lay outside where he could smell the woods though he was too blind and worn out to chase any more. Oh, that old hound was a gone Josie! There he made his bed under the eaves where the ground was a little dry, his ears sore, his eyes filmed over with white, his coat gray-streaked, scabby and bothered by flies. But he could still lift his head and wrinkle his nose when a fox or some other game passed between him and the river.

"C'm on, Sarge! C'm on!" Wyitt coaxed him to climb stiffly to his legs and stagger down the path after him. If he took Sarge along a piece, Sayward had no way but to think he wasn't going far. Once he got the old hound down in the woods, he sneaked back for his skins. The dog was waiting for him when he got to the path again. He struggled up and started to come after.

"Go back, Sarge! Go on back!" Wyitt mouthed at him. "You kain't go along where I'm a goin'."

The last he saw of him, the old hound was standing in the

path holding up his head high like he did of late, trying to gaze after through his blind spots, the drooped tip of his tail moving just inches between his legs.

It was a good thing he didn't take Sarge along, Wyitt told himself when he got there. An old hound wouldn't know how to act here, for he didn't himself right. He hardly knew the place when he saw it on ahead through the woods. Trees were down. A fattish boy, bigger than he was, and a hairy-faced giant had started putting up a pair of cabins. Wyitt watched them a while from safe back in the bushes. Oh, this was a tony place for a young woodsy to visit. Out there in the clearing a brush cabin had been set up first. This was the store. He could tell by the squaws sitting on the logs outside while their near-naked young ones rolled and raced around. Every once in a while the squaws would yell at one for getting too close to a lunging beast tied to a log. It was a gaunt, live wolf with a slobbered, rawhide muzzle on to keep him from biting his heavy strap through.

The Indian dogs left off worrying the wolf to bark at Wyitt and the squaws smiled broadly at him as he came up. Oh, they could tell the way he hung back he had never done anything like this before, hadn't ever seen the inside of a store up to now. But he was going to see this one. With his back stiff as a poking stick he went up to the brush door. Through the smoky gloom inside he made out a white man in a leather apron, red and cunning as a fox. That must be the trader, George Roebuck. Then he saw he would have to wait his turn, for a row of Shawanee men were ahead of him to try out this new trader's prices.

Holding up his small pack of skins so all could see he had business here, the boy slipped inside. The Shawanees turned their heads. They made like they didn't see him. Down in Pennsylvania the Indian looked up at a white boy like a dog would. Out here the Indian looked down on you like you were the dog. These Shawanees sat big as king's men on that log, taking long, slow puffs on their gift tobacco. One with bearclaws around his neck and scars all over his chest stood up with the post's yardstick. He'd point at something and the trader would tell him the price in skins. If the Indian bought it, he paid for it right off out of his roll of furs before he went on to something else. But first he had to heft and feel of it a long time.

Wyitt wished Sayward, Genny, Achsa and Sulie could see him here. Not that they ever would. Women folks couldn't walk in a post like a boy and stand with all the riches of the settlements piled up in front of them: bars of bright, new lead laid crosswise on powder kegs; red and green blankets and black ones with a broad white stripe that were the best; bolts of blue strouding and Turkey red goods; new fusils that had hardly been shot off yet; Indian vermilion for the paint bags; wooden buckets of beads, of bells for leggins, of rings for the nose and finger; and a half barrel that kept dripping from its tap in a wooden bowl, making the air sweet with whiskey. But what ran through the boy's blood like horses were those red tomahawks and shiny scalping knives stuck in a tree corner of the post.

He had plenty time to look at them today. He stood first on one leg and then the other, going out sometimes for a drink in the run or to put a tree between him and the squaws like a man. When old Bearclaws sat down, another stood up, and when the last sat down, the Shawanees started all over again with their best furs they had saved out for whiskey. Oh, they knew better than to mix their trading and dram-drinking. It was almost dark and the post candles had been lighted when those Indians got done and cleared out.

Wyitt pushed up.

"How much fur one a them knives?" he fetched out.

Maybe he shouldn't have bothered the trader right now, for wrinkles had to come between George Roebuck's eyes to hold his mind on the counting of his hairy gold. His lips moved as he laid out skins in piles—bear, beaver, otter, buck, doe, wolf, mink, redcross fox, fisher fox and coon. His quill had to tally these first in his tanned-leather account book. Then he held out a hand for Wyitt's scanty pack, looked the small skins over, threw them down behind him like they weren't worth putting in with the others, grunted and reached down a knife. From the trading Wyitt figured he ought to have a couple coon or rat skins left over. But once he got that knife in his fingers, with its round bone handle and blade heavy enough to strike flint with, he wouldn't hurt the feelings of the trader. Holding tight to that knife, he went out. The squaws had started fires and by their light he saw the trader's bound boy with two Shawanee boys laying for him outside the door.

"I kin knock you down and drag you out!" the bound boy bragged at him.

Wyitt stiffened.

"You kain't while I got this knife."

"Lemme see it!"

Wyitt put it behind him. His young face had turned hard and cruel. His freckles looked like rusty iron. Oh, he wasn't big as this bound boy but he'd go on his muscle before he'd let him touch his knife. The pair stood almost against each other, one scowling down and one scowling up, neither one giving way any more than two young bucks meeting in the path. The Shawanee boys watched with their black eyes glittering. They would be spited if no hitch between the two white boys came out of this.

The bound boy gave in first, for he was fattish and you could see he would be soft.

"I'll swap you knives!" he dared, stepping an inch to one side.

Wyitt went on, the victor, without saying anything. He could hear the whiskey taking hold of the Shawanees now. Already they were whooping and carrying on around the fires, dancing and singing some Indian catch that was the same thing all the time. Old Bearclaws was drinking with the big hairy-faced white runner, Jake Tench, and hollering over and over the only English he knew. Wyitt had to laugh, for it sounded like, "Dirty no good! Button up your britches!"

Wyitt's moccasins moved slowly. His eyes took everything in. Never had he seen post doings before and it might be a good while till he saw them again. He had no need to go home just yet. He'd wait a while. He lay out behind a big felled butt and watched the squaws carry their men's knives, tomahawks and guns to the woods to hide before harm was done.

Those Shawanees were getting good and wild now. They even took the wolf they had tied to a log. They wanted to skin it and trade its green hide for more whiskey. But that wolf was too quick for tipsy Indians. It twisted half out of its muzzle and bright red blood spat from a dull red arm. The squaws screeched and called down curses on it. They took limbs and wanted to beat and kill it, but the white runner held them back. He took one of their bankets and threw it over the wolf's head. Then he got some of the men to hold blanket and snarling beast fast while he started on the rear end with his knife.

The squaws and young ones yelled like penny trumpets when they found out what that white man aimed to do. They roared at their tipsy men trying to hold that lunging beast still. When one had to spit on his hands and grab dirt to hold a jerking leg that was smooth of hide or hair as a venison bone, the squaws doubled up with laughter.

Not in any of his born days, Wyitt told himself, had he seen a thing like this. His own Pap wasn't quicker or slicker with the knife. Jake Tench's hairy hand moved sure as death and never cut a hamstring. He peeled off the last of that pelt, shook off the blanket and let the live beast run. The little crowd gave. No such wolf had ever been seen in these woods before, stark naked of skin or fur. It made Wyitt's hair stand up to see it go. Like some red beast out of one of Sulie's nightmares, it ran across the clearing with the squaws and young ones screeching after. It staggered a little as if with rum. It jumped over a log, half fell, heaved up in the air and plopped out of sight in the run bush. And that was the last they saw of it. He wouldn't forget this easy, Wyitt told himself. He reckoned he had enough now. It was about time he went home.

Away from the fires the woods were black as a pit. He couldn't make out his hand before his face. Once his moccasins got wet, his feet helped keep him to the hard path. Hands and feet felt their way, through cold runs and wet places, through mud and over soft moss, around big butts and logs, through spice-wood and hazel patches, down hollows and uphill again. Far off he heard wolves howl and some cat beast cry like a woman. Closer to him noises came and went in the bushes. He told himself he would be plenty scared if he didn't have a hunting knife. He could slash around with that knife worse than a panther with its claw. He could even lay a beast open; in case he couldn't find in the dark a handy small butt to climb. On no account would he lose his wits and keep tramping all the way home through the woods like his Aunt Beriah did once with only a tin lantern between her and a yellow panther keeping abreast of her through the bushes.

He had no notion it was this far home. He felt he had walked half the night. He should have got to the cabin and back by this time. The path kept making strange turns this way and that. When he listened, the sounds of river and frolic came from the wrong directions. Where he was now, he had no more idea than a lamper eel in the mud except that he was lost. Once he thought he saw a faint light winking ahead. It was too early for firebugs. When he walked, that light walked too, blinking in and out from behind the butts of the trees. Then he crossed a small run and knew it was his Pap's oiled-paper window with the fire-light shining through for he heard old Sarge whining a welcome from the path.

Somebody pulled open the door. It was Genny. All his sisters were still up this time of night. He stood back, for it did him good to see the long faces they pulled thinking their only brother was still out in the woods. Then he stuck the knife in his belt and went in.

"Wyitt!" little Sulie cried at him. Never had she acted so glad to see him.

Genny stood back from the door to let him in.

"You'd catch it if Pappy was home!"

"I was just down to the post a tradin' my skins." He turned so all could take in the knife in his belt.

"Kin I see it, Wyitt!" Sulie shrilled.

Achsa and Genny tried to get their hands on it first, but he took it out and shrewdly gave it to Sayward who was eyeing him grimly. Her face didn't melt as she turned the knife over in her hands, feeling of the edge with her thumb as the others crowded around.

"Is that all you got?" Achsa jeered in her coarse boy's voice.

"Ain't that enough fur you!" Wyitt stiffened.

Sayward handed the knife on to Genny, the next oldest.

"Next time," she told Wyitt, "you better go a tradin' with your Pappy so you don't get skun."

"I wa'n't skun," he denied heatedly.

"And next time I ask you where you're a goin'," she said to him hard as could be, "you tell me! I don't want to set up half the night a frettin' some painter got you."

She was harsh, but he felt elated he had been fretted over.

Sayward drove them all to bed now. She was glad enough Wyitt was home. When she stepped outside she could faintly hear voices of a frolic down at the post. Now and then the night air fetched them clearer. She wouldn't have minded laying eyes on that post her own self, though the trader would not thank her to stick her head in.

It was good enough, she felt, just to know they had humans closer around them. Her bed leaves felt more comfortable tonight. They weren't set out any more in these woods only God Almighty knew how far. No, they had two improvements and a store around them. You might say they were living in a settlement now. She wished Jary could have hung on long enough to see it.

CHAPTER NINE

❋   ❋   ❋

A Noggin of Tea

Y OU COULD SEE Worth had something on his mind when he
came home this afternoon. He kept his eyes from Sayward getting ready to boil soap tomorrow in the big kettle outside. Oh, when he went out to the run to wash, he growled like
usual how they never boiled soap till they ran out. But after
supper he went and oiled his fine paper window, tallowed the
wooden hinges of the door so they'd stop their holding back and
screeching, and trimmed up a rock to fit the hole a log had
knocked in the fireplace wall.

"Don't you have any better shortgown than that 'ar?" he
came right out at supper time, looking critically at Sayward across
the trencher.

It made it plain even to little Sulie that something out of the
common run had come over their pappy. Once Genny opened her
mouth like she would ask him about it, but Sayward pulled down
her mouth at her and nodded her to go on and eat her supper. A
man's mind had stranger and darker ways than a beast in the
woods. You could poultice a body wound or a snakebite and it
would draw the poison out. But try and do that to a woodsy's
mind and you only drove it in. No, you had to bide your time and
go about your business. When it ripened like a melon, it would
come out of its ownself, if it was to come.

It passed through Sayward's head that her father might be
fixing to fetch a woman home to take Jary's place. But it had no
free white women in this country that she knew of, and hardly
would he spruce up his cabin for a Shawanee or Delaware wench.
It would be grand enough for her as it was. Before he went to bed
he poured fresh powder in his horn and told her he wanted his
breakfast early, for he failed to get meat that day. And yet long
after breakfast next morning, it seemed he couldn't take himself
off. Genny fetched word out to Sayward at her kettle that he still
squatted on his haunches by the fire, melting lead in his iron

ladle and pouring it in the funnel of his mould till it ran over. All the young ones had watched this so often they could tell their own selves by the change of color when the bullet had cooled and it was time to open the wooden handles, throw it out and pour in more. Later when those balls cooled a bit, he would cut off the sprues with his knife.

Well, Sayward told herself, he couldn't hold off and run balls all day. After while she saw him with his rifle, horn and bullet pouch coming from the cabin. Yes, he was heading her way. Now, like as not, this thing would come out. She moved around the kettle a speck and kept her back toward him, for the wrong look on her face might scare those words ready on his lips and drive them back in his mind.

"I come by those new squatters yesterday," he began roughly. "Just to bid them the time."

Sayward, calm as a June morning, went on stirring the soap with her paddle, while Genny and Sulie came up soundlessly to stand around with big ears.

"She gave me something she called tea," Worth said. "Oh, her man was there with her all the time," he added quickly to stop any wrong thoughts that might be in his eldest girl's head.

"You mean dittany?" Genny ventured.

"No, it was nothin' like that," Worth growled.

"Well, what fur thing was it?" Sayward asked him.

Worth's face grew heavy. "Near as I could make out, it was some kind of snack betwixt dinner and supper. It wasn't a meal and it wasn't a piece. A cup of tea went with it."

"What was it she gave you to eat?" Sayward put to him without looking up.

"I never paid no attention."

"Well, you have some idee."

Worth pondered. Had it been meat, he could have told you the kind of game, the part of the carcass cut from, whether young or old, and how long it had been hung to ripen. But this was woman's stuff. It made him feel kind of sheepish just to talk on it.

"It put me in mind," he said shortly, "of the playparty rations Jary had once when I came a courtin'."

"Could you take it up in your fingers?" Genny was keen to know. "Or did you need your knife to eat it with?"

Worth threw her a look from the whites of his eyes. "The tea, she said, come from Chiny. The rest was just this and that. I mind she had two kinds of breadstuffs. But never a bite of meat or gravy."

"What was her breadstuffs like?"

"Oh, I got nothin' for such," Worth stormed. "All I kin tell you it was cut up small and scanty like for little 'uns."

"The Chiny tea was tasty, I'll warrant," Genny said impressed.

"I'd as soon drunk water out of a spring some leaves fell in," he grunted.

"Did you notice the cup she gave you?"

"Oh, I took notice," Worth grumbled. "It was that thin crockery, I was afeard it'd break in my fingers."

Sayward made a face at them to jog at their father no more. Well she knew how woodsy men hated to get jockeyed into drinking tea or coffee, let alone talk about it. They claimed such slops never stuck to the ribs.

"Well, I'm off," he said shortly. At the big white oak he turned. "I mind now, Saird," he called back, "this woman ast about you. She said she might be up this way a visitin'—maybe today."

When the trees had swallowed him up, the young ones studied their eldest sister's face.

"I knew it all the time," little Sulie spoke up, wise as an owl.

Oh, her father could go, Sayward told herself, for it was out now. It was plain as the nose on his face why he wanted off this place today. She might have expected it had to do with these Covenhovens just up around the bend. The young ones said they were rich, and it must be, for they had three cows and two horses and had fetched a whole raft of plunder in hickory withe creels on those tamed beasts' backs. The young ones had lain up in the bushes and watched them unpack.

Genny said they had pewter and copper ware, a looking glass with a towel they hung on a tree, more pots and kettles than you could shake a stick at, a grind stone and a grubbing hoe. And that wasn't half of it. They had two chests; fine patched quilts; a big iron shovel and a small one Genny thought for the fire; a candle mould, reels, a flax and spinning wheel. And the woman had all the bushes airing with shirts, britches, petticoats, bedgowns and sheets like great folks had. The walls of the Luckett cabin, Sayward expected, would look mighty bare of clothes to such a woman.

"What rations kin you give a body so fine?" Genny wanted to know.

"I'll have to set my thinkin' cap," Sayward told her.

Standing over her big kettle she thought how handier than any time yet would her mother come in if she were living. Never could Worth mind anything save it had to do with the woods. But Jary could tell you all the houses she ever went in, the special victuals they gave her and how she figured they were made. The last year Jary puttered around like she didn't know her own name, but that old head was still a larder and storebin of most anything about folks and settlements you wanted to know. Jary would be a comfort to her oldest girl now. She would sit here and reel right off how to give this thing called tea in front of a lady.

But Jary wasn't here and it filled no kettles to wish her back. Sayward reckoned she would have to do it herself. She kept on cooking and stirring that soap till it dripped thick from her paddle. Then she went in and redd out the cabin. She was glad she had set sour dough to raise that morning. Only yesterday Wyitt said he knew where it had early yellow lady slippers and she had him fetch some for Genny to stick in cracks between the logs. She told him to fetch along fresh mint and cucumber tree leaves, for they made it smell good and welcome over a swept dirt floor. Now she washed her face, hands and feet at the run, combed her hair and put on her good shortgown. All she lacked was a pair of cowhide shoes, but since she had none she reckoned her feet would have to go naked.

"Some body a comin'!" Wyitt hissed in at the door a little while after dinner.

The young ones, even Genny big as she was, raced out and dove in the brush. Oh, Sayward knew they would manage to peek in through the cracks and see her and the visiting lady, but never would the lady see hide nor hair of them, nor would Sayward either, till it was all over with and the company gone.

She set the door open a speck and propped it with no fireplace log but a pretty white rock she had Sulie fetch in. This was a stylish way, Jary used to say, folks would do along the Conestoga.

After while she heard voices on the path.

"I don't believe any body's home," a woman's voice said.

"Now you come this far, you go on in," a man told her. "Smoke's a comin' from the chimney."

The woman must have stood out there a little while looking

around. Her steps, made plainly by cobbler's shoes with heels, crunched up to the door log. For the first time since that door had been swung, knuckles rapped on the heavy puncheons. You could tell this company wasn't a woodsy, for no woodsy would think themselves fine enough to knock on a door. Sayward waited for a seemly time to pass. Then with grave face and bare feet she moved to the door.

A genteel, pock-faced woman stood there in elegant blue calico with yellow flowers figured through, a plump little woman, light-footed and light complected although you couldn't see her hair under the fine sunbonnet. Sayward guessed she had worn it just to set herself off, for there was no sun in these woods.

The women took in each other with their eyes.

"I'm your neighbor up the river a piece," the caller said.

"Kain't you come in? Your man, too," Sayward added, although she knew by what he said he had taken the trouble to come down here just to show his woman the way.

"He has to go back and keep a watch on our things. We got a good many," Mrs. Covenhoven said delicately.

"I'd be proud if you set down and made yourself to home," Sayward told her.

The woman's blue calico rustled to a stool on one side of the room and Sayward took one on the other. Here they sat for a fitting time in sedate silence. It certain was a pleasant thing, Sayward told herself, to feel a woman's company in the cabin again.

"I thought we'd get rain a little while back," Mrs. Covenhoven spoke.

"Oh, we'll git some one a these times. You a gittin' settled all right?"

"Well, good as can be expected. It don't do no good to complain."

"No, you just got to juke till the storm's over."

"I had the idee you had brother and sisters?"

"I reckon they're off in the woods right now," Sayward told her gravely.

Outside you could hear a twig snap close to the cabin and Sayward expected those young ones were sneaking up to peek through a crack and make faces like the caller.

"Well," she said, "I'll start a gittin' you some tea—if it's all the same to you."

"Oh, I don't want you to go to any trouble," Mrs. Covenhoven told her.

"It's no trouble," Sayward said. "My big kettle has soap in. But I ain't a usin' the other."

"I could loan you one," the pock-faced lady offered.

"Oh, I kin do all I want with one."

Sayward took the small kettle and used it the first time to fry out bear's bacon for shortening she would need later on.

"Almost warm enough for a body to wash their hair," she said.

She used that kettle a second time to bake sour dough biscuits in, after she had poured the shortening in a gourd.

"You and your man have a mess of poke yit?" she made talk again. "It has plenty around."

When the biscuits were done, she used the kettle a third time to fry the shortcake in, first working the fresh shortening in the dough until it was ready.

"Pap got such a nice silver fox last winter," she said. "I wish you could a seed it."

Now she took the kettle a fourth time and used it as a bucket to draw and fetch water from the spring.

"I heerd your man's a puttin' up a double cabin?"

"Not that one room isn't big enough for us," Mrs. Covenhoven explained modestly.

"No, one room's got plenty room for the six of us," Sayward agreed.

When the kettle started to simmer, she used it a fifth time, as a teapot, putting in a lick of dittany and sassafras root shavings. Then she poured out a pair of steaming wooden cups and set them with her two breadstuffs on the table. Oh, if this woman could give Worth two kinds of breadstuffs at one time, Sayward would give her no less. In truth she would go her one better, for her sour dough biscuits were not fine and scanty but of a hearty size with a square of smoked bear's bacon set in the top of each to run down over the sides and bake with a tasty crust.

"Tea's done," she said gravely. "You kin draw up your stool."

This tea thing, Sayward told herself, wasn't as bad as she had looked for. The biscuits and shortcake were real good. The spicy dittany steam rose. Through it passed their women's talk with quiet spots between, for two neighbors living so close shouldn't tell all they knew or what they would have to talk about next time?

Dusk was running through the woods when she tramped part way home with her company. Her father, she told herself, would have to wait for his supper tonight. Oh, she knew he was back this long time. He could keep himself hid like the young ones but he couldn't keep the stink of his old clay pipe under some bush.

"Don't your sisters and brother stay out pretty late in the woods?" Mrs. Covenhoven wondered.

"Oh, they ain't that far off they kain't find their way home," Sayward said. In her mind she could see them in the cabin this minute fighting over the leavings of the tea.

Big John Covenhoven came through the woods to meet his woman.

"I need somebody to fetch home my cows," he said. "By the month. Maybe your brother'd want to talk to me about it."

"I had such a nice visit," Mrs. Covenhoven told Sayward. "Now don't wait till our cabin's up till you come over."

Sayward thought on the path home it was strange about new places and people. At first they had their strange look. Then gradually they changed. Later on when you thought about that first way they looked, it didn't seem like the same place or person any more. This neighbor woman she had known only one afternoon and already she had an old time look in Sayward's mind.

It was dark till she got to the cabin. She reckoned it must be true she took after her mother's side of the house, for a woman's comfort in another woman still lingered in her bones. Now after a fitting time she would take herself over some afternoon to return the visit. Likely she would see for herself those fine breadstuffs Worth talked about and the China tea that he said tasted no more than water in the fall when leaves fell into the spring.

CHAPTER TEN

❦   ❦   ❦

Mortal Sweet

GENNY WAS GETTING pretty as a picture.

You could see she wasn't a young one any more like the others. Oh, sometimes she'd rip and tear around with them, play fox and hounds, blow bubbles through Joe Pye weed in the run, or march up and down whistling through sharp blades of wood grass held tight between cupped hands.

And other times she spurned those young ones' company like they had just crawled out of their log cradles.

Today Achsa wanted her to race terrapins. But do you think Genny would? No, she had nothing for such doings today. She sat by herself on the cabin bench, her bare white legs twined around each other, singing to herself, the sadder the sweeter. Wyitt and Sulie hung around, for they could listen to their sister Genny's singing all day. Now Achsa didn't think so much of it.

"She's got one of her spells on again," she jeered in her man's voice to Sayward.

Genny paid her no notice. Achsa didn't care how hot were the coals she fetched to lay on her pet terrapin's back to make it run faster. Genny would sooner make music. A song or hymn stuck to her mind like rows of beggar lice to her skirt. Let her hear it once and she knew it by heart. When she didn't recollect a line, she made one up and nobody knew the difference. She didn't know herself any more which were the real words and which the made up.

"She's lonesome as a mournin' dove. I kain't even look at her," Achsa complained and went out.

Today Genny sang most everything she knew: "True Thomas" and "Sinclaire's Defeat," "Purty Polly," "Who's Afeared" and some others. "Fly Up" she sang over twice. That was a mighty short song but she liked it best.

> *Vilets in the holler,*
> *Poke greens in the dish.*

Blue bird, fly up,
Give me my wish.

Hay cocks in the meader,
Cherries in the dish.
Red bird, fly up,
Give me my wish.

Chestnuts in the treetops,
Punkin in the dish.
Brown bird, fly up,
Give me my wish.

Ice in the river,
Possum in the dish.
Snow bird, fly up,
Give me my wish.

Genny was thinking she would like to taste possum again. It had none here in these deep woods like it had close to the settlements. Then Achsa's face, dark as an Indian's was stuck in at the door.

"You got your wish," she jeered. "The bound boy's here again."

Genny slowly unwound her legs. You couldn't believe Achsa half the time, but when she peeked out of the door, Jake Tench and the bound boy were coming along the path. Jake had dressed up in a roram hat, and the bound boy's reddish hair was tied behind with a ribbon snipped off a bolt of blue strouding.

"Don't you dare tell where I'm at or I'll maul you!" Genny warned Achsa, and her white legs flew up the ladder to the loft. She threw herself out of sight on Sulie's bed, for that was the fartherest back from the hole so the littlest body of them all might not tumble down in the cabin should she roll in her sleep. The roof slanted down close above. You had to be careful how you raised up or you got a good smack on your head.

She could hear Jake Tench's moccasins scraping over the dirt floor. He came in their cabin of late like he owned it. Genny couldn't go him. He put her in mind of the black he-bear she and Sayward had once watched out in the woods trying to please a she-bear. He moved about playful and frolicsome on his legs. But his paws were powerful as all get out, and his little black eyes danced with the devilment he'd do once he got you in them.

She lay there hating to be penned up with him down there. Once she dragged herself to the loft hole to see if her oldest sister was all right. Sayward bent by the fire scraping back ashes to bake corn bread on the hearth. Jake was bragging how he fixed a copper snake. It had caught him on the shank so he held it down with a forked stick and spat tobacco spittle in its mouth. By night, Jake said, he had overed the spittle of the snake, but the copper snake was stiff as a poker. Yes, he could stand the poison of a copper snake, but the copper snake couldn't stand his.

Oh, he was feeling high today. When Sayward put the hot ashes back over her bread, he squirted tobacco juice half way across the cabin to that fire! Genny saw Sayward's face flush up, but she didn't say anything. If it had been Worth now, Genny thought, Sayward would have stopped him short enough.

She heard the bound boy coming to the door.

"Where's Ginny at, Saird?"

"Ain't she outside a matchin' terrypins?"

"I kain't see her."

"Well, you look on around a piece and see if you kain't find her."

Genny felt a glow of affection for Sayward. She stood by you. Wyitt would get streaks like his father. Achsa would turn on you like an Indian. Sulie was too little to be of much account. And Jary was half rotted away in her bury hole. But you could count on Sayward. She never went back on you.

She was far too good for Jake Tench. Oh, Genny knew well enough what he was coming around here for. First thing Sayward knew she'd have to live with him, whether she wanted to or no. Worth said already it had half-blood young ones in Shawanee-town they were blaming on Jake Tench. Genny wouldn't want to be around if Sayward ever had a young one by that old rip. To rock or tote such would go against her grain. Like as not it would have some deilish birthmark of its pappy, as the wolf Jake skinned alive or the wagoner's nose he claimed he bit off once in a fisticuff.

After while the bound boy came back to the door.

"I kain't find her nowheres, Saird," he complained.

Genny didn't like the sound of Jake Tench's laugh.

"Maybe she's up in the loft a waitin' for you," he said.

Oh, she knew now she should have lain still as a log in Sulie's bed and never dragged herself over to the loft hole. She heard the bound boy crossing the cabin. She raised up, and down that ladder she went, holding her dress low and tight between her white knees as she was able. Jake Tench and Will Beagle would get no look at her if she could help it. She had a glimpse of the bound boy stopping short and staring at her with brown, astonished eyes. Then out the door she went.

"Gin! Will Beagle's here!" Wyitt yelled from the chopping log.

"Ginny!" the bound boy called.

But Genny did not stop. She could hear someone running after. She looked back over her shoulder. The bound boy was coming fast as his feet could take him. She let her slim legs go.

Sometimes when she was out alone in the woods, she ran for pleasure. But never could she go like when a body chased her, if it was only the young ones. Something came in her thin white legs then and she didn't know any more she had any. She didn't need to try to run. An easy power buoyed her up like the wind and she felt she could sail off like a red bird if she wanted to.

Once when they were back in Pennsylvania, she dreamed she could fly. She hadn't any wings. She just held out her arms and floated from one mountain to another. The valley between had a square log house, a round log barn and redtop meadows. She flew over those meadows so close, the redtop waved in a breeze. The folks came out of that house to watch her. She could still feel how light her body was. Her bones felt hollow as a turkey's wing.

Today she ran till it felt good to walk, but she wasn't tired. The forest mould gave soft and springy under foot. Around her stood the thousand pillars of the woods, bidding her come on. The butts of the red oaks were coated with green but the moss would have nothing to do with the black oaks. Down by a run a young doe lifted its head and stared at her with eyes it was a shame to think a corbie would pick out some day. It had been drinking and the drops of water rained from its mouth. Back somewhere behind Genny the young ones yelled and the doe was off. It went through the trees in great effortless jumps, cut a half circle and when it came back to the ravine the run was in, it sailed over like a pheasant.

Genny could hear the bound boy calling to her now. It came over her she was a deer, too. The bound boy was hunting her like men always hunted women and wild things. Never would they let them be to live their own lives. No, men always came after, smelling and tracking them down. But the bound boy would never find her. She was a young doe. A delicious wildness came up in her. The woods looked different now. The trees and bushes, even the poison sumach, were friendly. They stood over and bent down at her and tried to hide her. You had to be a deer to know how the wild things felt when a man was after you.

A stick cracked close under the bound boy's foot and she was off like the doe. Her hair floated brown and soft behind her. Every deer she knew had its secret places where it slept out by day. She would go to her place now. Even Sayward didn't know where she hid herself when things around the cabin got too much to stand. She made a wide circle to throw the bound boy off the track. Then she headed for the river and something pure came into her face. This was a holy place. She had found it herself and never would she show it to any but her true love when he came.

First she tramped through a forest meadow of low fern that brushed soft as lace against her feet and legs. Then she came to a dark clump of pines. It hadn't many pines in this Northwest Territory and mostly they stood alone. But here in this spot they crowded everything else out like the hemlocks along a Pennsylvania stream. Always when she got this far, Genny kept her eyes religiously down. Would it mean as much to her as last time, she asked herself. Then when she raised her eyes she'd know this place would never fail her. It was dim with a kind of pine woods night and yet out there beyond the dark, scaly butts and branches the blinding sunlight came down, turning a ferny bank to golden, tender green and sparkling on the river with silver. Out there lay a new world. It was like something to come in her own life some day, something bright and shining on ahead.

She listened. All sound of pursuit had gone. She was alone in her secret bower. It had been warm running. The sweat seemed to stand over her body in fine beads. With a deft motion she slipped out of her single garment and lay white and cool on the ancient brown carpet of the place. She lay on her young belly with her chin propped up in her hands, looking out into this bright new world the like of which she'd go into some day. This was the door through which her true love would step in her life. He would carry no long woods rifle like her father but a fine government musket. No buckskins would he wear but bright green regimentals or those of blue and gold. He would take her by her lily white hand and lead her out of these dark woods. Not on foot would they go but riding a horse like the Covenhovens' or a river boat like George Roebuck's pole batteau. And when they got to the settlements they would stop. Here they would live where folks smoothed their stools and table with an adze. On toward evening she would dress like the other women and sit on her street porch to see those that went by. When she got tired she could lie on a lounge with a panther skin coverlet. And on the Sabbath she would prank herself out in a fine check apron and go to church.

All afternoon she lay in this mortal sweet place while a pheasant* stretched its neck this way and that above a log, trying to make out this white patch on the brown ground. It strutted up and down with its neck ruffed and its tail spread out, and all the golden spots on its feathers stood out brighter than they ever did on the birds that Worth fetched home in his hunting shirt. The pheasant got close as it dared. Then it clucked like a settlement biddy and ran to put trees between itself and this white thing before it rose.

It was dusk when Genny came down the cabin path, shy as a young she-fox. Through the open door she could see the bound boy and the young ones fooling in the cabin. Sayward and Jake were gone. After while they came through the early darkness together from the direction of the post. Genny felt herself harden toward Sayward. She didn't see how her eldest sister could do this and then go about getting supper like nothing had happened. Once in a while Sulie or Wyitt would come to the door and yell "Ginnee!" but Genny never stirred from her bush.

"She's a hidin' out'ar behind a log," Achsa told them.

Only when Jake and the bound boy had gone down the path with their shellbark flambeau bobbing in the black night did Genny come in.

"You'll git no supper now," Achsa jeered.

"I ain't a hungry," Genny said.

Wyitt fetched a lick of something yellow and sticky from the shelf and laid it in front of her on the table.

"Will Beagle brung it fur you but you wouldn't wait."

"What fur thing is it?" she wanted to know.

"It's a present he give you."

"What's it good fur?"

* Ruffed grouse were known for many years as pheasants by Pennsylvanians.

"It's a kind of sweet bob. It comes from Chiny or some far place," he said.

"You kin have it," Genny said and turned away while the others fought for it.

Neither would Genny eat any of the cold leavings Sayward offered to get for her this evening. That night she lay far from her oldest sister as she could in their bed together. It felt almost like she was laying down with Jake Tench herself. She twisted first on one side and then on the other but she couldn't sleep.

"What's a ailin' you?" Sayward broke out at last.

Genny turned her back.

"You needn't talk to me after what you done."

"Now I done something and don't know what it was," Sayward complained.

"You know good enough," Genny told her. "Jake Tench!"

She could feel Sayward shake with quiet laughter.

"Don't you fret about Jake. He mought make free with a Shawanee wench but he kain't with me."

"He mought marry you," Genny said.

Sayward's voice hardened.

"Not him," she told her shortly. "Nor any other man where spits in my fire when I got bread a bakin'."

CHAPTER ELEVEN

❄ ❄ ❄

Corpse Candles

THIS WOULD BE a strange summer, Worth gave out. All signs the past winter had been hindforemost. It had black frost early in October so that the axe couldn't chop the ground. And by New Year the little white butterflies ran on their wings through the naked woods. A dogwood bloomed on Old Christmas. Genny wanted to break off some branches and fetch them in the cabin for a nosegay, but Worth said sternly any tree that blossomed on the wrong side of the year had no good in it. Bees and flies that were foolish enough to come out now and suck its honey would die.

Up on the other side of the world where the North Pole stuck out of the ice like an old chestnut stub, it had plenty of winter. More than one evening they stood outside looking up through the bare branches at the Northern Lights. The Shawanees called them Dancing Ghosts, but any white person knew it was only the midnight sun shining on the ice and snow. Red hands kept reaching up to the middle of the heavens. One time they were here and one time yonder. Yes, it had plenty winter up in that far place, but by the time it came down here, the snow in the clouds had melted to rain. The trees stood black and dripping when they should have been white and froze stiff as pokers.

After most every rain the sun came out like April. Snakes crawled from their dens deep down in rocky places, and hoppy toads jumped from under your feet. You couldn't tell when spring came except for the leaves. Long before the turn of summer the woods were chockful of tiny things that buzzed and flew. Mosquitoes whined around your head like a water sawmill, and millers you didn't see as a rule till later came in clouds out of nowhere. The river was white with them.

"It was a black winter," Worth said. "Now we're a gittin' a white summer. No human knows how this'll end up."

It looked to Sayward that even years printed in an almanac must have off ones. Gray squirrels sometimes gave black ones. Once in a while you heard of a white crow. Worth had shot a deer one time pale as an ermine weasel. But such meat was tainted and he didn't fetch any of it home. Some said you could see a white deer running through the woods on the darkest night. The spoiled flesh glowed and glirred in the dark like fox fire.

Most every day now the white fog smoke lay over the bottoms. It came, Worth said, out of the wet ground and it fetched up with it all the fearsome swamp poisons. When water sinks in the ground it cleans itself of rot and stink, let it be green beforehand as a spotted rattlesnake's venom. So long as it keeps on sinking, it doesn't hurt any, not even the eels and slimy things that live in the mud, for the earth is deep and has fires down in the middle to burn out what is foul. That's how spring water comes out sweet and clear. But once swamp water is drawn back out of the ground, then it fetches all the poisons with it and everything that sucks breath has to watch out.

"It all comes from these plagued squatters!" Worth stormed. "The trees they burn make smoke. The smoke makes rain. And the rain draws out the fog."

The livelong day now you could hear some new squatter's axe or saw in the forest. Some hailed from Kentucky and came poling up the river with their six-foot rifles sticking out of one end of their boats and a half-wild hog sticking its snout out of the other. A few came off Zane's trace from the old states, beating what stock they had through the bush. It hadn't a cabin, Worth said, that didn't have some body sick in it. The swamp pestilence hung in the air night and day, and most everybody had it. Portius Wheeler, the young Bay State lawyer who bached somewhere beyond the post, gave out calomel pills till he didn't have any for himself, and now he shook on his bad days like any person who never went to school a day in his life. The Indians came for miles to see George Roebuck shake. When the trader felt a spell coming on, he took off his leather apron and stood in his bare chest and back and shook till the fever stood out on him.

This was the only time Sayward heard Worth speak Jary's name in a year. Jary, he said, would know what to do if she were alive. Jary always had her teas and herbs hanging in the cabin to doctor with when one got sick. She'd be piling covers on when they had their chills and dosing them with hot teas to get their fever over with. But Sayward felt glad her mother wasn't here. She wouldn't like to see that worn out body with one foot in the grave huddle against the table or log wall and shake till God Almighty would take a little pity and say she had enough.

She only wished she had had the sense to ask her mother how she used to make her moss and lemon tea. Moss lemonade, Jary would call it. Not a lemon did Jary have or see since she married Worth Luckett, unless it was the time she went back home on a visit, but you'd swear she had cut up a whole yellow fruit that had come across the sea in a frigate from Spain. Leastwise that's how Sayward and Genny reckoned a lemon would taste. Cold or hot, nothing could cool your fever quicker. And if you set it in the run to chill, it turned into moss jelly for an ailing person to eat with the spoon. Just to think of it made a body's mouth water. But the only part of the receipt Sayward remembered was that you had to wash the moss through five waters. What moss it was and what you did then was forever buried now under the big white oak.

Taking all together, Sayward thought they were luckier than most. They had their shakes every other day. Never were they all sick and down at the same time with nobody to tend them or cook their rations. Some were always up and around while the others lay in their beds. Achsa and Wyitt minded their sumach poison worse than their shakes. All night you could hear them squirming and scratching up in the loft. When Sayward found they were raw to their middles, she made Wyitt show himself to Worth and Worth took a mess of sang roots to Roebuck's to trade for salt. Salt was mighty dear to have on the table but for medicine he reckoned it wasn't too high. When he came back, Sayward took those two out and made them strip themselves. Then she sopped water that was salty as the sea on their legs and middles.

She told herself she hadn't noticed up to now how Achsa had been filling out. If she had to do it again, she'd have taken her out by herself. Not that it mattered for Achsa to see Wyitt, for Achsa had washed him more than once when he was little. A boy was nothing much to look at anyway. Now a girl almost filled out into a woman was different. But Wyitt never even looked at Achsa. He couldn't hold still long enough for Sayward to sop the rag on a second time. The first touch of that salt on his raw parts and he would run up and down the path for all he was worth, hollering at the top of his lungs, yelling anything that came into his mouth till the pain let up enough for Sayward to get close to him with the rag again.

But Achsa stood like a brown Shawanee and never let out a screech although she was scratched open the worse. And that, Sayward thought, was how it must have started. If Achsa had run and hollered and let the poison out like Wyitt, she might have been all right. All she did was shut her teeth and drive the poison in. Oh, it fooled them for a while. Sayward blamed herself she didn't catch on sooner. She might have ciphered it out next day. As a rule a body with the shakes could be down ready to die one time and not long after be up and sassy as a jaybird. But Achsa didn't get up after her shakes next day. She said she felt tired and expected she'd stay in her bed.

And that was the last time she ever had the shakes. She lay in her loft bed a spell and by the time Sayward fetched her down to her and Genny's bed, she was that gaunt her bones stuck out. Sayward boiled May apple tea and made her drink it scalding hot but it never fetched out a lick of sweat.

Next day she felt a little warmer and the next. She wouldn't take the tea now. She just lay and shut her teeth and her eyes sulled up at you defiant as a young Indian's. All she wanted was cold run water and that she couldn't have.

"Give her cold water and you'll kill her," Worth warned. "I mind when Jary was down with the fever, the Lancaster doctor wouldn't let her have a drop."

Although it was a warm day in the woods, he kept a brisk fire going in the cabin to burn the air clean for the sick. Every time Achsa moaned for water, his lips moved. By evening Achsa was the hottest Sayward had ever felt a body. The heat reared up and struck you in the face when you only came near her. Worth said he couldn't make out how flesh could get that hot and not fry or burn.

All through supper Achsa called for water.

"God Almighty, come down through the roof boards and fetch me some water!" she yelled once.

It made the young ones thirstier but Worth touched no water for himself this night. At last he pushed back his stool and said that before it got too dark he'd take himself down to Roebuck's for a speck of tobacco. Sayward knew he had plenty of tobacco in his minkskin pouch. He just couldn't sit by all night while Achsa bleated like a doe for water and out in the run gallons of it were running to waste.

When he went he motioned Sayward outside. He told her she better expect the worst. One night last week, he saw corpse candles. Not often had he seen such things in the summer time. Mostly they came in a wet spell in the late fall, for that was just before the winter season when old and young mostly died. These summer lights were over the old beaver gats. It had two of them bobbing up and down like fast to a string. He might have sneaked up close and seen faces in them. But he didn't want to know beforehand on whom Death had fastened its mark.

When Sayward came back in the cabin she sent the younger ones up the ladder to bed. Matters crossed her mind now she never let herself think of before. It wasn't for nothing that the little cheeping birds stayed away from these deep woods. Slimy, clammy things that crawled or hopped you could hear night and day. Bullfrogs bawled and tree frogs screeched. But Sayward couldn't mind hearing a woods robin all year. Mostly the token bird called. He started in the morning before it was hardly light. Owk-owk-owk-owk-owk he went and then flew to a new place in the woods to tell his bad news. You could hear him making all the rounds. He wasn't satisfied with the daytime. Sometimes he called like a Death Watch in the night.

She recollected how Jary used to say Death would take the strongest and let the weakest be. Death was like the pair of black wolves Worth had once watched from some elk rocks in the Seven Mountains. They started a small herd of deer and one of the does was poor. She couldn't go it with the others and fell behind. Those wolves could have got her without half trying but it wasn't such a one they were after. They never turned a foot right or left from the main herd till they cut off a strong young buck, ripped his ham strings and fetched him down in the snow.

Achsa was stout and hearty a young body as you'd want to find and yet here she was fetched down in her bed. It never bothered her to club the life out of a fox or coon caught in a trap. Now Genny had to turn her face some other way. Achsa could throw the young ones down on their backs and hold them with one foot on their breast. But hands and feet were not much good against Death. And if you ran off, Death was waiting for you behind a stump when you got there.

Once Worth had gone, Achsa didn't call for run water any more. She might work on her father till he gave her what wasn't good for her, but she had no such hopes with Sayward. She just lay like a lump of ore melting in a forge. Her cheeks were stained with pokeberry juice and she panted faster than a hound. Mostly she stared up with bright jelled eyes at the loft boards as if her bed up there was mighty far away, farther than she would ever go again. Sometimes she would leer at Sayward with bitter eyes. Oh, she would ask no favor of her oldest sister. Her mouth was shut hard. If die she must, die she would.

Worth didn't come home and Sayward woke up that night in his bed. Something was outside. The fire had died down. The cabin was black as charcoal but she could hear this thing crawling over the ground. It sounded heavy and clinked like a musket or kettle. She thought she had barred the door but now it opened and the thing came painfully in. Only when it crawled on the leaves of the other bed did it come over her what it was. If they wouldn't fetch her any water, Achsa must have reckoned she would take the small kettle and lug it to the run herself.

Sayward lay in her dark bed and spelled this out. It was no use locking the stable after the ox was stolen. Likely Achsa had already sucked her fill, pressing her hot face down in the cool run. Twice she heard her sucking greedily at the kettle. She thought, let her have her run water now. It was little enough while she lived. Worth could come home now and sleep in his bed. Achsa would not likely plague him for water again.

Sayward only meant to half-doze after that but when she woke it was late. Gray light came through the oiled-paper window. She saw what had roused her. Genny was backing down from the loft, staring around at the empty kettle beside Achsa's bed. Her face was mighty sober as if looking on a corpse.

A splinter in the ladder caught Genny's skirt and lifted it as she came down.

"The bound boy's a thinkin' of you, Gin!" Achsa jeered in her heavy voice.

Sayward expected she better get up. It sounded like Achsa would want some breakfast this morning. She wouldn't be surprised if Achsa overed it now. Only passing the bed you could smell that she was soaked with sweat and still sweating. There was one thing, it looked like, that could stand off Death. If your time hadn't come yet, it made you slick as an eel and Death couldn't hold you. Not even if you lay at Death's door burning up with a fever and swilled yourself with cold water at the run.

No, Achsa's time hadn't come yet. The Lord might have something he had in mind for her to do first.

CHAPTER TWELVE

❋　❋　❋

The Cabin in the Shumack

WYITT and Sulie seldom came this way if the cows were willing. They didn't talk much about it but it had a place on this path they hated to pass. You went down a long, dark hollow. A little run from a spring slimed across the path. Up that run stood a deserted cabin all grown up with sumach. Its logs were black with age and weather. Once there must have been a little clearing around it. One time smoke had pushed out of that chimney and human feet pattered about. Now you could hardly tell humans ever lived here. A pair of hickory saplings had rammed up through the bark roof like it belonged to them.

"No Injun ever set up that cabin," Worth told them. "Unless it was a white Injun."

"How kin you tell?" Wyitt wanted to know.

"It has a lilock tree in'ar."

"A lilock tree—away back here!" Genny's voice came out almost like Jary's.

"I stopped by today and seed it myself," Worth nodded. "The Shawanees say it's Louie Scurrah's place. You know the one where used to be with Simon Girty."

All the young ones stared. When they were back in Pennsylvania, Jary would say, don't you do this and that or Simon Girty will get you! Every young woodsy knew that Louie Scurrah was mighty near as bad, for hadn't he been a boy with Girty the time the Indians burned Colonel Crawford at the stake! Hadn't he used to stand as a little tyke white and naked in the Ohio River and call piteously for arks and keel boats to come to shore and pick him up? And all the time Girty and his Delawares lay behind trees waiting to massacre every one!

"They say Scurrah had a woman a livin' with him in that cabin," Worth went on. "The Shawanees called her the white-faced gal. He fetched her up from Virginny. She died on him one time he was off to the English Lakes. But her lilock tree's still a livin'."

Once Sulie let Wyitt go on with the cows and crawled through the sumach to see the lilac tree. The cabin stood still and dark as if no human had ever walked or talked inside. The door was down and a copper snake lay coiled up on the doorstep looking in, waiting for a deer mouse or some foolish small creature just off the nest. Sulie kept her eyes off its ugly arrow head so that it couldn't put a spell on her. She knew Wyitt would tell her she had ought to've killed that snake. Now she had let her worst enemy get away for a whole year to plague her. She wished she hadn't come, but she had to see that lilac tree. A stale dank breath came out of the cabin like out of the white-faced girl's grave.

Sulie didn't take a look around for any grave. It got dark

early in the woods and she'd heard tell of humans who came out when they couldn't rest in their bury hole. Not humans that lived good lives and did what was right. No, they would wait for resurrection morn. Nor folks that had worked hard and were all played out. No, they wanted a good long rest. You never saw Jary no matter how often one of them had to go out at night, and her grave only yonder from the cabin. Jary had been an old woman of thirty-seven and mighty near tuckered out. Now this white-faced girl was young and likely full of life when they put her underground, and such would get plenty tired lying in one place so long.

In the short time she stayed, Sulie didn't see any lilac tree. But she found a bush nearby choked back to the ground in front of the cabin. The little that was still green had smooth, tender leaves like none she had seen before. You could tell plain enough this wasn't a wild thing the way it stooped down and pined away out here. She smelled at the lone, scrawny bunch of flowers and reckoned this was what the white-faced girl had liked to smell. She wanted to break it off and take it along back for the rest to smell at. But the ugly old cabin watched her out of its dark eye. She was glad just to get out of the sumach herself and run after Wyitt and smell again the good stable smell of Mrs. Covenhoven's cows.

When she and Wyitt passed the old Scurrah place after that, Sulie's mind ran right to the lilac tree. She wondered was it still living. But she didn't go in to see. It was close enough just to pass on the path with Wyitt for company and all the cowbells chiming sociably on the smothery air. Most times when the cows fed up this far, Wyitt drove them home another way. Tonight it hadn't much daylight left and Sulie could see he was letting them take the short path home by the cabin in the sumach.

The cows saw it first. The black one with the bent horn stopped dead in the path and right away the bells slacked off and hung mighty still. Cows and young ones all stared. What they saw looked like a Shawanee with his rifle on ahead. The cows didn't want to go at all now and Wyitt's shock of sandy hair raised up defiantly at this body who knew no better than stand in the path and scare his cattle.

He had to lay the gad on hard to get the cows started again. They moved a little closer by fits and starts. Sulie could see now it was a white man standing easy and pert as if he didn't care if he turned your cows off in the brush or no. The rifle stock under his arm was of curly maple striped crosswise like a tiger cat. It was finished up fine with brass and Sulie reckoned Wyitt would stop to stare at it. But Wyitt's eyes were working on something else. Then she saw it, too. Through the trees faint gray smoke was rising like a wraith from the old chimney of Louie Scurrah's cabin.

"Whose cows are them?" the stranger wanted to know.

"Covenhoven's," Wyitt fetched out, not looking at him.

"I heerd it had a settlemint here." The man looked from one to the other with his light blue eyes. He was a stocky fellow, not as big as Worth, but his back was up and his chest out like a young cock pheasant. Anybody could see you didn't want to cross him. "Covenhoven, you say your name is?"

"My name's Luckett. So's her'n," Wyitt answered him.

All the time he was edging sidewise to get by and after the cows that had pushed through the brush. Behind him Sulie was doing the same. She had her head down and a body might expect she was out of her wits. But nobody could have measured the distance better so she was just out of reach of his grab. One move from him and she would dive in the brush like a rabbit. After that the wolf could run her hard as he liked but he would have to run harder than she could.

In a minute she was past him and, though she kept her face down, she hadn't missed a lick about him. Her father's hunting shirt was a loose frock that came half way down over his hams. More than once she had seen him work it on stiff and cold of a morning. It had sleeves full enough to make her a shift apiece, and it folded part way around itself when it belted. That's the way it was meant so the bosom had slack to stow away bread and jerk to eat and tow to clean the rifle barrel so the lead could sing true. But what this Scurrah had on was a shirt tight and fancy, caped and beaded, fringed and trimmed with fur that might have been mink and might have been, for all a person knew, the trimmings from the scalp of some poor white girl who had hair soft and brown as Genny's. The shiny buttons likely were melted down from pewter out of some great folks' cabin he and his Indians burnt. And his cape was lined with raveled cloth red as the humans' blood that had run plenty times from his knife.

"Is he a follerin'?" Wyitt asked when they were past a ways.

"I kain't hear nothin'," Sulie didn't turn her head to see. If it was Louie Scurrah, he could track them like an Indian and it didn't matter where he set his foot down. He could come through

dead leaves and you could no more hear or see him than a catamount that has hair growing on the balls of its paws to shush its
noise.

"We're off from him now," Wyitt told her. "You don't need
to be afeard."

But if Wyitt wasn't "afeard," what was he gadding the cows
so hard for? They went skyting and belling up hill and down.
Their heavy bags bounced this way and that. Mrs. Covenhoven
would give them jesse for churning buttermilk. No, neither of
them could get out of these woods fast enough tonight. Coven-
roven's log barn looked mighty good pushing gray and solid out
of the trees. Mrs. Covenhoven's round, pocked face was almost
pretty as she came sailing out with her two cedar milking buckets
on her arms.

"Don't say nothin'," Wyitt warned under his breath. "And
don't you run home till I'm ready."

Sulie waited first on one foot and then the other while he
put down the walnut bars, letting the bawling cows in the stumpy
barnyard.

"They must a smelt a painter tonight," he told Mrs. Covenhoven, grave as a man. "You couldn't hold them back." He put up
the bars. "I guess now me and her'll go to our supper."

He and Sulie walked off together, straight and sober in the
owl light. Once they were out of sight on the other side of the log
barn, their bare legs raced through the nettles and sweet anise on
the path to be the first to tell at home.

Worth listened to them a while.

"Go on and eat your supper," then he broke out. "I'll send
that king's man off purty quick if he comes around."

"Was he light or dark-complected, Sulie?" Achsa whispered
up in the loft that evening.

"He looked like he slept with a hex!" Sulie snapped.

"You don't need to act so high and mighty," Achsa stuck up
for him. "He was only a little tyke when the Delywares took him.
He did no more'n what they told him. I wouldn't mind gittin' a
good look at him."

Before juneberries were ripe, Achsa had her chance. They
were sitting down to supper. Sulie looked out of the door and saw
those fancy buckskins with the red-lined collar that some called a
cape coming up the path.

"It's him!" she hissed.

Worth, his stool half way up to the table, darkened. Most

of the young ones stiffened. Sayward went calmly along getting supper on the table. She could stoop over a fire half a day and when she raised up, her back would be straight as before. Now, since nobody else offered to, she went to the door her own self.

"Your pappy to home?" the light-complected man outside wanted to know.

"He's to home," Sayward said shortly.

Her coolness never abashed Louie Scurrah. His hair might be curly as a young one's, but his light blue eyes could get ice in them mighty quick. That ice said plain enough no girl or woman could keep him cooling his heels outside when he wanted in. He stepped onto the cabin floor and found Worth standing by the head of the stand table.

"How're you?" Scurrah said, strong and pleasant as a basket of chips.

"Evenin'," Worth answered him.

"George Roebuck said I mought come and see you."

Worth only made a grunting sound.

"I need some'un to put a clapboard roof on my cabin," Scurrah went on. "They said you had a frow and was handy with tools."

Worth shook his head warily.

"I got no time to spare you right now."

Sulie expected Louie Scurrah to flare up at that, for he was a fire eater if she ever saw one.

"I kin wait," he said, nice as could be, taking no offense.

Nobody spoke right away. The visitor stood inside the door easy and pert as if he could wait all day. Around the table the young ones didn't know whether or not to sit down to supper. The venison roast lay hot and smoking on its wooden platter. You could smell it all over the place. Oh, this was a hard spot for Worth to be in, for never did a woodsy turn a man away hungry from his door if he could help it.

"Rations are ready—kin you set down and eat?" he bid, but he said it so forbiddingly and gave such a cold glance through his growth of beard that no man could mistake his unwelcome.

"Thankee," Louie Scurrah said.

Worth motioned with his bearded chin for Achsa to give up her stool and squeeze on the bench. Then there were only the sounds of stools and bench legs being scraped up to the table and of air being drawn through wet, smacking lips and of hunting knives and wooden spoons on the split puncheons.

Worth ate with brief down jerks of his beard, stopping now and then to expertly carve out a fresh slice and hold it out on his hunting knife to some hungry body. Sitting in Jary's place at the other end of the table, Sayward bulked strong and solid as Bar's Hill that Sulie and Wyitt had fetched the cows over this day. Genny picked finicky at her rations like she always did while Achsa kept raising her dark young eyes at this man in the red-lined collar across the stand table.

Sulie watched him too while her young jaws worked on the piece of deer meat her father gave her. Here he was sitting at their own table, the white Indian who helped burn some of his own flesh and blood. Louie Scurrah was only a boy then, they said, but he'd danced and howled around the stake bad as the Delawares. Some claimed Scurrah and Girty hadn't dare to do any less in front of the Indians and that's why they stuck burning sticks under that naked white man's skin and helped run a red hot gun barrel into him and burned out his eyes so Crawford had to stumble around stark blind with the smoke coming out of his sockets. But they had done it, hadn't they? And now one of that wizzen-hearted pair had his legs under their table, eating Sayward's venison roast. If she had a knife like Wyitt, Sulie told herself, she'd reach right under this table where her pappy couldn't see her and fix that white Indian!

Supper over, he told Worth he wasn't a king's man any more. No, once he was big enough to know right from wrong, he had gone over to General Wayne's side. And Worth was taking it for gospel and giving in to him like he always did if a body worked on him long enough. Even Wyitt looked like he had taken the wrong sow by the ear and hadn't had need to run from him the other day if he hadn't wanted to. But Louie Scurrah couldn't take in Sulie. He tried to make up to her once, asking pleasant as could be how she got home that night with the cows. Her black eyes burned back at him like a wolf pup's. And when he laughed at her across the table, she made a face and bit her thumb at him.

She had no notion her father would do anything, but he pushed back his stool and rifted sternly through his hairy lips.

"You kin go to your bed, Sulie," he said.

She made no motion that she heard except that she kept looking at Sayward.

"Sulie!" he raised his voice.

She went for the loft ladder at that but her bare feet hung

back from rung to rung long as they dared, her eyes measuring shrewdly how quick she could leg it up if he made for her. Once in the loft, she threw herself down on Achsa's bed with her head by the loft hole.

"It's too hot up here!" she cried. "I kain't breathe!"

"Well, you kin come down if you mind," her father growled.

She told herself she would never go down, not if she had to be nice to that bloody-handed turncoat. She could see him pull his tobacco pouch from his hunting shirt and hand it to Worth. And her father was taking it like he hadn't any spunk at all. Now they were lighting their pipes with a coal from the fire. She hoped Louie Scurrah would burn his fingers. Now they were sitting back in a corner talking, and the smoke was swimming up over their heads like a white river that flowed up hill. It circled around the cabin getting higher and higher. The cabin was Pennsylvania and the white river was the Juniata that had to go up over the mountains to get out to the sea. The loft hole was the gap it had to come through. Now it came to the gap and flowed over the riffles of the loft boards. Here it went by her house. She could lay on the bank and drink from it. But it wasn't any of Louie Scurrah's river she drank from, only what came from the clay of her father.

They were telling hunting stories now and Louie Scurrah was bragging how he hunted out of some fort for General Wayne. The Indians had it bottled up but he kept the garrison in meat. The Indians were up in trees watching. They ambushed every man who left by daylight and they wanted to get him the most because he'd gone back on their side. But he went out of the saddle gate by night.

"Once I got in the woods without their seein' me, then I had as good chance as them," he said.

He'd stay out till he got game. It was winter time and he couldn't make an open fire at night or they'd see it. So he dug a hole in the ground with his tomahawk deep as the crown of his coonskin cap. He called it his coal pit. He filled it with crosswise layers of roth. He kindled a fire in the bark with the back of his hunting knife and a flint from his rifle. He slept sitting up with the coal pit between his legs and his blanket around him. The fire under him kept him warm and on the coldest night he could blow it up till it made him sweat.

From her place at the loft hole Sulie could see her father and Wyitt looking at him now with new respect and Genny had

moved across the cabin to listen. Louie Scurrah sat back easier
and went on. Before he drew a bead on a buck he always put a
bullet in his mouth. Then he'd load up quick to be ready if the
shot fetched an Indian. He'd drag his deer to a tree to dress it
with his back to the butt and his rifle leaning up handy. Oh, he
had been an Indian himself and knew how to give them the slip.
He'd pack the four quarters in the hide so he could sling it on his
back like a knapsack and tote it to the fort. The Indians found his
coal pits and what was left of his deer. They called him No-Man-
Can-Kill-Him. The Wyandots wanted to swap him squaws and
ponies for his rifle, but he wouldn't part with it.

He crossed the cabin to show that rifle to Worth. Not every
day, he boasted, could you see one with a raised cheek rest. The
cheek rest had to be cut out first, then the whole stock cut away
from it. Sulie wanted to call out loud, what scalped white man
did he take that off of? But her father would britch her for that.
Genny was looking at the rifle. Sulie reckoned she'd look at it,
too. She climbed down the ladder, but the raised cheek rest didn't
look like any great shakes to her, though the stock had a brass
patch box and hunter's moon inlaid in the curly maple.

She'd sooner look at Genny right now than any rifle. Never
had she seen her sister so mortal pretty. Her hair was soft and
brown as a pine marten tonight and her skin white as a town lady.
Even Achsa kept staring at her, but Genny didn't take notice. Her
bright eyes watched this Louie Scurrah in his pewter buttons and
hunting frock with the soldier cape. She listened to all he had to
say, and when he told how he hadn't the heart to kill a she-
panther and its kits he saw playing together like humans one day,
she leaned forward.

"Ahh!" she came out soft-hearted before she knew it.

"If you'd like a painter kit, I'll git you one some time,"
Scurrah said, looking across at her.

Genny shrank back on her stool and reckoned shyly she'd
like one if her pappy and Sayward wouldn't mind.

Sayward didn't say she would and didn't say she wouldn't.
She sat in a dark corner working the buckskin for Wyitt's new
britches soft and pliable in her hands. You couldn't read her face,
but Sulie remembered she was the only one hadn't gone forward
to make a fuss of the rifle. The little girl felt a sudden burst of
tenderness for her oldest sister. She went over and sat close beside her on her heels.

"How long till you go back up West?" Worth said.

"I aim to settle down," Scurrah told him. "They say it has a lawyer here from the Bay State. I want to see him about rights to my track out yonder. A purty place if you've seed it."

Sulie's young lip curled but Worth nodded gravely. Scurrah filled his pipe and passed his tobacco again to the older man.

"I'll stop by some day. One of your young'uns mought show me where he lives at?"

"The boy'll take you and welcome," Worth nodded, stuffing his dark clay.

"Thankee," Louie Scurrah said, touching his pipe with a bright coal so that the glow lighted up his bold young features. "If he's off with the cows, maybe Miss Ginny here kin show me?"

CHAPTER THIRTEEN

✻   ✻   ✻

The White Magnoly

WORTH told Louie Scurrah he needn't go home for a bed this night. No use doing that. It was a good ways out there through the woods after dark. Here was room on his own bed. Why didn't he sleep here and go on home tomorrow by daylight? And Louie said he might take him up on it.

Worth nodded, satisfied. It did him good that the younger man came in so often. These tree-slashing-and-burning squatters he couldn't go, but Louie was a woodsy like himself. He relished it when they sat back together and lighted up their clays and talked. Wyitt and Genny would pull up stools and listen. Last week Louie showed Wyitt how to make him a gigging light and spear. Today he threw down a spotted doe-fawn he had knocked over the head for Sayward to make a fawn roast. Oh, he wasn't a bad fellow for one raised by the Indians so long as you didn't give him fire to eat. This afternoon when Sulie kept at Genny and

Achsa to go visiting the MacWhirters like they planned, he said he'd go along through the woods for company.

Sulie and Achsa came home about dark.

"Whar's Ginny?" Worth wanted to know. Sulie looked up meaningly at Achsa.

"Him and her run off from us!" Achsa bawled in her heavy voice.

Worth looked in the fire. There were things he wanted to ask about this but he felt uneasy in front of Sayward. He ate his supper and when it got late and they hadn't come, he tapped his clay bowl and went outside. It must be close to full moon. A faint ghostly light drifted like fine smoke under the trees. He walked down the path to the river where he could look out. The moon lay upside down like a gold sovereign in the water and all the little riffles threw off yellow sparks. Yes, tomorrow night would be full moon, and he didn't know as he liked it. The old saying stuck in his mind. Women were dull in the dark of the moon, but when the moon was full they were bold and free.

"I'm a goin' to bed," he told them gruffly when he came back to the cabin. "You'uns better go, too."

"Maybe after dark they went to the Harbisons'," Wyitt stuck up for Louie.

"I expect," Sayward said easily, "they're just afeard to come in while it has light in the cabin."

The fire had hardly died down to coals when you could hear them nibbling on the latch string like a pair of wary young coons on the bait in one of Wyitt's snares. They came in on their toes.

"You kin stay," Genny urged him, whispering. "Pappy said so."

Louie took the knife from his belt, untied his moccasin strings and he was ready for bed. But Genny had to stoop at the fire and scrape ashes over the red coals till darkness swallowed her up. Then you could hear her taking down her hair and knotting it in braids, slipping off her shortgown and feeling around in the darkness for her bed gown till she found it and pulled it down over her and crawled in beside Sayward.

Worth lay on his back listening to the whippoorwill and thinking over many things before he could sleep tonight. It took something like this, he expected, to make him see he had another girl big enough for men to pester. Oh, he had little against his bedfellow. You couldn't help it if the Delawares took you when you were a little tyke and brought you up. Louie had his good points. He even stuck up for Simon Girty that every white person hated, saying he knew of Girty to buy off plenty white boys the Indians had slaving for them and to trade them off to the British.

No, it wasn't his living with the Indians he had against Louie Scurrah. It was his itchy foot. Once a man had such, it itched him all his life, and there was no help for it. It would itch to go from here off yonder and once it got there, it would itch for some other place. Nothing, likely, but the bury hole would cure it. Louie might reckon he was giving up and settling down, but an itchy foot wouldn't let him. If nothing else worked on him, the settlers would come in, the game and woods would move out, and a woodsy would have to move out with them.

Didn't he know? Wasn't he like Louie nigh onto twenty years back? Couldn't he see Jary now as he had seen her that first time along the Conestoga, young, white skinned and pretty as Genny today? Hadn't Jary's folks fought her for taking up with a woodsy like he was? He hadn't much use for them then, but he could see their side now. They wanted to spare their young one from being dragged off to some lonesome tract in the woods where they would never lay eyes on her again. But off to the woods she would go. And now where was she? If she had mam or pap left, they didn't even know she was dead and buried. When her birth time came around, like as not one grayhead would say to the other, "Jary's thirty-nine years old today. Wonder where she's at now!" They wouldn't reckon she was still thirty-seven lying deep in the black muck of this Northwest land. He hadn't liked much the time she had lit off for home when he went back to Wayne's army. But he was glad for it now. It gave her a visit with her folks, the only one she ever had. He recollected how little Genny had cried when he took them back to the woods. But if Jary shed any tears, she had done it in secret.

Now if Louie wanted a woman, Worth would like to see him get one. But he wasn't anxious for Genny to take the white-faced girl's place out in that lonesome cabin. Achsa was the better woman for him, if he only knew it. Achsa took after his mother who had Monsey blood, and her bare feet had tramped behind his father any place it pleased him to wander. Oh, he knew Louie took no more notice of Achsa than of little Sulie. These young fellows never would listen. Marrying wasn't like what you expected when you were young and foolish as a gandersnipe. Once you were married, you stayed married, unless one of you died or run off. And young ones came thick as squirrels on a hickory. A man and woman were a long time married but it didn't take long to get started. First thing you'd know, they'd be together.

His unshaven lips tightened in the darkness. He would put his foot down on this. He'd talk plain to Sayward in the morning. But next day when he called her out of the cabin, it wasn't easy as he had figured.

"You kin tell Ginny," he stormed, looking the other way, "she's too mortal young to be a sparkin'. And if she wa'n't, I still wouldn't want her a livin' way out somewhar in the bush by her lonesome."

Then he went off with his bag and rifle. He wasn't going for game today. This was summer time and they had fresh meat. He was out to dig sang, however far he'd have to go for it. He had dug out plenty hereabouts. The whole cabin was strung up with the drying roots.

Sayward felt for her father. He couldn't meet her eye but had to go right off. Oh, he knew well enough who it was had first taken in this Louie Scurrah and listened to his hunting stories and hefted his curly maple sporting rifle, and even gone out with his own frow and augur and fixed up that old cabin in the sumach till it was something more than for a coppersnake to live in. Yes, Worth knew who had egged this thing on. And now he was running off and telling her she had to break it up.

That was easier said than done, Sayward thought, as she redd up the stand table. You couldn't pen up humans in different coops like they did Gypsyfowl back in Pennsylvania. Humans were free as wild pigeons in the woods. You could talk all day to a young redbreast cock or a graybreast hen sitting up on a limb, but they would mate their own selves when the notion took them. And likely it would be deep in the woods somewhere far from your eyes and hearing.

Oh, she would tell Genny what her father had said. Let Genny think her jealous if she wanted to. But today when Genny came back from walking home a short piece with Louie, she looked too mortal sweet to heartscald right now. The last few days Genny had come out like the juneberry that is only slim and pale one day and the next is all blossoms and sightlier than anything else in the woods. Only Genny's skin was nearer like the tulip laurel that some call the white magnolia. She came back floating along the path like milkweed down. She could hardly have known what she was doing, for without being told she took the bedding out on the bushes to air.

Somewhere out there she swung on a creeper and her voice
kept lifting from the woods fresh as a bobwhite back in a Conestoga meadow.

> *Oh, the year was a risin' so bright and clear*
> *And the young gal sot in the old woman's cheer.*

It was too far to know what the verse was about, but when
she got to the chorus again, her voice sang out and you could
catch every word.

> *Oh, the year was a risin' so bright and clear*
> *And the young gal sot in the old woman's cheer.*

Sayward went to the door and stood a while looking out.
The pot was waiting for her to scrub it out with soap and sand.
Let it sit till she was ready. You didn't often see the woods more
still. They were atop of summer now. The leaves wouldn't get any
bigger or the days longer. The changing season had slowed down
till it nearly stopped. Now it would stay this way a while through
the dog days when you had to watch out for mad, slobber-jawed
wolves. The only leaves that moved were yonder where Genny
kept swinging on her creeper tied in a big loop for a seat. And at
the end of every verse you could hear her sing out:

> *Oh, the year was a risin' so bright and clear*
> *And the young gal sot in the old woman's cheer.*

What was that song about, Sayward wondered. She had a
notion, though she couldn't mind ever hearing it before. When
Genny came in a while later, Sayward reckoned she wasn't far
off, though this time Genny was singing another.

> *Oh, why have you put on your bonny blue suit,*
> *And why do you laugh so gay?*
> *I'm off to the Lancaster street fair, Mother.*
> *I'm off to the fair, I say.*

> *But the fair don't come off till June, Michael.*
> *You kain't dress now for that day.*
> *It's the May dance I'm off to, Mother, he said,*
> *It's the May dance I'm off to, I say.*

But the May dance is past, Michael, she said;
It was over with yesterday.
Then I'll go my Cousin Ellen to see,
Cousin Ellen to see, I say.

But Cousin Ellen's in Reading town, Michael,
And Reading town's far away.
Maybe she's back to her mansion house, Mother.
Maybe she's back, I say.

I fear it's another, Michael, my son,
Bright as a poppinjay.
But who would it be, Mother of mine,
Who would it be, I say?

Tell me it ain't the gypsy maid, Michael,
And this ain't your weddin' day?
It's rainin', Mother you better go in.
You better go in, I say.

Sayward's face was cruel as she bent over her black kettle where the bear grease had blackened and fastened. Louie Scurrah better be good to that girl, she thought. He better take care of their Genny. God help him if he thinks he can use her as he pleases and then run off to the English Lakes or some place and let her sit home lonesome as the white-faced girl in his cabin. If he reckons her folks won't do anything to stop him, she would change his mind shortly.

Next time he came, she would call him out in the woods alone and read the law off to him. If he couldn't make Genny any happier than he did his other woman, he better leave her alone. And if he ever had an Indian lover, he had better go back and stay with her. For every body knows an Indian lover never will give a white man up, but after seven years to the day will come back to face him with his child by the hand. It would give Genny a turn for him to go off now, but she would over it. It had plenty men in the woods for a girl like Genny and most of them, she expected, better than Louie Scurrah.

Next time he came over she would tell him. But that was a long ways off, although she didn't know it then.

CHAPTER FOURTEEN

❀ ❀ ❀

The Little Tyke

S AYWARD WISHED Buckman Tull had kept what day it was to himself. She would rather not have known that she and her father had made this out against Louie Scurrah on a Friday. The Tulls were bighead and always had to show they knew the most. They never let you forget they had an almanac and that it came all the way from the Bay State. Now Portius Wheeler came from down there himself and you'd never know it from him. But the Tulls couldn't pass the time without fetching in the day of the week.

"How are you, this fine Friday mornin'?" Buckman Tull had called out big as you please as he went by to the post.

Sayward didn't mind them telling her when it was the Lord's day. The better the day, the better the deed. Any washing she did on the Sabbath would be cleaner and sweeter-smelling and bleached whiter even though it had no sun handy to hang it in. But Fridays were not like other days of the week. No, Friday was the deil's day, for the Lord was massacred on it. Oh, it could be fair enough one place on a Friday, but other places in the world it would be black and bitter as death.

Never mind, Sayward told herself. If she couldn't change the day, she would have to let it go. It appeared fair enough here in this Northwest country today. Achsa's axe rang out like a man's while she chopped supper wood. Genny hummed while she roiled the leaves soft in their beds and lugged the bedding in. And Wyitt and Sulie ran off early on their chore of fetching the cows. When it got late and they didn't come in, Sayward didn't think much about it. She and the other girls pulled stools to their supper. But once it was dark, she reckoned she'd go over to the Covenhovens and see what was keeping them.

Then she looked up and saw Wyitt silent and pale as tallow at the door. His bare legs were black muddy to the knees.

"Whar's Sulie at?" Genny cried at him first.

"Ain't she here?" he said, but you could see the way his look went around the cabin that he didn't expect her.

"Whar'd you leave her?" Sayward asked sharply.

Wyitt stood just inside the doorway. He acted like he was scared to come in his own pappy's house. The cows, he said, had never been out so far. He and Sulie couldn't hear a bell till they climbed atop a sharp hill. Away down on the other side they found them in some gat brush off from the flies. But when they drove them out, the cows wouldn't make for the settlement. No, they had it in their heads to go the other way. He beat them over their stubborn horns with a club and still they would go away from home.

He promised Sulie they would get fagged after while and then he could turn them. But she was scared to go further in the Shawanee country. He could go on with them if he wanted, she said; she would take the path back and tell Mrs. Covenhoven.

The cows kept right on with Wyitt scrambling behind. They forded a river and wound through places he had never seen before. It was dark when he saw a light ahead. This was one of the Shawanee towns, he expected. He saw a strange log barn, and a strange white man came out with a light. Wyitt asked him could he tell him where he and his cows were at. The man looked at him. He said didn't he know where he was at? This was the Covenhoven improvement and these were their cows he had fetched home.

"It was Mister Covenhoven hisself!" Achsa jeered in her man's voice. "The cows fetched you home and you never knowed it."

"Then war's Sulie?" Genny cried.

"I expect Sulie kin take keer of her own self," Sayward said, holding her voice and face calm. "You and Achsa stay here. Wyitt kin eat his supper. Then me and him'll go out and git her. If he kin show me the way."

"I kin show you the way we went out," the boy said. "But I kain't the way the cows brung me home."

Before Wyitt got up from the table, big John Covenhoven came stooping in the door. His wife sent him over to see if Sulie had shown up. He said he better go along. Sayward dropped some dry candlewood and pine knots in her greasy leather apron. Wyitt lit a stick at the fireplace and went ahead. Sometimes he whirled around a pine knot or a sliver of candlewood and sometimes a bunch of shellbark torn off on the way.

More than once he stopped to make sure he wasn't turned around again. Sayward told herself that never had she seen any of this strange black woods before tonight. They went over runs and wet places, up hill and down and up again till Wyitt said this was the knoll he and Sulie had heard the bells from. He was sure as could be and if they couldn't find his and Sulie's barefoot tracks in the soft ground, it must be the deil had his foot over them.

They built a fire there atop the hill and kept it going to guide Sullie's little feet through the night. One time or another they would go to the end of the firelight.

"Whoooo-hoooo!" Sayward would send her strong call into the black woods.

"Suuuu-lieeee!" Wyitt would yell as if splitting his throat would fetch her in.

All that answered were echoes, and that, they knew, was the woods mocking them. Out in the darkness they could hear the night birds and beasts going about their business like nothing had happened. The big-eared owl some called the Hill Hooter bit off his hoots calm and steady as always and his barred relation dragged out the last of his arrogantly. Now and then wolves howled far off and once came a distant wail through the woods like a panther or catamount. Or it might have been only the red fox that Worth said could give you the worst scare of any beast in the woods when it wanted. Oh, the wild creatures gave no notice at all that they saw the red light of the fire up on this hill. They went prowling their rounds as if no little tyke had been lost in the woods and didn't know the way home in the dark to her pappy's.

It started to rain and in her mind Sayward could see little Sulie, a bedraggled mite somewhere out in this wide bush. Where was she at, she would be asking herself, and would ever she see sisters and brother again? She couldn't take her sopping wet clothes off her little body tonight and snuggle down safe and dry in her loft bed under the roof her pappy had made with his axe, frow and augur. No, she must crawl in a dead, hollow tree like a bear or up a live one like a marten. Up a tree she might be safe enough, should she but recollect she is no young gabby bird that can hold on to a limb with its toes while it sleeps. If she as much as half-dozed, down she might come. And if her young legs snapped like kindling, she would have to sit on a rock and wait till they came and fetched her.

John Covenhoven said hadn't they better go home on account of the rain?

"I ain't sugar and salt. I won't melt," Sayward told him.

She was all for pushing further on, but the rain put out their torches. They had to wait for daylight to look for the place Sulie and Wyitt had parted, and then Wyitt couldn't find the gat brush where the cows had stood off from the flies. When they got home to the cabin, no tuckered-out and brier-scratched little tyke was waiting for them, but Genny and Achsa hadn't lacked someone to talk to. When her man didn't come, Mrs. Covenhoven had bridled a horse and ridden over. And when he wasn't back by early dawn, she had ridden on to the Tulls and Harbisons to sound the alarm.

The settlers answered the summons like the blowing of a great hunting horn. No church bell could have drawn them as hard as such a heartbreak thing. Jake Tench and the bound boy, almost the last to hear, were the first to come. Billy Harbison fetched his hounds and tied them to a young dogwood from where they made it ring around the cabin. Tod Wylder rode his dun ox over with his wife on behind. A gaunt Kentucky woman came on foot with her man and her fourth baby. She was nursing it as she stepped dark as an Indian woman across the doorway, her breast white as milk beside the brown face, her eyes deep in their hollow sockets. Little Mathias and his boy came. The Mac-Whirters and the McFalls tramped together through the woods with all their five or six boys. And there were some the Lucketts had only heard about and never seen before.

It made you feel better with so many around, Sayward thought. The littlest ones didn't know what it was all about and ripped and tore like they were at a frolic. But the older ones stood here and yonder, grave as could be, the boys with their pappies, the girls with their mams in the cabin. The women had lots to ask about this thing. Each time a fresh one came, they listened to the story over again, and their eyes kept stirred up and glowing.

Outside the men stood in a hard knot, making men's talk, chewing off tobacco, telling of bodies they knew had been lost. Their eyes were alive in their sober faces, and now and then when one of them rubbed over his mouth with his hand, rumpling his beard if he had any and spitting copiously, he would cast around to see if his own youngest was all right, making like a grimace to cover it up, but there was no humor in it.

Jake Tench put a brighter face on them after the Mac-Whirters and the McFalls came.

"Never you mind, Saird," he called in at the door. "Jude

MacWhirter kin find a young'un for you. Now John Covenhoven couldn't find one behind his own choppin' block."

The men's mouths opened round to laugh at this joke on the childless Covenhovens. Judah MacWhirter had six or seven living and only God knew how many dead back in Kentucky. The women in the house laughed, too, pulling down their faces at each other, for behind the chopping log was where they told their youngest that babies came from. For a while now it was more like usual in the Luckett cabin and out. The men told lighter stories and slapped their legs. But the woods closed around this place too thick and dark to last. It hadn't a field here nor tame bush, not a clearing or patch of sky a human could call his own. No, this cabin was owned soul and body by the great woods that ran on and on to the prairies by the English Lakes and to the Spanish Settlements on the Illinois.

Buckman Tull was the first to hear and the last to come. Billy Harbison loosed his hounds and they were ready to start. It didn't seem they cared if Wyitt went along or not to show them the way. They would go out in the woods and find out for themselves what happened to this young one that she didn't come home. The women crowded out of the door to watch them go. They looked like Sinclair's army, men and boys, with rifles and clubs, in boots and bare feet, shoepacks and moccasins. Buckman Tull had on his soldier coat with his horn slung over one shoulder, and it was he who took charge.

"They'll fetch your young'un back," Ellen MacWhirter comforted Sayward. "If she hain't been killed by some wild creater."

But all they fetched back next day was news of a barefoot young one's track by a run. It might have been Sulie's toes in the black mud, and it might have been the youngest MacWhirter boy's. At the blast of the horn they had all run up and tramped it out before they could measure. The day after that they found nothing.

Oh where, Sayward cried in her mind, was her father? Why did he have to be off now when they needed him most? They were out of fresh meat with all these mouths to feed. And Sulie's bed in the loft was slept in by strangers. Didn't he know his favorite young one was lost out in the woods while he wandered around digging in the dirt for roots for the pigtail people!

When he did come home, she pitied him hard. The second evening little Hughie McFall ran in that a strange man was outside. Sayward thought one of the other women could talk to him. Then she looked up and Worth stood in the doorway, his bag of sang roots weighting his back, his rifle in his hand.

"What fetches all these folks?" he asked sternly of Genny who was nearest him in the crowded cabin.

When she shrank back and wouldn't answer, his eyes moved on past Wyitt and Achsa till he found Sayward at the fire.

"Whar's Sulie?" he asked louder.

"She never came home with the cows," Sayward told him.

He gave a start like a beast in a trap when it gets the first lick with the club.

"When was this?" And when Sayward told him, "She ain't out in the woods yit?"

The neighbor folks all watched, pitying him as Sayward told the story. She had told it so often, the words were worn to her tongue like Worth's pipestem to his teeth. Several times he groaned, and Sayward guessed he was thinking how it might have been different if he had stayed to home. She and John Covenhoven and Wyitt had done what they could that first night, but Worth could find his way through the woods like a lynx in the dark. That first night little Sulie couldn't have been far off. Now only God knew where she had wandered and to what end she had come.

When she finished, he looked like he had been dram drinking.

"Whar's Louie?" he wanted to know.

She didn't answer.

"You'd better git him." He wouldn't meet her eyes. "Louie mought know. He mought a seed her."

Louie Scurrah came early next morning. He wore a buck tail like it was some kind of frolic.

"So you wouldn't git me before!" the hard look he gave Sayward said.

Oh, you could see he knew he had been slighted and now they'd had to send for him. It made him cocky as all get out. He set himself in charge and told the men why they hadn't got anywhere. It was plain Buckman Tull didn't like this. Today, Louie said, they would stretch a line with every man and boy six poles apart. They would whoop at each other to keep the line straight and when somebody found a sign, Buckman Tull would blow his horn. Buckman Tull sat up and nodded. That, you could tell, satisfied him. And if they fired off their rifles, Louie went on, that would mean they had found the young one.

"Dead or alive," he said, looking hard at Sayward.

Wouldn't they need every human they could get?, Achsa put to him. You could see she hankered to go along. Every last man and boy, Louie told her. But not women and girls. They were no good in the woods. They only made it harder. If women found a sign, they would run ahead and screech for the young one till it would hide, if it were around. No, the place for a girl was women's work at home.

Achsa's black eyes burned back at him. You could tell she reckoned it easy enough to be a man and go out in the woods whooping to keep in line and beating the bushes for a little tyke in a red dress that by this time the brush must have whipped halfways off her back. You did no whooping at women's work. No, you stooped by the fire till your face singed and your leg muscles ached so folks got enough to eat. And you heard no horn. All you listened to was women's talk from daylight to dark.

The women hardly stirred foot outside the cabin, yet it hadn't one who didn't have her own notion why they hadn't found little Sulie. Tod Wylder's woman told about a boy called Chris that had been lost in the woods back in York state. This was in the olden times. When they found him, a panther had scratched leaves over what was left of him till it would get back that way again, and that's why it took so long to find him. Then Sally Harbison was acquainted with a lost girl it took four years to find down in Virginia. An Indian had shot her for a deer and buried her so the whites wouldn't find out. But her grave fell in and when they dug it up, they found the bullet in her breast bone.

God help you, getting lost in the woods was a fearsome thing, old Granny MacWhirter said. She had toothless gums and on the back of her head a white knit cap that was all yellow with age and hair grease. She was lost once herself for forty-eight hours.

"They's only one word for it," she bobbed her head, "and that's lostness. Even a growed woman keeps a runnin' and stumblin' till she's wore out. The smartest man gits fogged. He kain't see straight any more. He goes crazy with bein' lost, that's what he does. If he comes on a trace he tromped every day, he don't know it any more. Let him take it, and his craziness takes the wrong end. He thinks his own tracks an hour past are the tracks of some man he never seed or knowed. Let him hear man, woman or young'un a comin', and he runs and hides. He ain't a human no more. He's nothin' but a wild creater. Git him home and the whole world's turned around end for end. The sun's in the wrong place. It rises in the west and sets in the east. The North Star's away down yonder."

She knew a case once in Kentucky pitiful to tell. A young boy was lost seventeen days. They found him digging up acorns like a squirrel with its paws and wilder than anything in the woods. He tried to bite the thumb of his own pappy and run off. Once he was home, they reckoned he would come back to his old life, but he never owned his own sister or mother. He wouldn't sleep in a bed, and he dirtied the house like a hound. What end he came to she didn't hear, but the doctors knew nothing to do for a case like that.

"Sometimes," Granny MacWhirter bobbed her cap and worked her lips and drew down her face at you, "it's a good thing if you don't find a lost young'un!"

"Once they're out too long," Mrs. McFall said, wiping her eyes, "I'd as soon see them dead and buried. That's easier to stand than this waitin' around and never knowin'."

But Sayward reckoned different. She wouldn't mind if their little Sulie snapped at them like a pet fox for a while, just so they found her alive. She always snapped some anyhow. A little more would be of no account. And sooner never find her than see her dead and buried. So long as you never knew, you could keep on hoping, if it was a score of years. Once you saw a body put underground, that was an end to it and to a little part inside of you that died, too.

How many times the horn blew that day they didn't know, for it was too far to hear. The men must have camped out somewhere in the woods that night. You could see this wasn't going to be over and done with easy like Louie Scurrah thought. In the morning Achsa, Cora MacWhirter and some of the other big girls made the rounds of the improvements that had stock to tend. They fetched back food and bedding. The men did not come back that night either. But a few nights following, when they were all down on pallets on the floor like so many logs jammed side by each at a rolling, they heard a whooping. Genny's hands trembled so she could hardly pull on her shortgown. She thought they had Sulie.

It was old Hugh McFall and Hen Giddings whooping before they got to the cabin so the women and young ones wouldn't be scared. They had come back to see if the women folk were all right and the stock tended. They would take back some meal to the woods tomorrow. Sayward threw wood on the fire for light and got them rations. After their bellies were filled, they told what they knew.

No, they hadn't come on the young one yet. But that Louie Scurrah had a lynx eye in the woods. You needn't be out long to know he'd been raised by the Delawares. Between him and Worth they had no need of Billy Harbison's hounds. The first day Louie found spicewood chewed by some other creature than a deer, for it had teeth marks on the upper side of the twig. And Worth picked up a red thread torn off by a black haw.

Oh, those two could follow where you could see nothing. And every sign they came on, the young one was further and further from home. They found where she ate wild cherries and whortleberries and where she crossed the runs. You could see her foot plain as could be in the sand. The third day they came on a nest of old leaves where she spent the night. She must have camped here more than one day, for her little feet had beaten a path in a heavy stand of timber. Now what do you reckon she had in there?

Old Hugh, who was telling it, settled himself. He blinked solemn as an owl.

You'd never guess it, he said. Louie Scurrah found it himself and had Buckman Tull blow his horn. When they all came up, he took them in and asked did they see anything. So help him, if there wasn't a little bitty play house made of sticks in that big timber! It had bark on the roof and a doorway in the middle. Inside it had a bed of leaves and a block of wood for a trencher with a scrap off a young one's dress for a fancy trencher cloth. It even had a nosegay of flowers. Anybody could see right off a mite of a girl had done this. Away back here in the wilderness, far from any human's cabin, she had made herself a little house just like her pappy's. You might reckon a big hairy fellow like Jake Tench wouldn't mind looking at such. But when Worth raised up and called out to the woods, "Sulie! Sulie! Be you still alive?" Jake had to walk himself off in the bush.

Genny couldn't listen any more. She buried her head in the bed clothing. Achsa's brown face twisted up in cruel lumps. Sayward turned hard to the fire because like Jake she couldn't stop her eyes. "Sulie! Sulie! Be you still alive?" she called out in her mind with her father. Out there in the great woods, further than any of them had ever been except maybe one or two, their little

Sulie had built a play house to recollect how she and Wyitt and Genny and Achsa had run and played together by this cabin. Wasn't it just like her? Who but little Sulie would put a nosegay in a play house or make up a trencher with a fine red cloth? She was ever saying grand things that no one dared think of but she and her Granmam Powelly who lived in a story-and-a-half chipped-log house across the road from Granpappy's gunsmith shop along the Conestoga.

Sayward wished she could see for herself that little play house Sulie had made. She'd give all she had if Hugh McFall and Hen Giddings would take her back with them when they went. Those men would need a woman if ever they found Sulie. God knows that after all these days she would be a poor little bag of bones. She would need special waiting on. Men would not know how.

But old Hugh McFall and Hen Giddings went back to the woods without saying a word, no not a word. They went alone at daylight, and that was the last the women saw of them for a week.

Once upon a time Sayward wished she had a clock. Mrs. Covenhoven had one, and Portius Wheeler, the bound boy said, carried a pocket clock that struck the hours though it was no bigger around than his fist. A clock, Sayward reckoned, was almost human, for it had face, hands and sense to tell the time. No doubt it was a friendly face to have around and to hear it ticking sociably through the day and night. But a human could tell time the best, for some hours were fast and some were slow. Now you could tell nothing from Sayward's face, but the hours of this last week were the longest in all her born days. This was a time in her life, she thought, she would never want to go back to and live again.

You would expect, Genny said, that since they found Sulie's play house, it wouldn't take long till they found the little tyke herself. But it didn't work out that way. No, it seemed the deil had done it like this just to work up their hopes and then let them fall through. The men said there was a plain track of Sulie going into that place but none going out. Like a pack of hounds trying to find the lost scent, they made bigger and bigger circles around, but the one cold track was all they could find. It was almost like an eagle had swooped down by her play house and carried her off, leaving never a sign on the ground.

In worn-out bunches the men and boys straggled back. They

said they had done all mortal man could do. They had tramped the woods from Dan to Bersheba. They had tramped it further than any young one could travel on its own shanks. They had raked it with a fine tooth comb. All they had found were horse tracks and a place where some strange Indians had made fire for the night.

"The young'un's a gone Josie," Jude MacWhiter shook his shaggy head. "They ain't no use a huntin' what ain't thar."

Now little Sulie's bed up in the loft lay empty and lonesome again. Only Worth and Louie Scurrah had not come back. No, they had stuck to the woods like stubborn hounds that can't be clubbed into giving up the scent. There wasn't a fresh bone or dust of meal left in the cabin, but Sayward reckoned they could make out by their selves. The young ones could pick berries and fish the river with whang leather outlines. Wyitt could snare rabbits, and she could cut out the summer worms. Maybe, too, a body could take a rock and keep still long enough in the woods to call a turkey or kill a cock pheasant when he came strutting to his log.

But the hungry young ones were glad enough to lay eyes on Louie Scurrah at the cabin door one morning. Flowers sprang out on Genny's white cheeks though it would be an hour before she should taste the venison slung in a red summer hide on his back. No meat ever came in handier but Sayward begrudged him sorely that it wasn't their Sulie he had fetched back. Never would she forgive him that.

He said he and Worth had followed the tracks of the horseback Indians till they separated and petered out. Back on the Miami River he had to give up, but Worth wouldn't come home. No, he said he couldn't look at his cabin now with his littlest gone. Now that he was out this far, he would keep on beating the woods for her till he reached the grandaddy of rivers. Always had Worth wanted to lay eyes on that long river frozen in winter at one end while the other end has flowers and palm trees on either bank.

"He said one man could keep his cabin in meat till he got back," Louie told her.

Sayward's face was tight-lipped and cruel. She had not a word to say as she got a roast ready, for what could you say to a man who had beat the woods for your littlest sister that was likely dead, then fetched meat home for your living sisters and brother to eat. Oh, she would feed their empty bellies with smoking, hot flesh till their cheeks stuck out again, but it would be bitter enough meat to her. Dinner done she scrubbed what little she had to scrub and took herself off by her lonesome to the woods where she could work this thing off with her legs.

Everywhere she went the trees stood around her like a great herd of dark beasts. Up and up shot the heavy butts of the live ones. Down and down every which way on the forest floor lay the thick rotting butts of the dead ones. Alive or dead, they were mostly grown over with moss. The light that came down here was dim and green. All day even in the cabin you lived in a green light. At night that changed. By day you looked paler than you really were. By night the fire gave you a ruddy glow. She always waited for night time when little Sulie had looked to be ailing. Likely it was only the woods light. By firelight she would be well again.

Oh, it was a cruel thing for the trees to do this to a little girl who had never harmed them more than to shinny up their branches or swing on a creeper. Some claimed the trees were softhearted as humans. They said the pole of the cross had been cut from pine and that's why the pine was always bleeding. The crosspiece, they claimed, was from quaking ash. The quaking ash has shook ever since, and never can it live now more than the thirty-three years of the Lord.

Likely as not, Sayward told herself, a tree might tremble and bleed for the son of the Almighty who could heave it out by its roots with His breath or smack it down with His thunder. But neither pine nor quaking ash would give a hait for a poor little girl body wandering around lost in the woods crying for her sisters and pappy who never came to answer. And the birds and beasts would be as bad. Oh, she heard Genny sing a catch once where the birds and beasts covered up the lost Babes in the Woods with leaves. But that was just a pretty song. Any woodsy knew that the corbies would sit around in a ring waiting to pick out the poor little Babes in the Woods's eyes. And if any beast covered them up with leaves it would be the panther so he could come back and munch at their starved little hams another day.

Back along the Conestoga the trees seemed tame enough. Out here they were wild trees. Even in the daytime you could feel something was watching you. When you went through the woods it followed sly as a fox and stealthy as a Shawanee. Leave your cabin for a season and it would choke it around with brush. Likely you would find trees growing out of your bed when you got back.

Once Sayward thought she heard voices, but it was only

beetles in the air. The sound came stronger when she got to the riffles. Far off she swore she could hear Sulie calling. "Sairdy! Pappy!" her little voice came. Sayward knew it was no more than river water slopping and gargling over logs and stones, but it sounded real enough to make the sweat come and her knees to tremble.

She let her legs go till she reckoned she had tramped far enough. First thing she knew she'd be lost like Sulie. Back along the river she couldn't shut out those voices. Even the place was such as a little tyke like Sulie would hanker to play in. Fern grew like a garden all over the ground. You couldn't walk without it feeling soft and smelling sweet against your leg. Yonder was a row of fat pines you didn't often lay eyes on in this hardwood country.

Then she stood stock still.

It wasn't water voices she heard. A path wound here, worn by somebody's feet. It led straight under the dark of the pines. Out at the other end where the sun shone golden on the river, somebody was lying on the brown pine needles. Now she saw it was a girl and a man.

Still as a deer she stood there watching. Then sober and silent-footed she went back to the cabin.

CHAPTER FIFTEEN

* * *

Genny's Wide, Wide World

SAYWARD's bare toes gripped the sill log as she stood in the doorway. The cabin looked to be empty. Wyitt must have gone after the cows. But she knew Achsa lay in her bed. She could see the loft boards, that never would lay quite flat, rocking a little on their joists.

"You a ailin'?" she called calmly, blowing up the ashes and

laying on a stick or two so she wouldn't have to make fresh fire.

Achsa didn't give her an answer. She didn't need to, for Sayward knew she was sulling. Achsa didn't like it that Genny and Louie had gone off by themselves in the woods. Well, she would have to learn that two's company and three's a crowd.

Sayward let her body down on the wall bench. Once Mrs. Covenhoven had asked her if she wasn't tired, and Sayward had puzzled over it a long time afterward. If ever she was tired, she never knew it. Sometimes it felt good to sit down. It did today. She told herself she must have tramped further than she thought. But all the time she knew what it was. She had run from the wolf into the bear, and now the wolf had caught up to her again.

You could easy tell, she told herself harshly, that God Almighty was a man. He had favored man plenty when He made him up out of a fistful of dust and spittle. A man had no apron strings for things to get tied to. No, a man could gander around and have his pleasure and then wander off free as a hawk wherever he had a mind to. He could forget it by tomorrow and deny it a few months hence. But never could a woman deny it. She had to stay at home and take what came of it. She couldn't hope to outsmart God Almighty. No, it was the man who was usually "a willin' " and the woman "a sorryin'."

"What day have you sot to git married?" she asked the pair when they came in later.

There was a quick sound from the loft as Achsa came down the ladder, and Louie shot a sharp look at Sayward with his blue eyes that could blaze up like a sheet of wildfire. Sayward looked back at him so steady he went for a coal to light his pipe though anybody with eyes could see it was smoking.

"I hain't give it a thought," he said, flushing up. "It hasn't a squire or missionary nigher than the Ohio."

"You mought boat Ginny down," Sayward reckoned. "I don't allow she would mind."

Long afterward, Sayward was to remember the blinding look Genny flashed her and the cruel look from Achsa. No, you couldn't please two at one time. And you couldn't tell Achsa you'd rather it had been she. It wasn't what you'd rather in this world. If Genny would have him fair or cloudy, she'd better have him fair.

She would have liked to say a word to Louie Scurrah before he went off with his taken bride. He must recollect that Genny was a girl of tender age while he was a grown man. Let him flare up at that all he liked. Let him say, "Who's a doin' this, you or me?" She was not scared of him. But maybe the littlest said, the less Genny might have to put up with. You could but make trouble for a girl once she was some man's woman. From that time on she had to go it herself. When Sayward was a little tyke she thought the woods robins cruel for turning their backs on a young bird fresh out of the nest. Lonesome by itself in some strange bush they'd let it sit through the long dark of the first nights while the old ones roosted safe and high in the home tree. But when she got older Sayward reckoned the woods robins knew what they were doing.

Each day Genny was gone Sayward took herself down to the river. She told herself she wasn't fretting over Genny. No such thing. She just wondered, where was Genny now, when was she coming back, and would she come "a singin' or a weepin'?" What she went for was mostly to feel the breeze. The river was the oldest track through the woods there was, and the wind knew it. Things with wings knew it, too. Ducks flew up and down like bullets. Forest beasts had to cross it. Once she saw a bear splash over and once a fawn with a black wolf after. All the time the river flowed calm and slow. Specks of foam were liver marks on its face, but it kept its mind to itself. You couldn't tell what the river was thinking. Deep and shutmouth it was like most of these swarthy bodies. . . . Oh, but wasn't drowning a pitiful way for a young girl to die!

Not many brides in this world got a wedding trip, Genny told herself as she helped pole the boat home. Her man stood up to pole it from its hind end. Genny's pole was but light poplar that would callous her white hands no more than it had to. Louie's was a long hickory pole stouter than iron. When he heaved it back through his hands, she could hear the water churn like a flood tide under the front end. Sometimes in deep water he laid down his pole. Genny could not help him then, for he had whittled out only one paddle.

They had floated light as a leaf down this river, down past the forks, down past where the little river came in, down past the stockade to the Ohio where water was plenty as at the English Lakes and the settlements thick as blackberries. She and Louie had need only to pole the five or six days back, for the river had carried them down.

They were almost home now. That sweet chimney smoke

you could smell here on the water came from Buckman Tull's cabin hid yonder in the woods. You couldn't see from the trees that any humans lived on the upper reaches of this river. You could only hear Billy Harbison's hounds baying and the guinea hens of Buckman's younger sister, Idy, making like a rusty grindstone turning over and over and couldn't stop.

They hadn't far to go now. Never in her whole life before had Genny spent a night without her sisters and brother. Now she could hardly wait to see them again. Never had they laid eyes on Louie Scurrah's wife. No, she was only plain Genny Luckett then.

She expected she had better lay down her pole and put on her fine green stockings and her cowhide shoes. They were getting mighty nigh to home now. Behind her were the pines and ferns of her secret place. This here pied old buttonwood she had surely seen before. And yonder waterlogged butt was the one she and Wyitt had once fished behind or her eyes were a liar. Her pappy's cabin wasn't far off from here. Just around the bend and yonder through the woods a piece it stood if it hadn't burned down or been moved while she was off getting married. It wasn't more than a whoop and a holler. If she let out her voice, they might hear her by the fire.

"Hesh up!" Sayward would turn on the young ones. "That sounds like our Ginny a singin'."

She pulled on her fine stockings and her eyes felt bright as a coon's. She didn't know how Louie would take it. She better hum a little first. He might growl this was no way for a married woman to come home. But he paid her no attention, and her voice pitched out high and strong over the water.

> *Oh, the year was a risin' so bright and clear;*
> *And the young gal sot in the old woman's cheer.*

Some kind of body was up there by the landing log. It ran off and came back with another. They stood stock still as wild things watching this boat poling up the river. Genny's eyes moistened. She would know them anywhere in this wide world. They were Achsa, her own brown girl of a sister, and that rascal of a brother with his shagbark hair falling down his shoulders in back and standing up in front like a corn shock. Better had he not go north into scalping country with a head of hair like that, for he was the only brother she had living and never now could she get another.

Where was her oldest sister? She hoped nothing had happened to that Sayward while she was away. Once she had thought it was Sayward was against her, for never did she hear her oldest sister say a word for Louie Scurrah. Then that day she had said, "You mought boat Ginny down. I don't allow she would mind." Oh, she wouldn't mind would she! Why, she wouldn't have missed this wedding trip for all the skins in George Roebuck's store. She had gone out of these woods. She had been to the settlements of the Ohio. She had seen the wide, wide world again, that's what she had. And likely Louie wouldn't have thought of it had it not been for that yellow-headed bouncer of a sister she could see now taking her time through the trees.

All she could wish for on top of this would be her pappy leaning on his rifle and little Sulie running down the bank hollering what did Genny fetch her? Only last night in their camp she lay feeling it a sin to be so happy married while her littlest tyke of a sister was still lost somewhere out in the woods like a young gabby bird that fell out of its nest and never could find its way back.

But she daren't sniffle now. They'd expect something was wrong betwixt her and Louie. Here was Wyitt wading out to catch the front end and swing it up easy to the log so she could land dry-footed as a lady. And there was Achsa with a hard mouth staring at her fine, green, cotton stockings and her cowhide shoes. Now they all stood together on the bank, sisters and brother looking at her and she proudly at them. Never, Genny thought, had she felt so close as now when her man stood between them.

"Must say you're a lookin' good," Sayward made cheerful talk.

"You'd reckon I'd break the way Louie took keer of me," Genny said shyly, looking back at him.

"Are you married now?" Wyitt was watching her close.

"What do you expect they went off together for?" Achsa jeered, but her eyes were cool.

"Then your name ain't like ourn. You're Ginny Scurrah." Oh, you could see she was more in Wyitt's eyes now.

The path to the cabin was narrower than Genny remembered. They had to walk Indian file.

"Down to the Point," she told them, "they's a street so wide it has footpaths on ary side and a middle for carts. They even got the stumps out."

"Ain't the path good enough for you now that you went to the settlements?" Achsa mocked her.

Something flew up in Genny. She would show Achsa the path was good enough to race her back to the cabin. Even if she had shoes on. But she must recollect she was no giddy goosecap any more. No, she was a married woman now. When they got to the cabin, she sat down politely like it was a strange house and she, company. When Sayward started to get supper, she got up to do for her man. Her hands helped with the fire and lugged in fresh water and put it on to boil. When there was nothing more to do, she fetched in her and Louie's plunder from the boat.

"You kin put it thar," Sayward said, pointing to Worth's unused bed.

Genny turned her face from Achsa's hard stare. She could feel her face flush up at putting her and Louie's things together on a bed in front of all.

Halfway through supper, Jake Tench and the bound boy came. Jake said he knew they were home. Somebody had seen what looked like a bride and bridegroom poling up the river. He kept them all laughing and Genny in blushes. He told Louie now was the time for him to come to the aid of his country. All he had to do was feed himself gunpowder and it would be a soldier boy. Oh, Jake played the fool from first to last. Even Achsa forgot her sulling ways trying to keep her face straight. But the bound boy's eyes, sad and brown as a hound's, never stopped casting up across the table to Genny that she had gone off and given herself to another.

Genny had heard how great folks sat at the table long after their eating was done. Sayward would never stand for that before. If anybody wanted to talk, they could go somewhere else so she could redd off the table. But this was almost like a wedding night, and Sayward said nothing while Louie told what he saw down the river. He told it so good you could see the cabins at the forks as if you were there and the tavern where the little river came in. But these, he said, were only tomahawk settlements to the town on the point of Ohio. It had cleared fields to make a good-sized prairie and houses in rows like an Indian village. He reckoned at first it must be a public day, for all the women and girls were sitting out in clean aprons on their street porches. He saw young ones with neats leather shoes and a bigwig taking the air in a scallop-rimmed hat, blue coat, yellow britches and silver knee and shoe buckles.

A stranger hearing him tell it would have thought Louie had boated down there all by himself. The only time Louie let on that another went along was when he broke off at some marvel to say, "You kin ask Ginny thar'." But it was all right, for everybody knew what Louie had gone down the river for and who had gone with him. Genny was proud just to hear her name called by him and to say once in a while, "It's true as gospel" or "God kin strike me dead on this spot!"

While he talked Genny kept her eyes from the two beds in the cabin. That had been her father's bed and this one hers and Sayward's. But she would not sleep with Sayward now. No, she was something in this house tonight she never was before. All evening it lay in the back of her mind, never coming out and yet softly pleasing as a piece of sorghum taffy tucked back under her tongue. She could forget about it and sit here and listen. And after while such a mortal sweetness would come out all by itself she could hardly stand it. Ever since she had been a little tyke she had liked to keep something pleasant back in the mind like this, something on ahead and still to come. But never had it tasted honeyed as now.

Louie was telling how he wished he had fetched back a little gimcrack of quicksilver he had seen. It was painted with a fine brush so it would tell the heat and frost. It was no earthly use, for any human that isn't daft can tell for himself if the day is hot or cold, but he could have traded it to the Indians when he got tired of it. What he'd liked to keep for himself was a brandy bottle with a ripe peach in it. How it got in nobody knew, for the peach was many times bigger than the neck of the bottle. A doctor kept it in the window of his chemist shop so all could see it when they walked by. Oh, that big peach in a bottle was too deep for most. But Louie figured it out on the way home. The sharp doctor had put the bottle neck over the peach when it was a little green fellow. Then he had tied the bottle to the tree for the peach to fill out inside the glass.

Oh, Louie could reel off what he saw when he had a mind to. Genny felt warmed by the drone of his voice. The firelight played over these home logs and faces. It was good to be off, but it was good to be home again.

The night turned late. Some of them were yawning. Jake and the bound boy climbed up with Wyitt to sleep in the loft.

Sayward and Achsa went out in their shortgowns and back in their bedgowns, popping in bed quick as they could. While they were out, Louie had pulled off his buckskins and crawled under the light bedding where Genny showed him. But she was too shy to follow him right off for the first time in her pappy's cabin. She kept down by the firelight mending the tears in his buckskins.

Between the slow stitches of whang she let her eyes fall soft on every chink and peg she knew so well.

Her father's old hunting frock and Sulie's little patched bedgown still hung with the other clothing on the pins around the logs. Yonder was her three-legged stool with the signs she had carved on it. And there was the five-round ladder she had climbed plenty of times to the loft.

"Hain't you a comin' to bed a'tall?" after a while Louie flared out at her. "You won't want to git up in the mornin'."

Genny knew there was no putting this thing off any more. It was something had to be done. She could tell by their breathing that Achsa and Sayward were still awake. The others must be, too, for no snores came from the loft. She put her awl and whangs away. Stealthily she pushed the fire coals apart to make less light. Then she lit a splinter of candlewood, and when she came back in the cabin she was barefoot and in her bedgown. She set her shoes and stockings up on a stool off the dirt floor. Softly she nudged Louie to get over so she could lie at the outside, for she must be up and dressed before a man stirred. Now she wished she hadn't had him make all this noise. She should have stepped over him tonight and slept yonder against the logs and chinking.

The whippoorwill kept calling to her all the night. She reckoned it must be the whippoorwill kept her awake or else she had slept out in camp so long she couldn't sleep under a roof again. When she closed her eyes, she thought she was still in the boat or standing back in the grand room they were married in. The floor was of shaved boards. Shaved boards and doors nearly covered the fireplace side of the room. The wood was stained brown, and polished till you could see the candles in it. It had a high desk in that room with an iron noggin of ink and a quill in it. It couldn't have been either cooking or sleeping room, for there wasn't a pot on the hearth or a bed to sleep in. Even Louie couldn't lay his tongue on the right word to call that room. But they stood up in it just as big and pert as if they knew, Louie in his buckskins and she in her fine, new, green stockings and cowhide shoes.

She wished Sayward could have laid eyes on them then, for Sayward had never heard a bride and bridegroom say the solemn vows a dominie told them. She pitied her oldest sister lying over there in bed with nobody to sleep with but Achsa. Oh, Sayward never knew what it was to wake up at night with your man close beside you and maybe his arm slung over you in his sleep to tell you that if a bear or Indian came along no harm would befall you.

She pitied Wyitt and Achsa, too. Never hardly since they could remember had they been out of these woods like she had. No, they had never seen a blackamoor slave wench or Quaker with temple spectacles on his face. If they went in a house that had no logs inside, they would be dumfounded, that's what they'd be. They wouldn't know what to make of a room that had no joists or loft boards. The light from a whale oil lamp at night would mighty near blind them at first, so it would. And if they saw a house with real glass window lights, they would be liable to butt their heads against one like a wild pigeon, not knowing that anything but a hole was there.

She pitied any human tonight that wasn't lucky as she was. She had got herself a man, one that would keep her sisters and brother in meat till their father got home. She had a wedding trip. She had seen the wide, wide world again. Now tomorrow she and Louie would set up keeping house for their selves in their own cabin. Then her happiness better hold still for a while, for she couldn't hold any more. She would have her own roof over her head, her own bed for her and her man to sleep in, and her own place where she would keep that precious thing, fire, always smoldering under the ashes to blow up when she wanted to cook her man any tidbit his palate hankered for.

Not many were lucky to start off married life with as much as she had. Her cabin was all built and her father had unknowingly fixed it up with his own frow and augur. She had two pots and trammels to hang them on. Louie had traded English silver for them the same place he got her cowhide shoes and green stockings. In one of her pots were the lucky salt and pepper she'd carry first over her own doorsill. She had a bag of meal and Sayward, she knew, would give them more bedding when the nights started to freshen.

For the rest, the woods were there for the getting. It would not take her man long to whittle out quaiches or noggins, maybe even two-tined sassafras forks. She herself would go traipsing through the woods for gourds for water dippers and to hold grease and such. A few good clips with the axe would give all the clean plates they needed. Louie said he knew a chunk of soapstone he could fetch home and cut legs in with his knife. Now soapstone makes the best griddle of all. Frying meat or meal will not stick to it. And when the snow started to fly, she expected he would tan them a bearskin to lay on the dirt floor in front of the fire.

Oh, "her and him" would make their cabin a snug nest for themselves and for any young one they might find behind their chopping log some morning late next spring.

CHAPTER SIXTEEN

❋ ❋ ❋

Public Day

A YEAR to the month that Sulie was lost in, they heard about Worth. A keel boat pusher fetched the word up the Ohio. A packer left it at George Roebuck's. Talk reached the Luckett cabin that Worth was dead and some that Worth was living.

Sayward took her time and went about her business. This would keep. When her sang roots were dried, she took a grist of them in her apron and went to the post. It was just her luck that George Roebuck had gone to Shawaneetown looking for a pair of fusils stolen from his warehouse cabin. The bound boy was waiting on customers. He weighed up Sayward's roots. Then he put the salt she wanted on the steelyards, tapping the weight along the beam. Nobody had dare to walk across the puncheons while George Roebuck was at the steelyards, and the bound boy acted big as the trader. Twice he scraped salt off and once he put a pinch of the precious stuff back on.

And that's all Sayward got for her pains.

"I kain't tell you about your pappy," the bound boy said.

"Is he a livin' or dead?" Sayward wanted to know.

"I kain't tell you," Will Beagle kept saying. "George said he wanted to tell you hisself. You kin see him at the frolic."

Sayward held out her apron for the salt.

"He better stop by the cabin then," she told him with spirit. "We don't intend to go out celebratin' with our pap dead and buried."

The bound boy scraped up a few of the white grains he had spilled and licked them off his fingers.

"You kin go," he said without looking at her. "But don't give out I said anything."

Sayward's face did not change. Some said the settlement was giving itself airs already, taking notice of a public day in the middle of summer when work was plenty. But if they would give a frolic for Independence Day, Sayward wouldn't have liked to be the one to stay away.

She told Achsa that night they were going and Achsa was so tickled she wouldn't give up till Sayward tried something Sally Withers told her. You had to swallow a dry thimbleful of salt before you went to bed, then whoever gave you a drink of water in your dream, that would be your man.

"I got nothin' for that," Sayward said. "Salt's too high and skeerce for such foolishness."

But Achsa kept after her till she let her put some in her mouth. And now she hadn't dare drink any water till morning.

Some time during the night she woke up with a powerful thirst. She thought it was some place else. Everything stood out like real. She dreamed they were all in a stockade dying like dogs for water. Sulie and Worth lay with them and all their guts were dry as powder. But none could go out with the kettle, for the Indians lay outside. A soldier in a coonskin cap with three brass rings cut himself a long Joe Pye weed. He stuck that reed through a knothole and sucked water from the run. When he was sucked full, he motioned to Sayward she could drink from his reed.

Then she looked up and saw it was Portius Wheeler.

Sayward told herself she would say nothing in the morning to Achsa about this. It just went to show how daft a dream could be, for the Bay State lawyer was the last one she thought of when she was in her right senses. Never had she passed a word with him. Folks called him the solitary on account of him living out in the bush by his lonesome. Most times you just couldn't get any more talk out of him than a deaf and dumb mute.

But they said he came of a fine family and when Jake Tench got him dram-drinking the bound boy said he could recite anything he had a mind to out of the Bible, his poetry books or the Constitution. Jake said they were going to grease him up for a speech on Independence Day.

The morning of the frolic the three Lucketts went down the path in single file from the cabin. Wyitt tramped ahead, but when they came in sight of the folks gathered in Tull's shellbark grove, he hung back like Worth used to do. Sayward felt for him. Only a boy, he acted like he had lived in the woods longer than a lamper eel in the mud and never could he learn how to be sociable with his fellows. Now it was no trouble at all for her. She took after the Clays and the Powellys and liked neighbors nigher than the distance of a gunshot.

She had almost forgotten how it felt to get among a passel of folks on pleasure bent. The young ones were making high jack all over the place, wrestling and fighting, racing and wading, swinging on creepers, every last one yelling at the other and none listening. Some of the men were pulling a flag up on a high hickory limb. Others were laying meat over a pit of white oak coals to roast. This was one time, they said, when the he's would show the she's how to cook. The women didn't mind. They were glad to get out of it for once and go off to themselves yonder on some logs with nothing to do but lay their littlest ones on patches of moss and swap news among themselves.

Oh, this, Sayward told herself, was the only time the woods looked pretty to her. Sooner would she see colored shirts and shortgowns among the green than any buck's flag; sooner hear all these young ones fighting and swearing than the fattest gray moose cracking through the brush; sooner smell the soft pickled smell of human victuals in covered baskets and buckets mixed with the smell of the woods than a whole cabin side curing with beaver, otter and silver fox skins.

Genny hadn't come as yet. Sayward wondered if Louie could be mean enough not to fetch her. She couldn't see Jake Tench either. George Roebuck was here but Sayward wouldn't run after him. She had gone to him once. Now let him come to her, for he would want to tell it as bad as she would want to hear. For a long while she sat with the women, giving talk and taking it. When she looked up, George Roebuck was coming her way.

"I had news from your pappy, Saird," he said with the grave slant of his eyelids that meant serious talk, and the women hushed their gabbing and the littlest ones' crying to listen.

As a rule the trader was shortwinded in his post, but he took his time now with all the women watching. This wasn't business but a time to be sociable. He had his leather apron off for Independence Day and blue stockings on like the gentry. He wasn't a big man when you stood beside him. It was his bearing that made him seem so.

"He's away back at the French Settlements on the Mississippi."

"He's a livin' then?" Sayward nodded.

The trader's voice sounded a little nettled that she took it so "cam."

"He sent word for you to write him a letter. He wants to know how you all are, and did you ever hear from your Sulie? He'll pay the postage. I got the place he's at marked down in my ledger. All you need do is tell him if you need anything and he'll see that you get it."

"Worth must be a doin' purty good out'ar," Flora Greer put to him.

"He's skinnin' plenty wild bulls, they say," the trader answered shortly and walked off.

It was strange, Sayward pondered after he was gone, how just word from her father fetched him up in front of her eyes. Away off yonder he was with his rifle, slouching in his gray buckskins through the street of the French Settlements by that grandaddy of rivers that was mighty far to see across. And dark as thunder on the other side were those herds of wild bulls that some called buffalo, a curious kind of beast that didn't get up first behind and then in front like other cattle, but jumped to its all four legs from the ground.

He must be skinning more wild bulls than was good for him, Sayward thought, to send word for her to write him a letter. Certain he ought to mind that Jary had never got further with her and Genny than the alphabet. This was way back in Pennsylvania. More than once he had watched them on the sunny side of the old cabin where his hound, Rex, used to lie. Jary would chase the hound off and write a pothook in the dust with her finger. When Sayward and Genny had learned it by heart, she would rub it smooth and write another. The little "g," Sayward minded, had a long tail like a squirrel, and so had some of the others. This tail curled back one way and that tail another. A body had to be smart to tell them right off and to call out when an "s" had a tail up and down and when it hadn't. The printed "s" was easiest to mind because it looked like a trammel. The little "e" was only the cipher "3" turned around. Some of the big letters looked mighty foreign and hard to name. But Jary knew them all. She could make that old hound's bed talk with fine spelling and even rhymes when she had a mind to.

Yes, Worth must be getting up in the world to send such word to her. Perhaps he had taken some Frenchwoman for a wife and was shamed to own up in front of her that his oldest girl couldn't spell out a letter. Well, in that case she would fool him. Just sitting here she could rig out in her mind a letter she would get some body to write for her. She would make it read fine as one of George Roebuck's that the bound boy talked about.

I seek myself and take my quill in hand to write you the news. Billy Harbison promised Wyitt a hound pup next time his bitch came around. Achsa is growed up. You wouldn't hardly know her. Did you hear out where you're at that Genny has a man? I guess you know who. She was married lawful down at the Ohio settlements. I am good as usual.

Your obedient servant,
Sayward Luckett

By hokey day, if Worth dared her so big to write him a letter, she would take him up on it. He would be beat out, that's what he'd be. He would show off that letter to every body he knew. But to himself he would puzzle now who had spelled it out so fine and who had known how to fold it up and write on the smooth side so strangers would know where it had to go? And who was sharp enough to put on a couple licks of red sealing wax so all the nosey men that passed it on couldn't open it up and wear it out reading it for themselves?

Now where, Sayward asked herself, could she get a proper body to do this for her? Mrs. Covenhoven could spell like copperplate in the low Dutch language, but Worth would have a hard time finding a Dutchman in the French Settlements to make it out. Buckman Tull, they said, had a good "handwrite," but Sayward wasn't asking any favor from the Tulls. George Roebuck neither. He would write it short to suit himself if he was busy, and she would never know the difference. No, she wouldn't take it to him.

"Well, I didn't look for seein' that one here today." Mrs. Covenhoven spoke out suddenly.

Sayward sat up and her eyes beaded a little as she caught

sight of Jake Tench crossing the grove with Portius Wheeler. It perked her up to see how close he looked like he had in her dream. When last she saw him he was a dandy and no mistake in a ruffled shirt and his young face shaved smooth as a Quaker's. Now he wore a tangled beard and woodsy britches and his roram hat looked wooly as the coonskin cap with three brass rings she saw in her dream. Here, she told herself, might be a body to write her letter. Could anybody sharpen up a quill and make it scratch down sightly dabs and curleycues, it should be a Bay State lawyer.

By this time the woods were winking with pan flashes and echoing with small thunder. Those that had fowling pieces were shooting them off with as heavy charges as they durst. Powder smoke floated through the woods like a black fog. This was Independence Day for sure. Old Man Steffy marched around playing "Who's Afeared?" on his fife like they played it at Bunker's Hill, and those that had seen soldier service stood up plenty straight, sniffing the black powder like war horses. It spited Sayward that Genny wasn't here when they joined in singing. At places where the others held back, Genny would have sailed on clear and true as a redbird.

Buckman Tull and George Roebuck talked long and mighty earnest to the Bay State lawyer. Then Buckman quieted and addressed the crowd.

"We're lucky to have a speaker this Independence Day. I don't know as I need make you acquainted with him, but I'll call his name. It's Portius Wheeler, Esquire, and he hails from Massachusetts State, the same as my sister and me."

He and George Roebuck helped Portius up on the butt of a big log, and Jake Tench grinned from ear to ear as he stood handy by to catch him if he swayed too far and fell off. But once the Bay State lawyer was up, he stood steady as a brown forest hawk watching from some high chestnut stub. Only a burning in those gray-green eyes showed the brandy. Across the clearing Sayward saw the gaze of some Indian hangers-on fixed on him like on a chief's face.

"Patriots! Friends of the republic!" he began in a voice astonishingly deeper and stronger than his size. "I see a few soldiers present. I judge it only fair to warn them—" here his eyes flashed around—"that the subject of my oration will be, Hail to Civil Law, and Death and Damnation to Military Domination."

Buckman Tull flushed up and some of the older soldiers

scruched around on their logs or from one foot to the other. But Sayward felt a little tremor run through her. Oh, he was "afeard" of nothing! There he stood daring and double-daring most all the men in the grove, for the biggest part of them had seen army service one way or another and were prouder of it than a savage of his scalp stick.

"Some of the military say," Portius declared, "let's take Canada by arms. God forbid! If our American eagle wants to scream, let it scream over the fields, forests and workshops of its own white and red peoples for civil equality and justice!"

Oh, he could fetch out things that made the hair tingle at the back of your neck. Before he got half way through, some were firing off their rifles and fowling pieces already to show that they were with him, and Jake Tench had stopped grinning and was yelling loud as anybody.

Never had Sayward the chance to get a long look at Portius Wheeler up to now, and today she looked her fill. Of all the humans in these woods he was the strangest. What was he doing away back here where it had no call for lawyering? He didn't tramp the woods to hunt or fish. He didn't give a lick to trade. All he asked, they said, was to be left by himself in his cabin of buckeye logs that were easiest for a greenhorn to cut to length, out near the Fallen Timbers.

Once in a new moon, the bound boy told, he used to come down to George Roebuck's to ask for a letter that had never come. He didn't come any more, and what was to be in that letter and whom it was to come from, not even George Roebuck knew. Some thought the Solitary looked for money and some for pardon of a crime done back in the Bay State that preyed on his mind like the killing of a brother. But most believed that if that letter ever dropped out of the furry cap of some Ohio settlement runner, it would come in a woman's "handwrite." And this was Sayward's notion.

Today as she looked over his tangled young beard and woodsy britches and the bitter look in his eye, she thought that whoever that Bay State woman was and whatever she might be like, with her fine rings, her store scents and whalebone stays, it was time she sat down and wrote Portius Wheeler his letter. And she better do it soon.

What he said in the rest of his speech she didn't recollect for thinking of him and her letter. But she minded his toast. Speechmaking done, they had all hunted logs for their dinner. The women said the men hadn't done so bad with the meat. Anyhow they had plenty for all, venison, bear flesh, turkey and pigeons. Jake Tench went around with a jug for toast drinking. Sayward felt glad he didn't call on one of them. A Luckett would have hemmed and hawed and come out with some foolishment.

But you could tell George Roebuck had done this before.

"Long corns and short toes to the enemies of the republic!" he called out, and the men whooped and whistled.

Buckman Tull gave the shortest.

"The flag!" he said. Most every body yelled the hardest for that, especially the young ones, and Billy Harbison pulled on the rope till Old Glory and its fifteen stars waved fit to kill.

But Portius Wheeler gave the best, Sayward thought. He held up his wooden bowl and she reckoned how he looked like Captain Loudon who lived in the brick mansion house between her granmam's and Lancaster town.

"Northwest Territory!" he spoke, quiet as could be. "May we love her as a wife, but our home state as a mother!"

Most of the grownup faces went bleak at that, and plenty eyes watered as if here in these strange dark woods they could see for a minute the sunlight of those faraway places where they had been born.

It was the middle of the afternoon before Genny came. Sayward made them out first on the path, Louie ahead and Genny humble on behind as a woman should. Sayward had been getting her dander up against Louie, but now she was so glad to see Genny she didn't hold it against him any more. She watched her lovingly as she came over where the married women sat.

Genny gave her oldest sister shy greetings with her eyes.

"You got here ahead a me," was all she said and sat on the log beside her and let herself be stared at by two little girls going by who stopped stock still like she was some white flower of the woods to look at.

"You missed a good dinner, Ginny," Mrs. Covenhoven said.

"I ain't a hungry," Genny murmured. "The days go so fast out'ar, Louie and me plumb forgot what day it was till noon-time."

Oh, Genny would never complain it was Louie who wouldn't fetch her in, either here or to Sayward's cabin. No, when Wyitt went by out there with the cows she would always call after him to tell Sayward they'd be in one of these here days. And never would she come. Sayward would go out, but if Louie wasn't home, as happened mostly, he claimed she came to carry tales behind his back. Once when Wyitt stopped off after such a time, Genny tried to hide black and blue marks under her shortgown.

What all Louie had against Genny's oldest sister, Sayward wasn't certain. But it was plenty. He couldn't abide her, that she knew. And it didn't help any that he had to keep his woman's sister and family in meat. He wouldn't fetch it in the cabin any more but hung it on a dogberry back where none could see him when he came. They'd find it when one would go behind the cabin to see. Bad as she needed the meat sometimes, Sayward felt like taking it out and throwing it back in his face. But that would make it all the harder for Genny.

The sisters didn't talk much today. It felt good just to sit side by each. After a fitting time, Sayward told her the news from Worth. Genny didn't say anything. Her eyes were watching them clean off rotten logs for a dance ground. Her cowhide shoes tapped to the fast time of Old Man Steffy's fife and Billy Harbison's fiddle.

Jake Tench came up and asked Sayward to jig one off with him.

"Give the rest a chancet, Jake," she said.

What she wanted was some body to ask Genny. Heavens to Betsy, it was nothing out of the way for a man to jig or shuffle out in front of everybody with some other man's woman. That gaunt woman from Kentucky gave her babe to one of her young ones to hold and swung off with old Jude MacWhirter till her shortgown blew out like hogshead hoops and her black eyes glowed deep in her hollow sockets. Truth to tell, it had plenty who would like to ask Genny but they held back on account of Louie. Louie could fly up and get ugly over no reason at all. The bound boy stood around with his eyes bleeding on Genny and yet, even with Jake to back him, he didn't want bad feelings with Louie Scurrah.

Louie didn't take Genny out either. The only one he reeled with was Achsa.

"You don't many times see folks so brother-and-sister-like," Idy Tull had to go and say sweet as sap that has stood too long and started to work.

Nobody said anything to that, for they hadn't need to. Achsa hopped around with her sister's man as gaudy as a poppinjay in her blue shortgown. So that, Sayward thought, was why she had plagued for a kettle of burr oak dye. Sayward had told her red would look better on a dark-complected body like her. But Achsa had said, if Genny could wear blue, she could, too, so she could. Yes, any color would do for Achsa so long as it was blue, like Genny was married in.

After while, when Sayward looked around, her eyes couldn't light on Achsa or Louie, either one. Wherever they went, they stayed a long time. Achsa came back to the grove first from one side of the bush and Louie some time after from the other. Oh, Sayward's face kept tolerable calm but the set of her cheek bones warned Idy Tull she better make no more cracks now.

The day was at its short end when the frolic broke up. Those that had a long ways to go lit shellbark or candlewood at the coal pit so they wouldn't have to make fire for light on the way home. Genny caught sight of Louie waiting. He wouldn't come up where Sayward was but stood off by himself with a touchy face.

Genny slipped down off her log.

"Well, I expect me and Louie'll have to skedaddle for home." Her eyes met Sayward's for a moment.

"When are you a comin' in?" Sayward asked for something pleasant to say.

"Oh, Louie'll fetch me in some time I got the time. Why don't you come out? It's moughty nice out'ar. I sure like my cabin."

Achsa stood by hard as blacksmith nails, not saying anything. Wyitt had his shocked head down gravely. His eyes peered up like he was staring away out through the dark woods where his married sister had to go.

"Look fur me out'ar tomorry—if the cows come thataway!" Genny flashed back a radiant face.

"Goodby to you!" she called.

Sayward said no word to Achsa on the way home. When they got to the cabin the fire was out. Down under the ashes and all. The hearth felt stone cold.

"I won't make a fire till mornin'," she told them shortly. "You kin go to bed in the dark."

To herself she said she would like to take Achsa out and beat some sense in her. But that would do little good all around. No, it would only dare Achsa and double-dare Louie. Some you could talk to. Achsa would close up her face like a squaw. Even Worth couldn't get anything out of her then. Worth could be glad he was out in the French Settlements, not knowing anything about this.

Come to think on it, she guessed she wouldn't write him a letter after all. Let him go on thinking Genny was still single and things were all right in here. They didn't need anything, did they? No, they could make out. When she lay down in her lone bed she recollected her dream. Yes, that was all over with. She would have no excuse for striking up acquaintance with Portius Wheeler now. Well, it just went to show. She never had much for this telling fortunes anyhow.

CHAPTER SEVENTEEN

❊   ❊   ❊

The Ever Hunter

WYITT WISHED he had him a brother. He had one once, with the fairest hair they ever saw, but it never drew breath. Sayward slapped its little naked backside till her young hand stung, but this babe wouldn't squall or suck in any of the world of air just waiting around for living things to breathe on it.

That brother would come in handy now. He could tramp along through the woods listening for cowbells or help devil Tull's hogs when they ran across them wild as bear rooting up mast on the hills or anise root in the bottoms. He'd be company going out before daylight to the snares and fish baskets. At night on the loft they could lay on their backs together and make out what far parts they'd run off to. A brother stuck closer than a cockle burr. If some wild beast or human picked on one, he'd have to fight them both.

But the only brothers he had living now wore shortgowns. When his sisters were little he didn't know it had much difference betwixt a boy and girl except to look at. Achsa and Genny could race him, wrestle him, fight him any day. But once they got around twelve or thirteen, something came over them. They had to run the haw comb through their hair or wash their feet or oil up their feathers like gabby birds. They didn't even look at you the same any more. No, they knew they were girls now and you were a boy, and that's all there was to it.

He daren't as much as scratch his head at the table any more. A wild buck could rub his head against a tree whenever he had a mind to, but the minute Wyitt lifted a hand to his, he saw Sayward and Achsa watching him.

"He's a growin' hisself horns agin," Achsa jeered.

"Come over here by the fire and let me look at you," Sayward said.

"It's only the bed leaves," he flared up at her. "That fine dust itches my scalp."

"I'll tell you if its bed leaves," Sayward promised him.

But Wyitt wouldn't trust her. He moved himself handy to the door. Only when she paid him no more attention did he go back to his bench at the table. He'd wait till Sayward and Achsa went to their beds. They must be mighty tired, for they had worked all day cleaning out brush with the grubbing hoe in the Covenhoven corn patches. It was lucky the Covenhovens had no more heavy tools as these or they might have asked him. He wouldn't like to be caught working at such foolishness. Fast as you grubbed them out one place, the sprouts came up some place else. They wouldn't grow much any more this fall but early next spring they'd be up again all over the cleared land thicker than hair on a dog. If Worth was home, he'd bust his sides laughing at these settlers chopping down trees, burning them up, shovel-ploughing around the stumps and fighting the roots from spring to fall just to raise wheat and corn. All the wheat they got was sick wheat. The black ground was too rich. And the sick wheat made you vomit.

The only good part of it was the wages. Now they had Indian meal again. He could hug his belly tonight filled with hot mush and maple sweetening. He'd go to bed himself if he had a brother. It was lonesome for just one up in that loft. He had slept betwixt Achsa and Sulie too long. Sometimes he got awake in the night with the feeling that Sulie was still there. Not till he reached out his hand in the dark and found her bed empty would he give in that she had never come back with the cows.

He would stay down by the fire a while tonight. My, but he was gappy. He would lay his head on the table only for a minute. In a shake he thought that Jary was back. She looked a little like Mrs. Covenhoven but her hair and ways were Jary's. She was bent over tucking pine splints between the fire logs for light. Now she came puttering over and pulled his hair apart to peer down short-sighted at what she could find. She pulled so hard that it hurt.

He woke up and found pine splints burning between the fire logs and Sayward jerking the haw comb through his tangled hair.

"Look at 'em a tumblin' out!" she called angrily. The back of the comb dabbed fast here and there on the table, making fine cracks like the splitting of tiny hazel shells.

Wyitt was mad as a hawk to get found out.

"You let my hair alone!" he bawled although the quiet, righteous way Sayward turned her back on him for the clapboard shelves struck fear in his soul.

"I seed all I want to," she told him. "Now somebody got to burn your bed leaves and lay out your bed clothes so the wild things kin eat off the varmints."

She lifted down a gut of bear's lard and dished some out in a cracked gourd with a small paddle.

"What's that fur?" he demanded, bristling.

"Before you go to bed tonight," she said shortly, "you kin lard up your head."

Wyitt stared at the cold, greasy stuff. Always had he liked lean meat, never the fat. One lip stuck out over the other. She couldn't play off such a mean trick on him! Never would he slop that fat on his fine stand of hair till it lay down flat and bedraggled as a wolf sneaking out of the river.

When Sayward went out, he climbed up to the loft.

"He's abed without lardin' hisself!" Achsa sang out the door.

"You're a liar and don't know a bee from a bull's foot," Wyitt told her angrily, climbing down. His bed clothing was trailing on his arm. "If you want to tattle, I'll give you something to tattle about. If my hair and bed clothes don't suit, you kin tell Saird I'll sleep outside till they do."

Although the night was fresh, he dragged off to sleep on the ground under the leaning elm where he could shin up quick in the dark if there was reason. It felt like a frost till morning. More than once he wished himself back in his loft with his bare feet on the warm chimney. But he told himself oxen couldn't drag him back now.

Before daylight came right, he was up with the axe, making himself a half-faced cabin like hunters put up in the woods. Oh, he would build himself a house to fetch their eyes out! High enough in front it would be to sit up in and at the back down snug to an old beech log.

Achsa came out to watch a while and devil him with fool questions. But Sayward walked by only when her business took her. She gave it no more than a short glance. You could trust Sayward to keep her mouth shut except when he came in for his meals. And then all she said was to leave his fur cap off the pegs where her and Achsa's clothing hung. He could hang it on a bush outside. Every day he could see his cracked gourd of bear's lard waiting. Sayward would not give in about that, no not if the stars fell.

The front of his half-faced cabin was done from the first, for that side was left open to the weather. His side logs weren't very big. He could lift them up and notch them in himself. The cracks between he stuffed with moss. The roof poles he laid thick with bark to run the rain and snow water back over the beech log. In one of the side logs he set two pins. He could lay a clapboard on these if ever he had need of a shelf. A third pin he whittled out and set in its augur hole for a fine hat rack. He could tell you right now that never in his own house would his cap have to hang outside. Fresh green leaves he stripped and carried in till the place was snug with creature comforts as a wild thing's den. Now he could sit at home and scratch his head all he pleased, and no one around to hinder.

He wondered that he had not done this before. Lying here of an evening with his own roof overhead, with the beech log snug behind him and the light from his own fire shining in warm and red from in front, he could feel the woods like he never could shut up in the dark cubbyhole of the loft. Even at night something in him knew the woods and the woods knew him. Away out yonder where the forest was deep and wild, where it hadn't a path a white man had made, he could hear it calling to him.

"Come away!" it sounded like. "Come on away!"

It wasn't the loons and it wasn't the river. It wasn't the wind and it wasn't the hill hooters coasting silent as a sled of gray feathers over the soft moonlit tips of the forest. No, the trees stood quiet as if they heard something, too. Now they would listen. And now they would talk softly together like a flock of turkeys talk when settling down for the night, feather to feather and wattles to wattles, up in some wild roost.

From the time the first poplar leaf turned yellow back in the dog days, he could hear that horn although it was mighty faint then. It came a little plainer when the wind blew cool down the river. Away up on the far side of the English Lakes where that wind hailed from, it must be cold already for he could smell fall on the air. Soon it wouldn't need a wind to fetch fall from somewhere else, for fall would be here.

Now snakes were traveling across the path. The spotted rattler and coppersnake were the first to hole up and the last to come out in the spring. The water in the river was getting mighty chilly. You needn't wash yourself all over any more till next May. Ringtail coons ran heavy with fat. Wild pigeons feasted on the acorn trees. Fox grapes turned blue along the runs and skunks smelled fine and sweet on the evening air.

Now it was cold and wet, and the rainy spell hung on. Around the change of the seasons you could look for bad weather in the full of the moon. And now one fine morning the gums by the river were red as blood, the hickory ridges yellow. Directly the whole woods were burning up. The young beeches on the north side of the hills were the only thing left green among the hardwoods. Colored leaves floated in the spring and run. You had to fish them out of the kettle when you dipped water. All through the night you could hear nuts and acorns come rattling down.

Hardly could Wyitt stand any more lying in his half-faced cabin night after night, smelling the turned leaves and waiting for Louie. Oh, he and Louie had a secret between them. When he went out to Genny's, she told him Louie said it wouldn't be long now. Then one day he didn't go out and that evening when he fetched the cows, Mrs. Covenhoven told him Louie had left word for him to come.

That night on his pallet he lay first on one side and then on the other. He kept twisting like one of those horsehairs that get alive when they fall in the spring. Long before daybreak he was up but it was plenty light till he reached the cabin in the sumach. Louie and Genny still lay abed. It was good, Wyitt told himself, Sayward didn't know about this. Genny unbarred the door and the boy came in slowly, his eyes ransacking the room. There was Louie's brassbound, curly-maple, sporting rifle in a corner and that's all. There wasn't any more. He could see the whole cabin.

"You was warm when you come in and never knowed it," Genny told him.

He fetched himself around. On two pins over the door stretched a long rifle, its wood and metal the same rusty color. A patched powder horn hung over it. The rifle was tied together at one place with tow, and the stock had a dent like it had been clubbed over the head of a bear. Or it might have been where a wolf chewed it.

He stood on a stool and lifted it down. It was two heads taller than he. Never had he lifted anything so heavy.

"I kin handle it," he said quickly before they might take it away.

"You kin be glad it ain't curly maple like mine," Louie said when he had pulled on his leggins. "I got to keep a takin' my bor'l off. It rusts from the acid. Now walnut has nothin' in it to rust a bor'l."

Wyitt nodded. Louie needn't talk up the gun to him. Walnut might be the commonest tree in the woods but it was plenty good enough for him, just so he had a rifle. The flint on this one was set in buckskin and somebody must have hunted a long time in the woods to find a hickory whip for such a long, straight ramrod.

"I'll show you somethin' you never seed," Louie said. He loosed the tow, unbreeched the gun and took a stained, brown paper from between barrel and walnut. It had faded writing on it.

"What's that fur?" Wyitt wanted to know.

"Wait till I tell you," Louie said testily. "George Roebuck hisself couldn't read it. He said it was Dutch so I took it to Mrs. Covenhoven."

"Tell him what it says," Genny urged.

Louie held up the paper and made as though he could spell it out.

" 'Who hunts with this gun will be lucky,' " he read off.

Wyitt stared.

"A witch master wrote that," Louie told him. "You're lucky, for a witch kin never spoil your aim now."

Wyitt raised up understandingly. He recollected how his father never would let a strange woman lay hands on his rifle. Louie put the paper back.

"I paid two buckskins down. You'll have to fix the rest with the skins you git."

Wyitt nodded. Oh, he'd soon have all the trees around his place curing with hides! George Roebuck had better put up a new shed room, for he and his rifle would fill that old hide cabin from dirt to rafters.

"You said nothin' to home?" Louie wouldn't mention Say-ward's name but you could tell by the sudden, hard look on his face whom he meant. "Well, you want to do like I said now. If you git meat with it, you kin take it home. If you don't, you want to hide it out somewheres till you do, or she'll make you take it back."

Genny told her brother to wait for breakfast. She'd start fire and have meat frying in three shakes. But Wyitt wasn't hungry. No, he couldn't eat a bite, not if it was spiced with pepper. He had to go now. Oh, he knew how to load that rifle. Hadn't he watched his pappy load his since he was knee high to a coon! The old powder horn patched with buckskin he slung over his shoulder. The seven balls Louie passed him he counted and kept knotted in the rag Genny said he better take along. He said she wouldn't need to have done that. He could have cut off some of his shirt if he couldn't find some old hornets' nest in the woods for patching.

"I'll tell you what I git," he nodded and, staggering under the rifle, went forth from the cabin.

That was a time he'd always recollect, when Genny's door closed behind him and the boy found himself alone outside with his rifle in his hands. All around him, still as a burning secret, lay the great woods making not a move and yet beckoning him on. Just to see the tangled colored leaves, the oak rusty as a deer's coat, the gum red as its heartblood, the hickories yellow as pelts' gold and all the creeper coverts where wild fowl and beasts could hide, went through and over him like nothing else could. Near and clear now and sweeter than a hound dog after a fox blew that old hunting horn in his ears. Every leaf sailing down set him off like a squirrel's barking rattle. He was drunk on powder, that's what he was. Any old log today might hide a bear behind it. A splash of rusty leaves near the ground might be a fox in hiding.

Up in a little grove of white walnuts he pulled his first trigger. Snap went the flint down on the steel frizzen. Pish went the blinding white flash of powder from the pan. Then the whole woods to the English Lakes roared to his thunder. It threw him back like a rag. Before he was down right he had picked himself up and run to the foot of the tree. No stump-ear squirrel could he find lying in the leaves though he scratched the black ground bare with his moccasins like a turkey after mast. No, he guessed at last, he'd have to wait till next time to lift his game up by the tail and feel it soft inside his hunting shirt with the red blood trickling warm against his belly.

He tramped the woods all day through that golden haze but it wasn't as easy as he had reckoned. One after the other, those seven precious balls lost themselves yonder in the woods, all except the last that cut off a runbush limb and buried itself in a poplar, just missing a black squirrel spread-eagled upside down with head and tail jerking. Oh, he reckoned he'd have to wait a while before he could bark squirrels like his father, breaking the high branch they sat on so it knocked them stunned to the ground and not a mark on them from ears to vent.

He turned back figuring out what to say to Louie. Where could he hide his rifle? How could he get him lead for next time? As if he wasn't down far enough in the mouth, close to a run he jumped two bucks. The young one went sailing over a hazel patch, but the old one held up his rack of horns and watched him. Spit on a boy like him! his looks said. What could a boy do to him? And there was Wyitt without a ball in his rifle.

It was at this time he recollected the spent ball back in the poplar.

He had to dig mighty hard for that lead. The runbush limb had slowed it down some but the soft white wood of the poplar had let it in easy. It was a good thing, Wyitt reckoned, that black squirrel wasn't on a hard hickory or his ball might have flattened out like a ball of mud. Now he pounded it a little between two rocks, and shaved it round again with his knife till it rolled free in his rifle bore. This time he poured heavy powder in the barrel and in the pan, too. He set the patching on the muzzle, the spent ball on top and pushed it in. He cut around the patching with his knife as carefully as Sayward cutting out a new shortgown, and rammed that ball home till the thin hickory liked to dance in his fingers.

Both bucks were gone till he got back to the hazel patch, but they mightn't be far off. This was feeding time. He could follow the young one a ways. Under the leaves his tracks cut deep in the black earth at every jump and slid like a mud boat at the

wet places. It was getting along toward dark now, time long since
to have gone for the cows. Well, Achsa could chase cow tails
tonight. Dark came early to the woods in the fall. Now the color
was fading fast from the leaves. A while ago when it was still
light he had a bead on a buck and no ball. Now he had a ball and
nothing to draw a bead on.

Forty or fifty paces further on some shadow feeding in a
spicewood thicket raised a head. If this wasn't the old buck,
Wyitt told himself, it was his twin brother.

The boy's hand trembled as he opened the set screw on the
hammer and turned the flint to a fresh side. He scraped his
thumb nail down the frizzen channels. Never, he told himself, did
he need a spark like now. Oh, he wasn't tired. He could hold his
arms steady as a rock and yet that long rifle sagged and shook
like a fit of the aguers. He crawled to a log and propped his
barrel so he could draw a bead. Then he set his mouth and pulled
the old blacksmith trigger.

The long white flash from the priming pan liked to burn his
eyes out, but he held fast as a glut in a log. That was a green
hand's trouble with flintlock, dodging and flinching and spoiling
the aim. The rifle when it went off shook the earth. He felt blind
and deaf as he crawled up to the spicewood thicket. He told
himself that old buck had never held still all the time between the
hammer snap and gun discharge. No, when the pan flashed, if not
before, it had reared up and sailed away like a pheasant over the
tallest bushes.

Ahead was a brown log he hadn't seen before, and when he
looked hard, that brown log was the buck lying there in the
spicewood thicket.

Was or wasn't that buck lying? Now it must have woke up
that he was close and now it was trying to get up. He had to cut
its throat quick if he wanted to keep it down. Oh, he better stay
out of the way of its bad front feet. He straddled the neck from
behind but before he could get his knife out, that old buck was
up in back and front with him on top. And now he had to leave
that knife in his belt, grab fur on the cape and hang like grim
death on Billy Allen's blind pony.

That buck's hair was turning all the wrong way. It whipped
around like a crazy thing, bucking and kicking and running in
circles. It bumped against this and that. It scraped every place it
could to get him off. It dragged him through prickly haw thickets.
One of his legs or the other it kept whacking against trees. How

his knife stayed on he didn't know. His powder horn went, his leggins got torn to rags on thorns and brush and the roots and branches of windfalls. He could feel warm blood now but it was his own trickling down his legs that were wrapped like death around the deer's belly. No man could tell how this would come out. All he knew was his first buck wasn't going to get away easy.

"It kin throw me," he told himself, "but I won't stay throwed. It kin kill me but it kain't whup me."

Once it started to go, the hurt buck fagged fast. It was going down now in the black night. Wyitt pulled his knife and felt his way to finish it. He stood a while still straddling it while the dark trees went around. Half his clothes were torn from his body. The sticky blood kept drying on his shoulders, sides and legs.

"That paper was true," he thought like a shaft of golden lightning in the woods. His lips repeated silently, "Who carries this rifle will be lucky."

He took out a flint and struck sparks from the back of his hunting knife. Now he blew up a fire. By its light he worked carefully. Not even his father had ever skinned a buck as smooth and even as he would this one. After while he would cook him a venison steak on a green stick. He would hang up the hind quarters for the night and make him a great fire to keep off the wolves. Last he would make him a nest in the leaves and lay down with that warm hide over him, bloody side up, till day. Then he would have plenty time and light to go back over his tracks and pick up his powder horn and rifle.

When Wyitt didn't come home for supper, Sayward put his victuals on the hearth to keep them warm. When it got late without him, she and Achsa lighted candlewood and went over to the Covenhovens. The Covenhovens were both in bed but big John came to the door with his great coat around him, his bare legs and feet sticking out below.

"He never showed up for the cows," he told her a little angrily. "They had to come home themselves. Long after dark."

Sayward didn't make excuses for Wyitt, nor did she flinch from John Covenhoven.

"I don't think any harm's come to him," Mrs. Covenhoven called from her bed. "Louie left word yesterday he wanted to see him."

Achsa's black eyes were mighty bright in the torch light as if she knew something and couldn't tell.

"If he don't show up," Sayward said with dignity, "Achsa'll git your cows tomorry." To herself she added that if Achsa hid out around this time, she'd fetch the cows her own self.

She asked nothing what Achsa knew on the way home. The best way was to go to bed now. If Achsa wanted to keep back, she could.

It was noon next day when Wyitt turned up at the cabin. He must have moved mighty quiet on the path. The door was open and still they didn't hear him till he stood on the log step, powder horn slung over one shoulder and over the other a long rifle with barrel shoved through a great knot of hide so heavy it hung down and dragged on the ground behind.

Achsa jumped up but Sayward stayed sitting.

"Whar was you last even?" Achsa said to him in her coarse voice. "If you reckon I'd fetch your cows, you're fooled."

"I don't keer about any cows," Wyitt said. "I was out a gittin' you some meat." He staggered in and slung the heavily packed hide to the floor. "I shot it my own self," he told them. Now he held his rifle in front of him so they could plainly see.

Achsa shot a quick look at Sayward to see how she'd take it, but she sat there looking at Wyitt's shirt and leggins. From the front you couldn't see much but both sides had been cut to ribbons.

"Whose gun you got?" she asked.

"Mine." He stood there straight as he could like Louie. Oh, you could see he was mighty proud of being a man today.

"Whar'd you git it?"

"George Roebuck's."

"Louie's you mean, don't you?" she asked him a little sharply.

Now how did Sayward know of that? He bristled at her defiantly.

"Louie said I was big enough for a rifle this long time. Ginny says so, too."

If Sayward felt a twinge inside of her for Genny, her face gave no sign. So that was it, she told herself stolidly. She had wondered how long Louie could stay put with his woman's folks to keep in meat when all around him the woods and prairies ran a thousand miles for his itchy foot to wander. Oh, he would scheme out some way to get him free, if it meant sneaking a gun to an eleven year old boy and getting him half killed by a buck many times bigger than he was. For Achsa, Louie gone would be good riddance, but she didn't like to think it might be the last time they'd lay eyes on Genny.

She climbed a stool and lifted down a bundle of dry boneset hanging from a joist.

"I'll make tea and you kin wash out them hurts of yourn," she told him.

Wyitt stood there, trying not to show the whooping in his mind. Hadn't she as much as said now he could keep his rifle, for she hadn't said he couldn't He set his gun by the door where the best light would fall on it. Then he came over so she could see his hurts.

"I'll let you wash me off your own self if you want to," he told her, noble as could be. "I'll keep you in meat, Saird. You better have Achsa fetch the cows from now on, for I won't have the time. I'll git you calico for a fine shortgown, if you want one."

"It'll take all your skins to buy powder and lead," Sayward said shortly.

"Oh, no it won't. I'll have more skins a curin' around here than a body'll know what to do with."

He stood stiff and still while she peeled torn shirt and leggins off him. His arms and legs were a mass of gore as if a bear had clawed him. A dull resentment for Louie Scurrah rose in Sayward. Wyitt was watching her face.

"You kin tell easy who I take after. Kain't you?" he said eagerly.

Sayward sopped the wet rag over his hard, naked, young body. When the caked blood washed off, you could see deep cuts in plenty places. He would carry scars and welts from this. Oh, she knew a long time whom he took after. He'd grow up a hunter like his pappy, following the woods, moving on with the game. If it was in him, it would come out. There was no stopping such kind.

She could see him in her mind, yonder through the ups and downs of life, skinning deer and trap-drowned mink and otter, giving a rap over the head to foxes that hid in bushes ashamed to be caught and to coons that sat up as big as you please on a log as if they didn't have a trap and clog hanging to one paw. Snared panthers would shed real tears when he pulled out his hunting knife, and beaver would swim out of their smashed houses and find he had left no ice for them to come up and breathe under. No, they would have to come out on the bank where he would take them by a back foot to bleed them. If he took them by a front foot, they would bite him.

That shock of sandy hair would be farther down over his shoulders then and his young face that had hardly fuzz on it as yet would be covered thick with a sandy beard. His buckskins would be bloody where he wiped his hands, and his hair would be full of nits. Not often would he wash, least of all his itchy feet. Where those feet would take him, a sister had no means of knowing and no business if she had. Didn't Worth say once he hadn't seen his brothers after he was fourteen? And Jary and her sister never heard from each other again.

She better wash him tender whilst she had the chance. Later she'd think of this many a time when he had gone off yonder with none perhaps but an Indian woman to tend him and a gray moose cow for milk. For all she'd know then, her brother Wyitt might as well be dead and buried, deep in some woods or plains she never saw and never would see.

"Now stand up to the fire and dry yourself warm," she told him. "I'll git something on you till I fix you a new frock and leggins."

CHAPTER EIGHTEEN

❊ ❊ ❊

Out on the Tract

THAT first winter Wyitt had his rifle, they had tracking snow from Martinmas till Maytime. The cold stood on end longer than anybody could mind. Even in late spring the frost held. The new leaves had to push through cold and snow. Skins stayed prime for six months, more or less, and if game got scarce, wolf skins still fetched nigh as much as panther hides at Roebuck's.

They came around the cabins at sundown thick as corbies by day, the little brown curs that yelped and barked and the big

gray and black night dogs that howled their heads off. Wyitt
and the bound boy couldn't hear hardly a word of what the other
said all the way home from the post one moonlight evening. When
dark came, Wyitt would build a fire and lay in his half-faced
cabin waiting for a pair of eyes to shine. But Sayward would
make him mad. As soon as they got to carrying on good and loud
around the place and it wouldn't be long now till he got a shot,
she would come out of her door and whack a clapboard against
the side of the cabin till they'd stop.

Oh, he knew why she was touchy, though it made him mad
just the same. She was thinking of Genny out yonder in the
woods where the drifts piled deep as leaves in the fall. For Genny
would not come in as long as Louie was on the outs with Sayward, and Sayward would not make it harder for Genny by
traipsing out. Sometimes Achsa went, sliding the crust or breaking
through, to see how her sister Genny was making out, for Louie
had naught against Achsa.

But now Achsa wasn't to home. She was off helping out
Sally Withers with her work and none was left to go but himself.

Yesterday he had shot his first deer since Achsa went, and
already Sayward was making him tote a haunch out to Genny's.
He had to hang it on a tree in the woods and go in first and see
that Louie wasn't to home. For if Louie was there, he would flare
up like a priming pan that anybody save himself thought he had
to keep Genny in meat.

He didn't need to hang it in the woods today. Louie must be
still off somewheres. He could hear Genny chopping wood by the
cabin, keeping herself company with that catch she used to sing
at home. Genny might be a married woman now, but still nobody
he ever heard could touch her for singing.

> *Oh, the year was a risin' so bright and clear*
> *And the young gal sot in the old woman's cheer.*

The boy stood there in the path listening, his furcapped
head a little to one side, the haunch tied with leatherwood and
swinging from his rifle barrel. A skift of snow had fallen during
the night and though it was May, it hadn't melted much out here
as yet. It hung on the young leaves that were all curled up with
cold. And it showed up all the dead and ancient logs that lay this
way and that, almost one against the other as far down the hol-

low as you could see, as if this was the deepest and wildest woods
the deer ever ran in. The butts of the live trees standing up
looked old and shaggy as the dead ones lying down. It gave the
boy a queer feeling to hear a woman singing away back here.

He hollered so it wouldn't give her a turn to see some body
coming through the trees.

"Wyitt!" she said when he got close, and you could see the
soft pleasure in her face.

"I fotched back your shawl," he said, pulling out of his
hunting shift the knit throw she had given Achsa to wear home
the last time she was out.

"Achsa could a kep' it a while yit," Genny murmured.
"Kain't you come on in?"

His eyes took in the bare ash that had blown over a while
back and still leaned against the cabin. Maybe Louie was letting
it dry out for firewood. Likely he didn't know what Worth used
to say, that "ash cut green is fire for a queen." Not that Wyitt
would ever dare tell him. Nor would he tell Sayward that if the
ash had stood a pole further off, it would have fetched down
Genny's roof and Genny, too, if she was inside. What Sayward
didn't know wouldn't hurt her.

He hung the haunch on the meat pin in a cold corner.

"You're always a sendin' out meat," Genny said in a low
voice. "Louie leaves me plenty." She dropped her eyes. "But now
since you fotched it, I'll keep it and thankee."

Wyitt saw a little meal in the bottom of a grain bag, but if
Genny had any meat around, his eyes could not find it.

"It looks like young doe and moughty tender," she praised.
"Kain't I cook some for your dinner?"

The faint sweat of pride showed on Wyitt's face. He went to
the door.

"I'll chop a speck at your woodpile and git me warm," he
said, grateful.

Oh, Genny needn't fret he'd chop too much. Not he! He
wouldn't give Louie the chance to flare up at Genny that her
brother reckoned he had to come around and keep Louie Scurrah
in firewood. No, he'd only chop so much.

He fetched in two logs when she called him for dinner. She
told him to sit down in Louie's place. Every now and then he
could feel her raise her eyes softly over him across the table. You
could tell she was glad he came. He was somebody in Genny's
house, as welcome as the flowers in May. Hadn't Genny cooked

for him special? She did no more for Louie when he came home.

He had meant to go back early to hunt along Black Run, but he couldn't leave her alone so soon today.

"I'll lug in the rest of your wood."

"I like something to do my own self, Wyitt," she murmured. "I'd ruther if you just set a while."

Oh, he could tell she was hungry for company, though never would she say it. He took his stool by the fire and watched the little red tongues lick up along the snowy log he had fetched in. All would grow dark in the cabin and you expected the fire was out. Then like wild things sneaking out from under the log, the red flames would lick up over the bark. There they came again quick as a toad's tongue after a fly.

Now and then Genny would say something.

"Saird a keepin' good?"

He nodded. He might have been at Black Run by this time. The spicewood was always green there first. He had passed more than one track leading that way.

"What's she a doin'?"

He tried to think. All he could fetch to mind was her making Achsa a new shortgown. Achsa had plagued the life out of her for it. He himself had given her the skins to trade at Roebuck's for the goods.

"I wish she'd come out. So I could see it," Genny said.

"She ain't home now. She's out a helpin' at Sally Withers's. Did you know Sally had twin young'uns?"

Now how should Genny know that when he was the first human she had seen or talked with in four or five days! Her face lighted up with pleasure.

"Boys or gals? . . . Ain't some folks lucky?"

Wyitt looked at her, for most people had said, wasn't that just the way—with meat and meal scarce, a woman had to get two to feed at one time!

When one log burned up, he put on another. He was a fool to have hung around so long. It was too late for him to hunt back by Black Run now.

"Well, I reckon I got to go, if I want to git home by daylight."

He didn't get up yet. That was just breaking the ground for the time he would have to go. Genny knew it as well as he. She sat as if making the most of every minute now.

"Well, it's a gittin' late," he said again, and this time he rose. He stood there by the fire fingering his fur cap. After a while he made his way across the dirt floor.

He put on his cap and opened the door. You could see the day was waning fast. The woods looked mighty different than the time he had first got his rifle. Then they had burned like fire. Now they stood dark and cold and mighty still. He could tell Genny was looking over his shoulder. She couldn't go home to Sayward's like he could. No, she had to stay here by herself.

"I'll catch you a young gabby bird this summer," he told her roughly. "You kin learn it to talk. That'll make you company."

"Oh, I ain't a lonesome," she said, after a little. "I guess Achsa told you Louie was home a couple days or so back. He seed she got back to your place that day I give her the shawl."

Wyitt bent down to tie his moccasin strings. No, Achsa had said nothing about Louie seeing her home. Sayward wouldn't like that, Genny giving Achsa her shawl to keep her warm while Louie kept her company through the woods. She would raise jesse if she knew that.

"Well, it'll be dark if I don't git off soon," he said.

"I'll go with you a piece," Genny murmured.

She put on the shawl, and brother and sister walked wordlessly down the path. When they came to the old chestnut stub, Wyitt stopped.

"You better go back now," he told her, stern like Worth.

Genny's eyes lingered on him tenderly.

"Say obliged to Saird for me," she said and her unwilling feet turned.

He went on with alacrity now. But when he looked back from the bend, she hadn't gone. She was still standing there peering after him. Just the way she held her head and stood there in her faded shortgown with the shawl tight around her shoulders, made him turn quickly as if he didn't want her to know he had spied on her.

Once out of sight, he stole slowly back and watched till the lone figure picked up a log at the woodpile and went to the cabin. The door closed behind her. He told himself he could go his way. She was safe now. Maybe Louie would come home tonight and surprise her.

Genny bent over and dropped her log easy on the fire so it wouldn't dust her clean dirt floor. The cabin looked dark as al-

ways when the fire was low, for it had no window. But tonight
the dark had a kind of golden light that humans make between
them when they visit together. There on that stool her only
brother had sat. The cabin still felt warm with him like a river
rock feels warm long after the sun has gone. No doubt Wyitt
reckoned he had come by himself this day, but he had fetched
Sayward along. Worth, Sulie and even her dead mam had come
visiting her, too. She could feel them all tonight as plain as if they
had just slept in her bed and eaten off her table. Even Achsa.
Wasn't that a surprise she was out at Sally Withers's, rocking two
girl babies to sleep and likely trying to sing in her rough man's
voice that could never keep a tune?

> Up she goes,
> Little yaller-haired baby!
> Hi dum a diddle and a heidy O.
> Hold on tight
> Just as long as you're able,
> Hi dum a diddle and a heidy O.

Never had Genny laid eyes on more than one baby born the
same night to the same mother like two fawns are sometimes
born to a doe. What wouldn't she give to see those babes so much
alike that their own mother would have to hang a loop of whang
leather around one mite's neck to tell it from the other!

It was mortal strange about babies. Some women were favored and tried to stop them before they came. Some let them live
unwanted. And some got neither chick nor child though they
hunched down on their knees and prayed to God Almighty till
the tears dried to salt on their faces. Next time Louie came home
she would ask if he'd take her out to Sally Withers's. He wouldn't
mind going there, for Louie had naught against Achsa.

Genny thought she would steep herself some dittany tonight, for this was a big day. She took a lick of Indian meal from
the bag, mixed it with water and patted it in her hands. She
swept a spot clean on the hearth and laid the johnnycake there.
The rich warm smell of baking meal rose through the cabin. This
would taste good. Wyitt's fresh meat had woke up her appetite.
She was lucky to have meat and meal off and on this hard winter
that hadn't as yet melted into spring.

She was up mighty late tonight. As a rule when Louie was
off, she went to bed with daylight. She opened the door wide
enough to peek out. All was black as Egypt. Through the woods

she could hear night dogs howl like the cold weather wasn't over yet. She hoped Wyitt had got home safe and sound and was sitting there now telling Sayward about his visit. Sayward wouldn't say much, but Genny could feel her plain as she went to bed.

She woke up with the chink of dried clay falling down her fireplace. She sat up in her bed leaves. Something was trying to come down her chimney like it was a hollow tree in the woods. Likely it had smelled her fresh meat. She jumped out on the dirt floor in her bed gown. For a spell she couldn't tell whether those two red spots were the eyes of some beast glaring at her from her fireplace. Then she found herself over there, piling bark and chips on those two red coals and blowing on them till they shot into flame.

When fire and smoke roared up the flue, the clawing stopped, but she could tell the beast, whatever it was, did not go away. Oh, these wild brutes got mighty bold sometimes when they had young in their dens. Billy Harbison knew a charcoal burner who came home one night and found one of those big black wolves with long dragging tails they called the deil's dogs inside his cabin. It must have run up a windfall, like the leaning ash ran up her cabin, and jumped down the chimney, but it couldn't get back out. And Granny MacWhirter told how when she was a babe, a panther had come in her father's cabin, picked her out of the cradle and ran a good ways with her till they shot it. This was back in Pennsylvania before the MacWhirters went to Kentucky. Granny could still take off her white cap and show you the mark left by the beast's teeth in her head.

She could be glad, she told herself, her father had made the roof that was keeping this beast out of her cabin. He had cast away Louie's old bark roof and fixed up this new one with his axe, frow and augur. Those clapboards he had split thick and stout. The straightest grained butts were none too good for him. He had set the iron blade of his frow in the logs and pounded it with the battered maul he had hacked out of gum. Not many cracks had he left up there for snow or rain to come through.

Through one of these cracks now she could hear the beast giving long snuffs like a hound. Oh, it could smell well enough there was only a woman down here. It could lay one eye at the hole and see no more than a slip of a girl with neither rifle nor shotgun across her knees. But it couldn't come down so long as she kept a fire roaring up the chimney.

She wrenched a clapboard from the pins and stood on a

stool and pounded up against the roof till her arms shook like she had the ague. But the beast did not jump down and run off. She could see a place by the chimney where the roof boards gave and shifted with a heavy weight as if a long, tawny, cat thing or a black, shaggy, dog thing lay there to wait.

Wasn't it pitiful, she told herself, she hadn't let Wyitt fetch in all the wood like he wanted! This was her last log and she had a long ways to go till morning.

For a week off and on Sayward questioned Wyitt about Genny. It gave her comfort to know Genny looked so hearty. But she had nothing for Louie letting her by herself so much this winter.

She was real glad that afternoon when the bound boy came. He took her mind off things, this lump of a boy little bigger than Wyitt but old as Achsa and with eyes soft and brown as a hound's. His hands, that looked like fried pieces of bear's fat, could make anything they turned to—a man doll whittled out of soft wood, a water wheel to turn in some run, or a lady's box of hickory bark taken off in the spring when bark would run and lapped and sewed neat as a woman. Wyitt said he even made ropes out of linn bark for George Roebuck to tie up his skins when he took them down the river.

Yes, the bound boy's hands were mighty quick though the rest of his body was heavy. Along side of him Genny used to seem light as a feather. When Genny ran, it was like a young doe sailing over a log. But the bound boy ran like a fat yearling bear that was furred heavy down to its claws, bending from side to side and puffing at every stride.

Sayward judged he had been running today. Sweat showed on his face like dew on a gourd. He looked around for Wyitt and when he couldn't find him, came in and took the bench Sayward bid him. There he sat hardly making a word. A lump of tobacco, stolen likely from George Roebuck, pushed out his cheek. If he had anything on his mind, he did not say it. When Sayward looked up from her work she would find his soft, brown eyes settled painfully on her as if there was something in his thoughts he couldn't quite make out.

Dark fell before Wyitt came home. It was ten days since he'd had meat to take out to Genny's and still he had nothing over his shoulder but his rifle and nothing in his hunting shirt but an empty belly. The three of them supped with hardly a word between them, then Wyitt and the bound boy went off to the half-faced cabin. When Sayward went out before going to bed, she could see their fire red among the trees. But they did not come in that night.

It wasn't nearly light yet when she heard somebody open the unbarred door and stand beside her bed.

"That you, Wyitt?" she said but she knew who it was. Now, she told herself, whatever this was, she would hear about it.

"It's me," Wyitt spoke. "Will said he didn't tell you."

Sayward waited. She could feel him standing there, bracing himself in the dark.

"Some'un told George Roebuck he seed Louie on the trace to the English Lakes."

Still Sayward didn't say anything. The boy stood silent a good while as if he couldn't come out with this thing unless Sayward helped him. Then he spoke low.

"He said some other body was with Louie. I reckoned you ought to know."

Sayward pricked up her ears.

"Somebody we know?"

"Oh, me and you know this body all right."

"Were they a comin' or a goin'?"

"They were a goin'," Wyitt said shortly.

"Not Ginny?"

"No, it wa'n't Ginny. You know now."

Sayward lay unmoving in the form her body had made in her bed leaves, though a fine sweat rose on her upper lip. She told herself she wouldn't take this to heart yet. A mess of tittle tattle had she heard in her born days that never held water. Her voice was steady when it came.

"When did you see Achsa out by Withers's last?"

"I ain't been out thataway a tall," Wyitt said shortly.

"Well, I want you to go out this mornin'," Sayward told him. "You kin give Achsa the flannel patch I give you for her chest. Say no more than I said she's to wear it. If it should happen she ain't thar, you kin come back and tell me."

She got out on the cold floor with her bare feet and felt her way across the cabin. She heard Wyitt talk low to the bound boy who must have stood listening just outside the door. Then both started off in the early morning blackness, not waiting for something to eat.

Before it was light right they were back.

"You wa'n't out'ar in this time!" Sayward told him.

"We didn't have to," Wyitt had the red flannel patch in his

hand. "We seed Adam a comin' in to Tulls' to maul rails. He said Achsa never came around his place a tall. They had to git some body else."

Sayward stood there on her dirt floor, the faint gray light from the open door on her face. It was true then. Clear as through spring water she could see Achsa that morning she left, they reckoned, for Sally Withers's. Not many times could you see brier roses in Achsa's cheeks that were brown as a young squaw's nor her hard body as sightly as this in her new red shortgown against her coal black hair. She would take off her new shortgown when she got there but she said she wanted it to wear out. She had filled out a good deal lately, a little plenty to suit Sayward. Her plunder was down off her pegs and rolled up under her arm. She must have known then to what far parts she was going, but never did she say goodby. No, she played it to the last, tramping on at the bend in the path without a look back, although she might never see this cabin again or her oldest sister standing on the step looking after. That was Achsa all over.

"You kin eat now," she told the two boys, her face bitter as boneset. "Then, Will, you better run home before George Roebuck gives you a britchin'. Wyitt, you kin come on out to Ginny's and help lug in her plunder. I'll go on a while."

Yes, she cast up to herself as she went down the path, she could go out to Genny's now, for no more could she spoil Genny's marriage with Louie Scurrah. Many's the time had she wanted to go when it was still sweet. Now she must go when it was sour. Oh, she would give plenty had she tended Louie when she had the chance, given him what he had such a long time coming. Till she got through, he would have had to hide his face in the bushes when he heard folks coming along the path.

But then, when this came, she would have blamed it on herself. She would have reckoned that she was the one who had baited him to run off with his own woman's sister. Maybe this was best, though it spited her what she hadn't done. Either way, God Almighty knew, the hell gates were open and Genny must go through.

The sun was rising as she passed the MacWhirter place. It came up red as Shawanee vermilion. It slanted through the half-leafed deep woods like late afternoon. Down here on the dark ground, the tree butts and dead leaves were splotched with a strange coppery glow as if the deil's candles were lighting the way.

It was a long piece out to Genny's. Wyitt caught up to her crossing the footlog over Marsh Run. Oh, he let her keep the lead. He didn't want to get there first this time. Sayward would hold back for nothing today. Her cheek bones stuck out like hickory gluts when she laid eyes at last on Louie Scurrah's cabin. There it stood, choked with brush and black with rain and weather. You had to look sharp to see it wasn't part of the dark woods. A windfall leaned against the roof and mighty near covered it. Almost the house could have been one of these monster logs laying around it. This was where their Genny had to live.

No smoke came from the chimney. Sayward didn't like that. But where else could Genny be but here? She might have let her fire burn down to coals or stepped in the bushes. Her latch string hung out. No, she was to home. You could hear her talking in the cabin. Now who could Genny be talking to out here?

Sayward stood silent at the door till she made out the words.

> *The soldier took his sword*
> *And made for it to rattle.*
> *And the lady held the horse*
> *While the soldier fit the battle.*
>
> *The soldier took his sword*
> *And made for it to rattle.*
> *And the lady held the horse*
> *While the soldier fit the battle.*
>
> *The soldier took his sword—*

Over and over the low voice went with the same words like one of the bound boy's water wheels, racing now and then when a spurt of water came, running everything together, all the time going on and on without a letup. The short hairs on the back of Sayward's head wanted to stand on end. You could tell now there was nobody in there listening to Genny. She was talking to herself. Wyitt stood with his fur-capped head forward, stiff as a poker. Sayward raised up and pulled the latch string. Then she went in.

The cabin was bare as a deaf nut. Stools, table, even the clapboard shelves Worth had made were gone. There were only a pile of fresh firewood in the chimney corner and on Genny's bed a strange gaunt woman sitting with her bed quilts around her. Her hair was down and out of it two eyes stared at them without recognition.

Sayward's face grew cruel as death when she saw her.

"Ginny!" she called out.

Something in that strong cry stirred life under the wasted skin. Genny fumbled to lay back the quilts and get up. The skirt of her rumpled shortgown was up to her middle showing no more than white bones for haunches before it fell, but Genny, who was always mighty careful about such things even in front of Sayward and Achsa, did not seem to know what she was doing.

"I didn't hear nobody," she apologized to these people who had pushed in her door. She came up, puttering for all the world like Jary, and peered at Sayward.

"She don't know you," Wyitt muttered.

She came up to Wyitt at that and peered at him as if half blind from living in a dark world.

"Oh, I know you," she told him. Then she nodded toward Sayward. "I know her, too. She ain't been out this way in a long while."

He agreed mutely.

"Oh, I know the both of you," Genny said triumphantly. "I kain't mind your names. But I knowed the minute you come in I'd seed you before."

She stood there bobbing and smirking. Wyitt's face was screwed up cruelly. Sayward looked around the cabin to hide her feelings.

"Whar's all your house goods?" she asked harshly.

A frightened look came in Genny's face.

"It was up on my roof," she said. "A tryin' to come down my chimley."

"Was it a painter?" Wyitt asked.

Genny's hand shook.

"It was trees." She watched them close from one to the other. "Oh, it wa'n't day trees. It was night trees. When it gits dark you kin hear them come a hissin' around like a coppersnake and a rappin' on the door like a human. I went out once and told one to stop and it hit me in the face."

Wyitt looked at Sayward.

"She means it was a blowin'."

"Oh, no it wa'n't a blowin'. Not that night. It was still as death. I could hear it a clawin' my roof."

"It was a painter," Wyitt said.

Genny began to whimper though she hadn't a tear in her eye. Those eyes didn't look at you now. No, they looked on and beyond and you could see back through them like an open window to a fearsome country you had never laid eyes on before.

"Let her be," Sayward said. "She kin tell it her own self."

"It wa'n't my man's fault," Genny said anxiously. "You know that don't you? He'd a never gone off if he'd knowed."

Sayward's face hardened at that. Genny grew alarmed.

"You wouldn't tell him what I done?"

"She don't know what you done to tell," Wyitt interposed.

"I didn't do nothin'," Genny whimpered. "I wouldn't a burned my own stools and stand table."

Sayward gave Wyitt a shove to keep him quiet. Genny would tell it her own way if you only let her go. Her bony hands had begun plaiting, unplaiting and tearing at her brown hair. A string of talk was coming from her mouth about her fresh meat and the lady that held the horse while the soldier fought the battle.

"Would I now!" she begged Sayward. "No, never would I a done such a thing. Not if I didn't have to. But the thing was a waitin' up on my roof. It wanted down my chimley. Wa'n't it pitiful I hadn't left him fetch in my wood? That was my last log and I had a long ways to go till mornin'. Thar was Ginny all alone and her man too far off to hinder. Did you know I had to burn up my own chinkin' board shelvin'? I had to stand thar and see the fire eat my own stool and table. Never could I burn up my man's stool, for it wa'n't mine to burn. I sat down and cried my fill and every tear would turn a mill. Slowly, slowly I rose up. My table fit me. It didn't want to go to the fire. Kin you see them fine quilts on my bed? My sister give them to me after I was married. Wa'n't it pitiful a havin' to burn them! I had them at the fire, but the thing jumped down off the roof. I heerd it. I looked out a crack and seed it was daylight, and all the trees a standin' back in their places."

Sayward heard it through with a granite face.

"Now we're a goin' home," she said. "And you're a goin' with."

Genny drew back.

"Oh, I kain't leave my house. My man wouldn't like that when he comes back."

"He ain't a comin' back. He's run off with our Achsa," Sayward said cruelly, for it had to be said some time and might as well be now.

"Oh, no he ain't," Genny told her craftily. "You kain't fool me. Achsa never could run off with her twin gal babies."

"Take what you kin," Sayward said in a low voice to Wyitt. "I'll take the rest and we'll git her out o' this."

Wyitt took the pots and axe with his rifle. Sayward rolled up Genny's scrimpy bunch of clothes. She took the quilts and clothes in one arm and Genny's in the other. Then they went out in the dark hollow. When she looked back the lilac was like a little body looking after them. It stood there so pitiful at having to stay behind. Oh, any body could see this wasn't a wild jit of the woods. No, it was a tame thing and needed the patter of sociable human feet around it to bloom and thrive.

"Go back and dig that lilock out with the axe," she told Wyitt. "I'll plant it for Ginny by our doorsill."

All the way home the woods lay dark and dripping. The heavy butts of trees nearest the path moved furtively behind them as they tramped, but the furthest ones stood off watching them go. Oh, those wild trees stood stock still like they hated to see Genny get pulled out of their clutches. They thought they had her fast like they had little Sulie.

Not that Genny was clear of them yet. It hadn't a breath of wind today and yet they heard a tree off in the woods somewhere crack and fall till the ground thundered. More than once Genny would try to stop.

"What's that'ar?" she would cry, pointing a gaunt finger. "Up in that tree. It's a lookin' at me. Kain't you see it!"

Sayward had no time for such, but as she yanked Genny on she would take a look at what her sister saw, something shaped up like a kind of beast, a wolf, a bear or even a tame house cat. Oh she knew it was only dried oak leaves on the branch, that you would see nothing if you stood on the other side. And yet as she stared at the thing it would turn realer and realer here in the dim forest light, and over her would come that fearsome feeling her father told about till her hair wanted to raise and her feet to run.

Never had it felt so good at last to see a cloud of white shining ahead through the dark trees. That white was sky you could tell long before you came out in the open fields of the MacWhirter improvement. The sky hung free and light overhead. The only thing of the woods left here were the black stumps in the tame wheat patch. The eye could look unhindered now. It could look across to where a log house, barn and shed stood gray and sociable together like a small settlement in the sun. You could smell cows and manure. A guinea hen kept calling through its nose. A door banged and two young MacWhirters came out of the house yonder, quarreling and fighting with each other, a mighty pleasant sound to hear. After the long gloom of the woods, this, Sayward told herself, was as mortal bright and sweet a place as a body could wish for.

CHAPTER NINETEEN

❈ ❈ ❈

It Came A Tuesday

LITTLE did Sayward know what she had ahead of her this day. Now who would have expected the strange way things had of working around.

Life wasn't easy like it used to be. No, Sayward had hardly anybody to cook or sew, dye or boil soap or chop wood for but herself any more. First to go had been Jary under the white oak, and then little Sulie never came home with the cows. Worth had to track off to the French Settlements. Wyitt took himself out to sleep in his half-faced cabin. Achsa was up somewheres around the English Lakes. And now Genny, who came home a while, was off again, working by the year over at Covenhoven's. Oh, Genny had got fair to middling since she had humans to live with again. Her arms and haunches had filled out nice and plump for her. Yes, Genny was real good now except she had got out of the way of singing. When folks asked, she said she couldn't mind how the tune or words went any more.

By rights, Sayward told herself, she ought to feel she was in clover. Wasn't it good to have Genny back in her right mind?

Didn't Wyitt keep her kettles in meat when he came home from the woods? Hadn't she a stout roof over her head, more than one bed to sleep in and a run that never went dry just a piece from her door? What more could a body want? Hadn't she done the best for her family she knew how? Now why couldn't she sit down and take it easy?

By hokey day, she'd do it, too; if it killed her, she told herself. But little did she know what she had ahead of her this day as she went down the trace with Mrs. Covenhoven and Genny. Some might expect that Genny would have enough of hearing a man say how he would cleave to his woman till death did them part. But Sayward guessed that Genny would go as many times as a marrying came around, crying a little in the skirt of her shortgown, wondering to herself where Louie and Achsa were by this time and had Achsa her child? Yes, a wedding was an old story to Genny, though it was new enough to the settlement. This was the first they ever had hereabouts.

The settlers came a long ways to Flora Greer's cabin. The men that couldn't get in stood up to one door, and the women and young ones that came late worked themselves in the other. For a long time Sayward had wanted to see these two doors in one cabin. Jake Tench said Flora had her first man put in the second door so, when she heard Linus coming in the back way, some other man could go out the front. Come to think of it, this was an uncommon cabin all around. Linus Greer hadn't notched and saddled his logs one against the other but laid them full end on end and pinned, leaving a span of chinking between each log wide as the timber itself. It made a cabin look grand, Sayward thought, with white stripes as broad as the gray.

The bridegroom had plenty whiskey for the men in one new cedar keg and some that was watered and sweetened for the women and young ones in another. The wooden cups went round and round, but they couldn't stir up much life, it looked like.

"It ain't whiskey makes a weddin'," Jake Tench said with his hairy lips at Granny MacWhirter's ear. He ought to know, for he had emptied half the keg and was still sullen as a bear.

"Na, na!" she agreed in her deaf, toothless, old voice and bobbing her white-capped head. "What ye need ain't a halfways old man and woman that's been a livin' together since her man made a die of it up in the Western Reserve."

"Not so loud, Granny!" Cora MacWhirter tried to hush her.

"Wha?" Granny raised her voice. "It's true, hain't it? They're only married lawful because the squire got his papers last week. Oh, I'm nothin' agin it if they want. But if this would a happened most places, some would a fetched along cow horns today to shame 'em." She nodded triumphantly at Jake. "And if they had hosses, they'd have to use 'em a while with their manes and tails roached."

Cora MacWhirter had taken off hastily.

"You go and talk as loud as you please," Jake Tench baited her on.

"Wha? Yeh. Sure I will," Granny nodded. "When I was a bride, ye could hear 'em carry on over the mountain. Fourteen men raced two mile to be the one to take the black bottle out of my hand. One broke his leg over a log, but he had as good time as anybody."

She sat there silent a while in her gray wrapper, alternately shaking and bobbing her head in answer to her own thoughts.

"Na, na!" she said. "What ye need for a weddin' is a pair of younger 'uns. Two that's never been in sin." She chuckled and nodded to herself in approval. "Turtle doves is best. Many's the time I seed the gals take the bride up the loft and put on her bedgown and tuck her in. Then the men would fetch up the bridegroom and put him in with her." Her alive black eyes danced around the group. "That's a genuwine weddin'. None a these tame ways like some that's come up since the Revolution. Once in awhile ye take meat and drink up to 'em. Oh ye don't forget a time like that easy."

Jake went over to the keg only to find it empty. He sent it off with the bound boy to Roebuck's for more. He wasn't sulling now. His beady black eyes had a secret look in them. He said something to Billy Harbison and they stood a long while side by each. When the bound boy came, the other men mustered around the keg and listened with their heads together.

"What's Jake up to now?" Mrs. Covenhoven asked the bound boy.

"Oh, nothin' much, I reckon," he said, wiping his sweaty face with a sleeve. But he wouldn't meet her eyes.

"It don't look like nothin' to me," Mrs. Covenhoven told him out of the sharp side of her mouth.

After a while Mary Harbison came scuttling over.

"Did you hear the deviltry afoot? Jake's a hatchin' out a new match. Two that's never courted. They say they're a goin' out in the bush to fetch in the Solitary and see if Idy'll have him."

The women looked at each other and Idy Tull acted like she would swoon.

"I could have married more than him if I had wanted to!" she called out to all who would listen.

Sayward turned her back and stood watching Sally Withers nurse one of her twin babes that already were getting too big for one woman to lug around. The other kicked and screeched to have to wait on the second table. It did Sayward good to hear it drown out Idy, for what was more natural in a cabin than a baby crying. The greedy little shaver. It would have plenty left when its sister got through. A woman's breasts weren't the foolish doodad they looked like. No, they had more sense than some humans. If one babe came, that one had plenty and running over. If two came, they still had a dug apiece. And if three came like she heard of already, they could all three take turns without getting starved out. An old maid like Idy Tull might have a hard time filling the hard little bellies of three at one time. But a stout, hearty girl like herself could make out, and some to spare. Never would she have to step down in favor of some old tame mooly or gray moose cow.

She turned back now and listened to the women. Some reckoned this was going too far but most allowed Jake Tench would go through with it. Flora Greer thought it a sin and a shame. It was making high jack of mighty serious business. Decent women should step in and stop it, that's what they should. Sayward kept listening and never said a word, no not a word. If it had a woman here who would stop it, she didn't know her. There wasn't one but who could hardly wait to see what would come out of this.

Sayward walked herself outside. The Greer improvement was on a hill. With the trees cut, she could look out fine. It was toward evening when the air clears like springwater and she could see down to the post and away out over those lonesome waves of woods that swallowed up the Solitary's cabin. More than once since Genny was back with humans again, Sayward had thought about Portius Wheeler still living out with the bears and panthers. When first he came, he was a dandy with a whole casson, they said, of shirts and fixings. The last time Sayward saw him, he looked like an old bushnipple. You would never have reckoned this shaggy woodsy in shoe-packs and an old brush-whipped roaram was the young Bay State lawyer.

Oh, a man might stand it a little longer than a woman out in the woods by his lonesome, seldom seeing a human face save his own staring up at him from some wild run; seldom hearing a human voice save his own croaking back at him from some wild thicket. But sooner or later the woods would get him like they had Genny.

Hadn't she seen with her own eyes two solitaries back in Pennsylvania! One, they said, had been cheated by his own brothers. He lived in a house of rails he stole from settlers' fences. You could wind him like a fox when he passed. He had greasy white hair, was bent nearly double, and never would he lift his eyes at you when he went by with a load of pumpkins on his back and all the young neighborhood hooting after.

The other lived somewhere in a cave. He had been a fine clerk in a counting house when he was young. His family came and tried to fetch him back to town, but he said he had turned his back on the world too long. To most folks he never returned the time. When he had the notion he would stop and talk to Granpap Powelly in his gunsmith shop. He would take hold of Granpap's wamus in front with his two hands and all the time a spittle of tobacco juice bubbling between his lips and coming out fine as mist in Granpap's face so he'd have to wash it off after the Solitary had hunted his cave.

No, Sayward didn't reckon this notion of Jake Tench's such a sin and a shame. If he could talk the Solitary into coming out of the woods and taking a woman, the Solitary couldn't be much worse and he might be a good ways better off.

When Sayward came back in the cabin, Idy Tull was still carrying on. Oh, she had the chance for attention now and wouldn't give up telling how she'd never take the Solitary. Sayward listened, drawing down the corners of her mouth. Idy might be stuck-up and bighead, but she was an old maid. She wouldn't let any man slip through her fingers at this date, let alone a Bay State lawyer. No, she'd jump out of her shortgown for a man who could read and write like herself. And the Solitary would have nothing to say once Jake Tench and his pack had him in tow and skinful of grog.

Now Sayward reckoned she had heard Idy enough. She moved up where the men hemmed in that pretty white and red staved cedar keg.

"You kin fetch him to my cabin, Jake," she said strong and knowing her own mind. "I'll marry with him if he's a willin'."

Oh, Sayward needed no one to talk for her. She could fend for herself. Genny and Mrs. Covenhoven hurried after as she went firm and stout-willed out the front door. Mrs. Covenhoven looked sober when they caught up outside a ways and Genny had a scared look on her face.

"Now don't you fret, Ginny," Sayward calmed her as she stooped to take off her shoepacks and make herself comfortable in her strong, bare feet on the path home. "I ain't afeard a this. I had my mind on him this long time."

"I only hope, Saird," Genny murmured, "the full moon ain't got you."

Sayward turned her face to the east as she stooped. Here in the open hill patches Linus Greer had cleared, she could see a blob of yellow moon rising from the woods, and it was round and full. That gave her pause, for the moon can bend humans to strange ways. You could always tell on Jake when the moon was full or near it, for then he'd act the fool the worst, bellowing crazy jokes to folks half a mile off through the woods.

Could the moon have worked on her tonight? In her mind drifted something the bound boy said once of the time he heard a voice in the woods near the Fallen Timbers. He was picking blackberries and crept through the bush till he saw the Solitary sitting alone at the open door of his hut. He had a book in his hand and was reading it out loud in that lonesome place. The words at the end of every line made rhyme, but the bound boy couldn't make out a lick of it. When he got back to the post, George Roebuck told him that Portius Wheeler had books in Latin and Greek that nobody but himself could read, and it must be the bound boy had been listening to one of those.

Sayward straightened up with her shoepacks in her hand. She wouldn't take it to heart if the moon worked on her or not. She had set her triggers for Portius Wheeler and freely would she be his wife, for no man with such fine booklearning should bury himself out in the bush.

Jake must have talked to Squire Chew, for the squire came in good time though you could see he didn't think much of it.

"You certain you want to go on with this, Saird?" he asked.

Oh, she might be sinful and out of her head, Sayward told herself, but she would go on with it. And when she saw the bridegroom that Jake and his cronies fetched to the door, she felt she had done right, for it made her mad some wilful body hadn't the sense to do this long ago. His ruffled linen shirt was pied with doeskin patches. His home-seamed buckskin britches had got wet and stretched some time or other till he had cut the legs down to suit. Then they had shrank and dried hard as iron, and now they clapped like clapboards when he moved. Oh, you would never have told this bushnipple for a master hand to read out of a Latin book or climb a stump and give speeches to a crowd or jury.

There he stood shaggy as a bear that for a short while would mind most anything Jake Tench told him. His high forehead was held gentle and tender to one side, but his eyes could still flash young and gray-green out of his briery beard, for hardly even did he shave any more.

"Don't crowd him so close!" Sayward told them angrily. "He ain't a greased hog. He kin come in without you a helpin'."

They fetched him in near the chimney corner and had him stand where the bridegroom ought to be. Squire Chew gave a kind of hard-put look around, then fixed himself so the firelight fell on his pages, for Sayward had no candles. Jake kept close. You might have reckoned he was the one getting married. Portius stood there taking no more notice of her than that York State bride and bridegroom took of each other, the ones Mrs. Covenhoven told about, who as soon as they were man and wife walked one out of one door and the other out of the other, and never did they see each other again except mayhap on the far side of the earth where they were still trying to get farther off from the other.

From where she stood, Sayward couldn't see the wedding company, for they were behind her. All she could lay eyes on were Genny and Mrs. Covenhoven tending the meat at the fire so it wouldn't burn on them. But she could feel that a good many waited uneasy for the time when the Solitary would have to speak out. Hardly a word had he said since they got him here. Would he make his vows when the time came or would he get balky as an ox and shame her? Or might the grog thicken his tongue and cause him to say some untoward thing that folks would always laugh about and say behind her back?

Well, she told herself, they would mighty soon find out, for the Solitary's speaking-out place wasn't far off now. Squire Chew was lifting his book higher to the firelight.

"Portius Wheeler," he read, "do you take this woman, Saird Luckett, as your lawful married wife? Do you promise to live with her in holy wedlock, protect and guide her, forsaking all others so long as you may live?" He looked over the temple spectacles he got with the book. "The answer is, 'I do, so help me God.'"

You could tell the squire hadn't done this but once before. He hemmed and hawed as he said it and mixed up some hims for hers. But never for a lick did Sayward wish it could have been different. The minute he stumbled and got a word wrong, she saw Portius cock his head as if something had caught in the back of his Bay State lawyer mind. From then on he listened close and when the squire got done, the bridegroom looked around in the master way he had that day on the log and his voice came out deep and schooled as a lawyer at the bar.

"I, Portius Wheeler," he said, and everybody turned so quiet that between words you could hear the death ticks in the logs, "a citizen of this territory, do take Miss Luckett as my lawfully married wife, vowing to protect and assuage her, to guide and direct her, and, living with her in the state of holy wedlock, to forsake all others so long as the twain of us may live or take our breath, so help me God." No, he hadn't taken the easy way of the book. All the squire's words he had kept in his head and added more to them, making it still more solemn and majestic than the book, and all rolling out sure and easy as breathing till he came to the end.

It was still the grog greasing him, Sayward knew, for this was the way he had held them spellbound for a while that Independence Day. And yet a feeling ran up her spine and over her limbs that she couldn't recollect before. It seemed she stood high above the trees where she could look out over a vasty sea of leaves. She heard the squire ask would she cleave to Portius, serve and obey him, comfort and help him through sickness and trouble till death did them part? And away down in the cabin she heard her own voice firm and knowing her own mind say she would, so help her God.

The squire closed his book and said that by the power given him by the governor of Northwest Territory, Portius Wheeler and Sayward Luckett were now man and wife. Sayward saw Wyitt looking at her like she was somebody he had never had a good look at before. Through her cruelly triumphant mind ran that whoever that Bay State woman was and whatever she was like with her store scents, her fine rings and her whalebone stays, it was too late for her to sharpen a quill and write Portius Wheeler his letter now.

Before the wedding supper was ready right, the younger women came to whisper in Sayward's ear and drag her up the ladder. Everybody looked on, laughing and calling after. Genny fetched Sayward's bedgown from its peg behind the door. Up in the loft they offed with her shortgown, pinching at her bare skin and making screeches and giggles at what they saw in the half-light. Then they pulled on the bedgown and put her in Achsa's, Wyitt's and Sulie's old bed which she had laid over with two clean-washed yarn blankets. In most of this Genny took the lead. When the others went laughing and whispering down, it was Genny who stayed up a bit to give her some married woman's talk. Oh, you would reckon Genny was the older sister and Sayward the baby of the family being married off the way Genny busied herself about and the knowing airs she gave herself.

Warm air lifted through the loft hole again after they all were down. But the loft shutter was open and a skift of cool air flowed across the bed. The roof shelved close and comfortable over Sayward's head. It was a mighty peaceful place up here beside all the gabbing and taking on down in the cabin.

You could tell they were pulling Portius for the ladder now. Everybody called out good will words to him. The men said plenty to make the women blush. The women called he might as well get used to climbing that ladder, for many's the time he would have to, but Sayward told herself that she and him would make their bed down in the cabin after tonight. The only ones that would sleep up here would be their young ones, if God Almighty was good to her and him and sent them a loftful.

They were pushing Portius up first. She pulled the blanket up over her breasts. It was just as good, she told herself, they hadn't candles like the Tulls and Covenhovens. The firelight from the loft hole would make it plain enough for those men's sharp eyes to see by. She would close hers all but the lashes so as not to shame her man while they pulled his clothes off, all save his buckskin patched linen shirt. That would be his bed shirt.

Now the rungs of the old ladder were creaking. And now Portius stood with his head and shoulders up in the loft. And now the gray-green eyes in that tangled brier of beard were staring at her cold sober, as whose eyes wouldn't be to find his woman lying softly waiting for him in their bridal bed.

So far he had come easy enough. Further, no man could fetch him. One minute he was here and the next he was gone. She could hear the women and young ones pile out after him under her loft shutter and Jake Tench curse like a grenadier while the men beat the dark bushes.

Now who would have looked for a thing like this when all had been going so good! Sayward lay still as could be, studying up at the roof. Well, that's what she got for reckoning she could get a Bay State lawyer man who never courted her. It would have to be faced now and put up with.

When the women came back in the cabin, they found Sayward down and dressed, taking the meat off the fire.

"No use me a sayin' anything," she passed it off, hands and feet moving fast with her chore. "Every time the sheep baas, it loses a mouthful. Lucky he didn't run off with our supper."

Jake Tench came in, the devil raging out of his black hairy face.

"I'll learn that tarnal dolt he's a married man now!" he swore.

"You don't need to call him no names," Sayward said shortly. "He didn't call none at you."

The others tried to put a better face on it for her sake.

"You know how men are, Saird," Mary Harbison told her. "They never know where they'll roost from one night to the other."

"Don't you mind, Saird," Mrs. McFall said kindly. "I heerd a rhyme once. No goose so gray and none so late that at last she gits an honest gander for a mate."

Genny looked sick. Wyitt sneaked off shamed to his half-faced cabin. But Sayward laughed and talked all that wedding supper like nothing had gone wrong. Never had they heard her raise such a sight of fun and chatter.

Had the bridegroom not run off, the wedding frolic would have run till morning. The company would have danced and made high jack all night and gone home by daylight. Now already some said they hated to leave so soon but they had to. Others waited around while Jake and his cronies wiped the supper grease from their lips and went out with torches to the Solitary's hut to see if he had come home. When they did not come back, the rest took light and reckoned they had to go, too. Genny told Sayward she'd stay with her this night, but Sayward said aside to Mrs. Covenhoven it would be easier on her mind and Genny's, too, if Genny were off in her bed at the Covenhovens' away from all this.

When the last party took off, Sayward stood at the door

and watched them down the path till all you could see were their lights floating through the woods like corpse candles over some boggy place fetching bad luck to them that saw it. Truth to tell, they hardly needed a light tonight for the full moon almost let you see the path.

Could that full moon, Sayward pondered, be why they had all acted tonight like they were touched in the head? You hadn't dare wash and warp wool in a waning moon or it would shrink, like it would stretch if the moon were waxing. You hadn't dare lay roof boards when the moon was tipped up at one end or it would turn up those solid oak clapboards easy as the toe of a boot. But a moon blown up full of air as a bladder raised the most mischief of all for it made you lightheaded as itself. You couldn't see it here by the cabin. Yet you knew that somewhere up yonder above the trees it must be and all the heavy-raftered, leaf-thatched roof of the woods couldn't keep it out. No, if it hadn't places for it to shine down whole, it would come down in fine pieces and drift like spook smoke under the dark trees. It turned all night things false as a gypsy. Plain leaves looked like they were fine calico quilt patches and many-pointed stars.

Quietly she turned back indoors and redded up the cabin. Her splint broom scraped and hackled the bones, gristle, bed leaves and black boot dirt off the hard clay floor. The hearth she swept clean with a turkey wing. Her old buckskin rag wiped dust off logs and chinking. The clean-washed blankets she lugged down from the marriage bed and spread them over the everyday place she slept in. Last she fetched out a choice slice of roast venison she had saved back for her man if he came home, and set a place at the table.

The moon was down somewhere in the black forest when she heard them come. Yes, the moon was down now and so were their didoes. When she went to the door, there was Portius limping between them. Oh, anybody could tell he was sober now. His green-gray eyes blazed out of his briery beard. His face and hands were raw from thorns and his shirt ripped till a woman would be hard put to mend it. A couple hounds slunk in the shadows behind them. So they had gone and tried to track him with Billy Harbison's dogs, like he was a bear that had robbed somebody's hogpen!

Jake gave him a shove in the cabin.

"Leave him alone!" Sayward flared at him. "Don't you reckon you dogged him enough tonight?"

Jake stared at her in surprise, then at his cronies. His look said, "That's what we git for all we done for her!"

"You kin be glad we didn't shoot and skin him," he said.

Sayward's eyes told him he better not say any more right now.

"Keep tab on him, Saird," Billy Harbison spoke out. "First time you turn your back, he'll be off from you like a gadd."

"Then he kin light off right now!" Sayward said. "I ain't a holdin' him."

She swung the door wide and stood there in her bare legs and feet, a strong figure dependent on no one or nothing. Out that door was the forest, cold, black and still. Around him inside, Portius Wheeler could see the firelight dancing cheerfully over the rubbed logs and scrubbed table set for one body to eat. A stool had been pulled up to it. On the poplar chip was a plump piece of brown-roasted meat. Beside it lay a cabin knife to eat it with, and a noggin stood for tea. The mint flavor of the steeped dittany filled the room.

She waited, but the only move Portius Wheeler made was to shiver, for he was soaked to the skin from runs and wet places.

When Jake and his cronies had gone, Sayward closed the door. She did not trouble to lay the stout hickory bar across.

"Set up to the table—if you're a hungry, Portius," she told him, filling his noggin with tea.

Oh, she didn't sit up with him or lean behind his stool asking him how it tasted or could she get him anything more he wanted. No, she let him eat while she went about mixing a sponge of sour dough to rise till morning. Should he take a notion to jump up from the table and run, he could go. She wouldn't hold him. It might be she stole a look at him once in a while, for it did her good to see how hearty he ate her rations. But never did she let him know. When he was done, he waited for her to pester him and when she kept about her business, he threw her a sharp look under his heavy young eyebrows. And when she paid him no more attention than before, he came over and warmed himself at the fire.

His teeth still chattered, and she walked over to a peg and took down her father's old linsey hunting frock that had hung there since he went off looking for Sulie and never came home.

"I expect you better put this on till you dry your shirt and britches," she told him.

She turned her back on him now and went on mixing her

dough. Oh, she could tell he didn't know for a good while whether he would do this thing or no. But when she set the dough by the fire to rise, his patched shirt and wet buckskin britches were laying on a stool and he was standing there with Worth's hunting frock down over him till it nigh onto touched his knees.

She gave those knees and the shanks below a sharp look.

"When was it you washed all over last?" she put to him, and before he could answer. "Is that how they learned you back in the Bay State?"

She fetched the wash trough Worth had hollowed out of a poplar log up to the fire and dipped hot water from the big kettle, using the gourd with the long handle. Then she laid out a sop rag and a gourd of soft soap.

"Don't you reckon you better wash that dirt off before you git in your bed?" she said shortly.

She had his wet britches over her shoulder. His eyes flashed her a hard look out of his briery young beard but she went on redding off her table and making a long ado of washing his knife and noggin. Once or twice she couldn't help looking after she heard him splash, and found him gaunt as a gutted deer. His haunches were all ham bone.

He had done with washing and stood drying himself with his front side to the fire when she took her bedgown from its pin and went to the door.

"Now I want to tell you something, Portius," she said. "You don't need to run off from me. Any time you want to go, just you say so. I'll see your clothes are mended and your belly full of fresh cooked meat for you to travel on."

Then she went out and when she came in, she saw he had pulled on Worth's frock again and crawled between the blankets of the bed she had made. She didn't know as she liked this so much, his going ahead and getting in first. For her to get in now would be the bride running after the bridegroom. He should have waited and let the bride in first. Then if he had enough grit to come after, that would be no more than befitting a bridegroom.

She made to fix the fire for the night but what she was doing was making up her mind. No, he had left her no other way now but to lay a pallet for herself where her and Genny's old bed used to be. Never, since he ran off from her, would she run a foot after him.

Then she saw he was holding back the top blanket so she

could get in, and his eyes had a gentle look toward her as to a lady. She had heard how sometimes men of the gentry did mortal polite things such as this or helping their woman over a log like she was a helpless young one.

"Sayward," he spoke in his deep Bay State voice, " 'let's not to the marriage of true minds admit impediment.' "

Now what, Sayward thought, did he mean by that jawbreaking mouthful? Then he smiled and she judged it must be fine words out of one of his books, and it pleased her. She didn't know for sure whether or not she liked the way he spoke her name, Say-ward. Making two words of it like that seemed too high-toned and big-sounding for her. But if he wanted to say it that way, she expected he could. Like as not she'd get used to it in time, should he stay that long.

CHAPTER TWENTY

❋ ❋ ❋

Black Land

WHAT she had ahead wasn't woman's work, Sayward told herself, but she could do it. No, it wouldn't be the light chore of grubbing sprouts out of cleared ground. An axe in a woman's hand was a scant tool against wild butts thick as oxen and hard as skull bone. A woman would have to whack at one till the ground lay white with chips, and still the big butt would stand there, hardly more than flitched right. But give her time and she could fetch it down.

She ground both axes over at Covenhovens' the afternoon Portius went out for his casson. She had Wyitt turn till he'd liked to drop in his tracks. The spittle she blobbed on the stone ran red with rusty steel. That round stone had made Worth laugh the first time he saw it. It had tickled him that the Covenhovens had lugged a rock in a withe creel on the back of a horse all the way from York State when the woods out here lay full of rocks. But Sayward would take it any time to one of Worth's spit-and-rub stones. A long while she stood over it, grinding out all the nicks that had been clubbed in since away back yonder. She had to keep a close tab on Wyitt or he would have skinned off to the woods.

When she came home, Portius had been out and back with his chest of books and small fixings. His eye fell on those two axes shiny from the stone as new hard money in her hand, and he cast a keen inquiring glance at her. But Sayward only asked if he had found all his plunder and went about getting supper, saying nothing of the axes she set in a cabin corner.

How could she tell him what was on her mind? She didn't dare come out to herself right that what she aimed for was a little cabin patch planted with tame seeds that had in them the strange power to grow and bear their kind as the wild ones did theirs. Her people on both sides as far back as she knew had always been hunters and gunsmiths to hunters. She couldn't look at these dark woods growing up to her doorstep and ever reckon potato vines, roasting ears and flax growing there in the sun. The great butts stood thick one against the other so that in places a yoke of oxen would have a hard time getting through. Worth had cut only the little fellows here and yonder for cabin logs. The big ones he had no use for and let stand.

No, Sayward would say nothing, for he didn't have to help if he didn't hanker to. She wouldn't want her neighbors to say she had lost no time putting her bridegroom to work, unless it wasn't true. Then she didn't care how many said it. No, Sayward would rather tell Portius nothing unless he asked her. And hardly would he do that. He was no dolt to ask what he could figure out for himself.

Afterward she reckoned he knew all the time as good as she did what she was after. Maybe he had a bone to pick with the woods. Maybe he had lain around so long he was glad enough for something to turn a hand to. Next morning she took one axe and went out. After a while when he heard the chopping, she saw him coming with the other.

Oh, she hated to do this to him, for he was soft as a buck fawn. The hickories stood like iron and the oaks so hard their bark looked like the flaking off of the stubborn, gritty old wood itself. Thirty, forty, fifty feet off the ground the heavy butts went, holding their thickness like hogsheads. Even some of the grapevines were a couple feet through. The working side of Portius's hands broke out with blisters. His fine lawyer forehead strained like this was the hardest case he ever took. You could have wrung water out of him like he tripped in the run. More than once when he went for a drink, Sayward expected this was the last she'd see of him. But not for good looks, she reckoned, did a young Bay Stater have a beard on him tangled and spunky as a brier patch. Give him time to callous up those burning hands of his, and he'd get there, so he would, if he didn't run off.

Oh, she and Portius knew when it came Sunday now. They were turning their hands together to it better, too. One would sink his bit deep in the flesh of the butt and the other clip the chip off like clockwork. Sometimes they hardly spoke for half a day, unless you'd call axe grunts speaking. A doe could bleat out that the wolves had it. Pretty soon that bleating would stop, and it was hardly likely that with their axes going they would have heard the last pitiful call for help of that wild thing. Here was plenty chance for Sayward to lean on her axe and find out about that Bay State woman and the letter that never came. But Sayward and Portius could live together till their heads silvered, and never would she ask him that. What he kept in the back of his mind was his own business.

The chips spun like square tops. The smell of fresh sap and leaves curing on the felled stems hung in the woods like Conestoga hay. It took Sayward back to the time her father set up this cabin. Sometimes she had the notion little Sulie still played around somewhere in this bush and that Jary would come puttering to yon door any minute. But when one of the big butts came thumping down near the white oak, then she knew plain enough where Jary was and hoped her mother didn't rest uneasy with all this shaking and bouncing around her bury hole.

It took a long while to make a clearing in these bottoms. She and Portius would leave off work in the dark and go in to supper and bed a little pleased with themselves. And next morning when they went out, it seemed like all the big butts had stood themselves up again and had to be hacked through another time. For meat a man need only take his rifle and wander through the woods where it pleased him. But he had to stay in one place and work like an ox for a year or two to get a patch of roasting ears or a little ground bursting with potatoes.

One time Buckman Tull came up from the trace.

"Why don't you ring those trees and let them die their own

selves?" he said. "That's the way Billy Harbison got his patch."

Sayward nodded gravely at his unasked advice and went on chopping, softly at first not to insult him and then hard as usual. And after a little, Portius, not to stand by while his woman chored, fell in, too. Sayward had nothing to say against Billy Harbison. No, Buckman Tull could have a fine sunny field of grain among his low-cut stumps, but she and Portius could have a scrubby corn patch like Billy Harbison's with the ugly skeletons of trees standing over and the sun shining down pale and scrimpy through all the dead bones.

"You kin go look at Billy Harbison's patch," she told Portius when Buckman Tull had gone, "and see how you like it."

She thought his gray-green eyes glinted at her but all he said was short and pleasant.

" 'I'm with you in any plot against those aristocrats.' "

Now where, she wondered, did he pick up that saying? She had a notion she knew where the glint in his eye came from. That was for her having her own way without ever saying a word of what she wanted. Oh, she had vowed to the squire never to lead her man around by the nose or tell him what to do. And never would she break it. But if he was sharp enough to read in her mind what she didn't say, that was her own business.

For a long while they couldn't see they were getting anywhere. The more they cut, the thicker the woods closed around them. Then one Sabbath afternoon she and Portius walked up on Bar's Hill and stopped to look down from the devil's rocks. Already, she thought, the settlement looked like Lancaster town, with twelve or fourteen houses, not counting barns and outhouses. All had paths or at least a line of flitched trees running between so women and young ones wouldn't get lost visiting a neighbor.

But what gave Sayward pause was their own cabin down there like a Noah's ark in a small sea of logs and brush, with blue smoke rising from the chimney and the sun shining on the wet clapboard roof like quicksilver.

"A clearin' sets a cabin off, don't you think, Portius?" she asked him.

He nodded and broke from their view a tremendous oaken branch with no more than the arms that had helped perform that piece of miracle below.

"Never could you even tell it had folks down there before," Sayward murmured.

All that fall the big butts lay round curing in the sun. They lay every-which-way, with the river and crossways to it, sidelong and slopewise, atop one another and bedded like giant brothers side by side. They straddled the run and choked off the path. Sayward and Portius axed off the limbs and light top logs, but they could see no sense hacking the big butts through a second time to clear the path. Something could eat through them handier than axes. Meanwhile she and her man weren't so old and stiff they couldn't go around or climb over.

The butts that lay against each other they niggered themselves, building fires beneath and between as soon as the sun had sucked the sap out of the brush and limbs they fired with. All winter the air around the cabin was dyed a fine color with hardwood smoke. Day after day they lived in a blue world so that on a rainy morning with the fires out, the clear colorless air looked thin and strange. Lying in bed most any night they could peek through a crack and see a lick of red flames in the dark, working while they slept. So long as two butts touched each other with fire between, they smouldered night and day, green though they might be. But once they burned off from each other, they turned cold and the fire at their hearts went out.

By the Pawpawing Days in late February they had burned and niggered off into lengths all that two bodies could, and still the ground lay thick with the giant carcasses. Most of them had been straight as a handspike, some thirty feet without a knot and so almighty thick you could hardly look over them at the butt. Black walnut, white ash, three kinds of oak and plenty more, all worthless, good for nothing, cluttering up the black land. Now how could you raise anything to keep body and soul together with all these no account wild butts in the way?

Soon as it froze up again, Sayward and Portius named the day for their log rolling. It was a true March day when it came, with a high wind blowing across the river, chasing white clouds in a blue sky. Shadow and sunlight raced after each other across the clearing. So fast did they go and so close on each other's heels that it was gloomy, blinding bright and gloomy again before you could say Jeems's cousin. Mrs. McFall complained it made her lightheaded on the trace.

John Covenhoven fetched his two-horse team with bright worn chain dragging behind. Others that had them fetched oxen. Jake Tench claimed the keg of brandy he fetched on his back would move more logs than all the beasts. Most every man came shouldering his own axe and handspike. Oh, Sayward knew these men had plenty trees of their own to fell and burn so their scanty fields could nose a short ways further into these woods that had no ending. But they all had a day for Portius and Sayward, they said.

All except Buckman Tull. He sent word he was ailing and Idy had to stay and tend him. That was as good excuse as any other, for Idy and Sayward never hit it off together. No, they were better some distance apart. All they saw of the Tulls that day was Buckman's half-wild boar, savage for mast he could not root up out of the frozen ground and smelling cooking a long ways off.

"Buckman didn't want to strain his back so he sent his deputy," Jake Tench said, running off the hog from the meat with a handspike.

Jake said it was too bad Sayward had meat for all hands, for he surely hated not to butcher that hog. Oh, Wyitt had turned the woods inside out for a month, and she had most everything except the meat of bears which still slept off winter in a hollow tree with a paw in their mouths so they could suck out their stored-up fat. At such times panther roasts were good living, white and tasty as a woods hen's breast. But it was hard roasting any kind of meat outside today. The wind blew the ashes up over the flesh lying on green poles across the fire. It blew cold on the top side while it roasted on the bottom. Even inside the cabin where the turkeys hung over the hearth, the wind nearly sucked the live coals up the chimney.

That old wind made the men and teams step lively. The beasts snaked away and the men prodded their handspikes under the heavy logs to roll them in piles. The lighter logs they carried with many a handspike under and a man on each handspike end. That's when you found out who was a man and who wasn't. By the middle of the afternoon the patch was clean except for the stumps and log heaps. The wind had gone halfway down. Fires were started. The brush crackled in the heat. The men went around with begrimed hands, holding their faces toward the ground when they got close to pile on more. Portius was a sight with his face streaked and his eyes red from smoke as some old cinnamon bear. You could smell singed beard and hair on him or any other man that came close.

When all was done for now, the men started acting the fool. Somebody ran John Covenhoven's horses over Jake's whiskey keg, smashing it up, and Jake had to go for more. It came out afterward that George Roebuck had nothing but barrels when Jake got there, so Jake went back where he had seen Buckman Tull's hog and killed it, skinning it whole, tying together the few broken pieces and taking the bone from the root of the tail for the neck of his hairy bottle. But George Roebuck guessed whose hog that was when he saw it and would give him no wet goods to fill it. Oh, George didn't want to get mixed up in any trouble. He knew Buckman would eat fire when he found out what happened to his boar.

Back at the burning bee they never missed the whiskey. Those that were begrimed went around blacking the other faces. The women screeched and the boys ran after the yelping girls. They blacked the white spots on the oxen and even the faces of the littlest ones lying in a row on Sayward's and Portius's bed, though some of the mothers got mad as hops. As soon as one body got blacked, the others gathered around to laugh and rally him on how he looked. Then one would grab and hold somebody else for the rest to work on. Sayward didn't know half her neighbors any more unless she looked close. Before they got done, she felt she was a blackamoor and this was a blackamoors' frolic.

"You won't have no soap left till they git through, Saird," Mary Harbison felt for her.

But most of the men went home black-faced and black-handed. They said they'd go while it was still daylight and scare the insides out of any Shawanee they met on the trace. It was too mighty cold and windy anyhow to sit around the fires and swap tales tonight. Sayward and Portius would have to keep rolling the leavings together as they burned apart.

Portius said much obliged to each family as it left. Sayward felt beholden to them as much as he did to see all their logs piled up and the long rows of fire eating at them. But she hadn't the gift of gab to say it. Portius was the one for that. Not many could make words talk like he could when he wanted to. You could see they all liked Portius. Their faces would light up at him.

"Good night to you!" he would call what she couldn't for wishing a body good night would be too much putting on coming from a woodsy.

"Don't burn yerselves up, Portius!" Jude MacWhirter, who had the biggest family in the woods, yelled back. "But we got room for ye if ye do."

Sayward and Portius stayed up that night, taking turns tending the fires. For a long time those log piles burned. Sayward boiled lye from the ashes and black salts from the lye, and Portius took them to Roebuck's to trade for silver which he would trade later on for seed and blacksmith-made grubbing hoe irons. He himself would make the handles. By the time it thawed and set in raining, all that was left of their summer fallow were plenty stumps, a few charred butts too big to burn up in one winter and gray patches on the ground where the fires had been.

Next time John Covenhoven came over, Portius told him how a man named Vergil gave a rule in a book for testing your ground. All you need do was dig a hole. If the dirt you took out went back in with room to spare, your ground would grow most anything. And Big John, not to be outdone told Portius the rule that when a man could go out in his fields and put down his britches and the air would not feel cold on his bare parts, then it was time to seed corn. He said as soon as it dried off a little now, he better plough and drag their patch for them. He would fetch his team over next week. It took a pile of geeing and hawing to sidle around the stumps and charred butts with his shovel plough. But when it was done and the seed put in, the ground lay quiet and waiting around the cabin.

It was no ordinary day when the wild ground gave birth to its first tame crop. The wind stood off. The clouds hung like summer. The tender sky came right down in the clearing, softening everything with a veil finer than spider skeins. A little ways there in the woods, Sayward knew the air still hung chill and dim. But here in the clearing, the four sides of the forest held summer in like the banks of a pond. Flies and beetles hummed in the bright warmth. The soil breathed up a sweet rank smell of sprouting and growing. And here and yonder the first tiny green shoots of the baby corn had pushed overnight through the black ground. You could just make out the faint, mortal young rows bending around the stumps.

Sayward and Portius could see now to grub out the wild sprouts without hurting the tame crop they planted. Before they got far, Jake Tench came out of the woods. He took a paper from his hat and said Buckman Tull had left it at the post for him. You knew he'd had George Roebuck read it to him but now Portius had to read it to him all over. It said that Jacob Tench had with malice aforethought killed and skinned Buckman Tull's boar, and now he had to answer for it Saturday evening in front of Squire Chew.

You might expect that Jake would be in an ugly mood, but Sayward never saw him more pleased with himself. Here he was in the middle of a lawsuit where he would have to brag under oath to all who came to hear him how quick and slick he had skinned that hog.

"I want you to lawyer me, Portius," he said.

Portius stood there straight and telling in his buckskin britches as a Bay State lawyer in brown velvet small clothes.

"Come in the house and we'll talk it over," he said with grave restraint.

When they had gone, Sayward chored on by herself. Her grubbing hoe kept cutting off the woody sprouts. You could look back now and see the corn rows plain, with nothing to hide or choke them. Oh, those corn grains had been drops of crinkled gold that could make more of themselves just by lying and rotting in the ground. She had made Wyitt take his rifle and watch that the squirrels and other vermin hadn't dug them up. Early next fall when the ears were pushing, he'd have to sleep here in the patch with his hound pup to keep off the coons and foxes.

She grubbed deftly, moving among the dismembered carcasses of the trees, a strong woman's figure with a single garment on, her bare feet, her calm face bent over the sweet-smelling earth. This was a mighty different world than a woodsy like her knew. Folks of this world didn't need to wander off to the woods for wild crops and beasts. No, they had their own tame crops and beasts at home. Give her and Portius time, and they too would have their tame beasts to give them milk and hides and a sweet kind of tamed meat they called beef.

She found she was singing tunelessly to herself far back in her throat like some of the married women did when their hearts and hands were at peace. Her voice fitted in with the humming of the flies and the droning of the woods beetles. Oh, it was hard beating back the woods. You had to fight the wild trees and their sprouts tooth and nail. But life was sweet sometimes, too.

Only yesterday she had seen a golden fly at the dogberry flowers. Portius said that was a good sign. Where the honey bee went, the white man's fields and orchards weren't far behind. Soon the small singing birds would find their way to these corn and wheat patches. They would wake up some fine morning and hear a robin redbreast in the dogberry.

Let the good come, Sayward thought, for the bad would come of its own self. Never again would they see the face of their little Sulie, for if she wasn't dead, some Indians far off in this vasty Northwest country had her. But a young one of her own was on the way, and if it came a girl, they could call her Sulie and look on her face. That's how life was, death and birth, grub and harvest, rain and clearing, winter and summer. You had to take one with the other, for that's the way it ran.

* * *

A NOTE ABOUT THE AUTHOR

CONRAD RICHTER was born in Pennsylvania, the son, grandson, nephew, and great-nephew of clergymen. He was intended for the ministry, but at thirteen he declined a scholarship and left preparatory school for high school, from which he was graduated at fifteen. After graduation he went to work. His family on his mother's side was identified with the early American scene, and from boyhood on he was saturated with tales and the color of Eastern pioneer days. In 1928 he and his small family moved to New Mexico, where his heart and mind were soon captured by the Southwest. From this time on he devoted himself to fiction. *The Sea of Grass* and *The Trees* were awarded the gold medal of the Societies of Libraries of New York University in 1942. *The Town* received the Pulitzer Prize in 1951, and *The Waters of Kronos* won the 1960 National Book Award for fiction. His other novels include *The Light in the Forest* (1953), *The Lady* (1957), *The Grandfathers* (1964), *A Country of Strangers* (1966), and *The Aristocrat*, published a month before Mr. Richter's death in 1968.